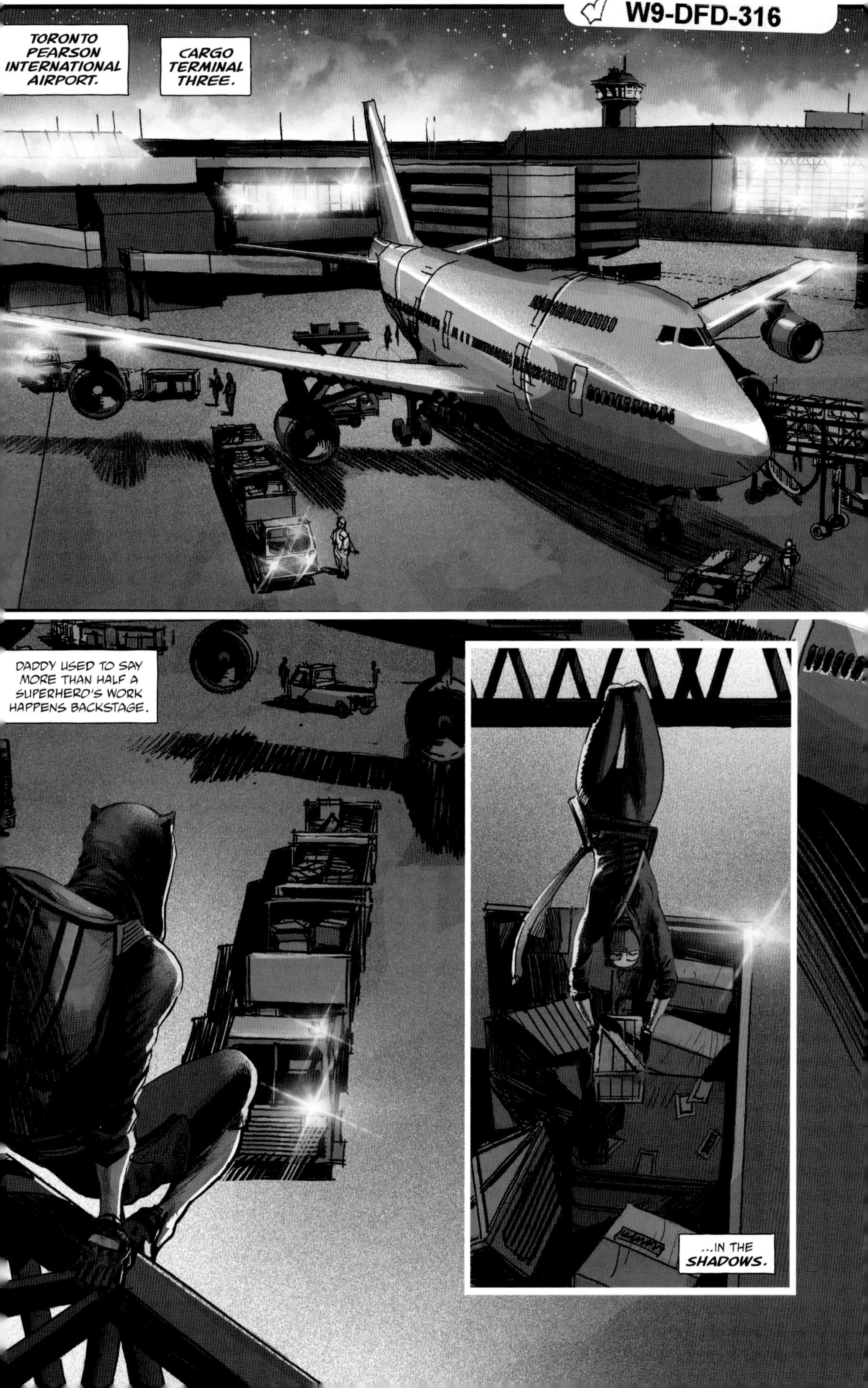
TORONTO PEARSON INTERNATIONAL AIRPORT.
CARGO TERMINAL THREE.
DADDY USED TO SAY MORE THAN HALF A SUPERHERO'S WORK HAPPENS BACKSTAGE.
...IN THE SHADOWS.

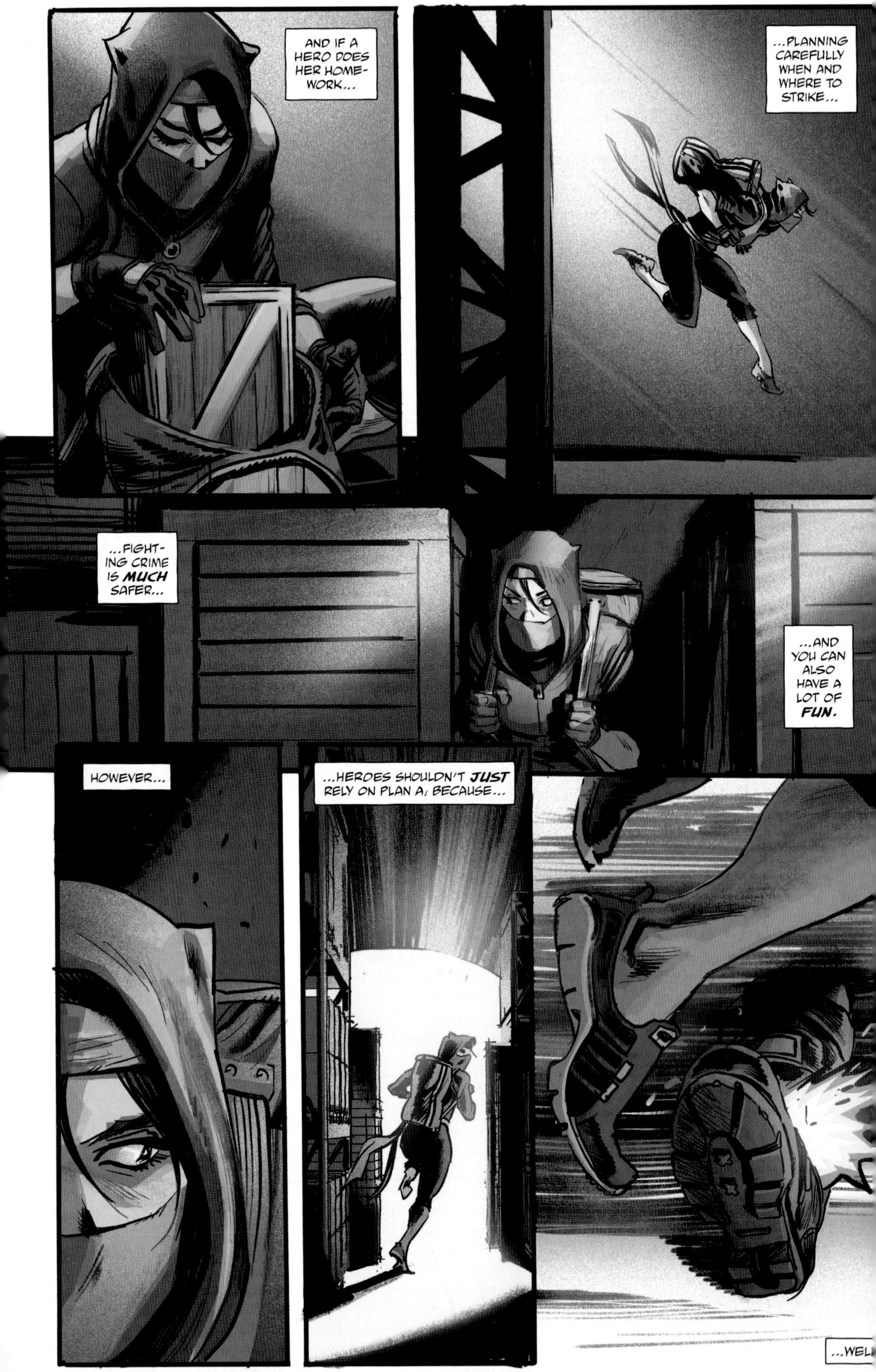
AND IF A HERO DOES HER HOME-WORK...
...PLANNING CAREFULLY WHEN AND WHERE TO STRIKE...
...FIGHT-ING CRIME IS MUCH SAFER...
...AND YOU CAN ALSO HAVE A LOT OF FUN.
HOWEVER...
...HEROES SHOULDN'T JUST RELY ON PLAN A, BECAUSE...
...WEL

HIT-GIRL
IN ROME

RAFAEL ALBUQUERQUE ARTIST AND WRITER

RAFAEL SCAVONE WRITER

MARCELO MAIOLO COLORIST

CLEM ROBINS LETTERER

MELINA MIKULIC DESIGN AND PRODUCTION

RACHAEL FULTON EDITOR

HIT-GIRL and **KICK-ASS** created by **MARK MILLAR** and **JOHN ROMITA JR.**

IMAGE COMICS, INC.

Robert Kirkman — Chief Operating Officer
Erik Larsen — Chief Financial Officer
Todd McFarlane — President
Marc Silvestri — Chief Executive Officer
Jim Valentino — Vice President

Eric Stephenson — Publisher / Chief Creative Officer
Corey Hart — Director of Sales
Jeff Boison — Director of Publishing Planning
   & Book Trade Sales
Chris Ross — Director of Digital Sales
Jeff Stang — Director of Specialty Sales
Kat Salazar — Director of PR & Marketing
Drew Gill — Art Director
Heather Doornink — Production Director
Nicole Lapalme — Controller

IMAGECOMICS.COM

ONE

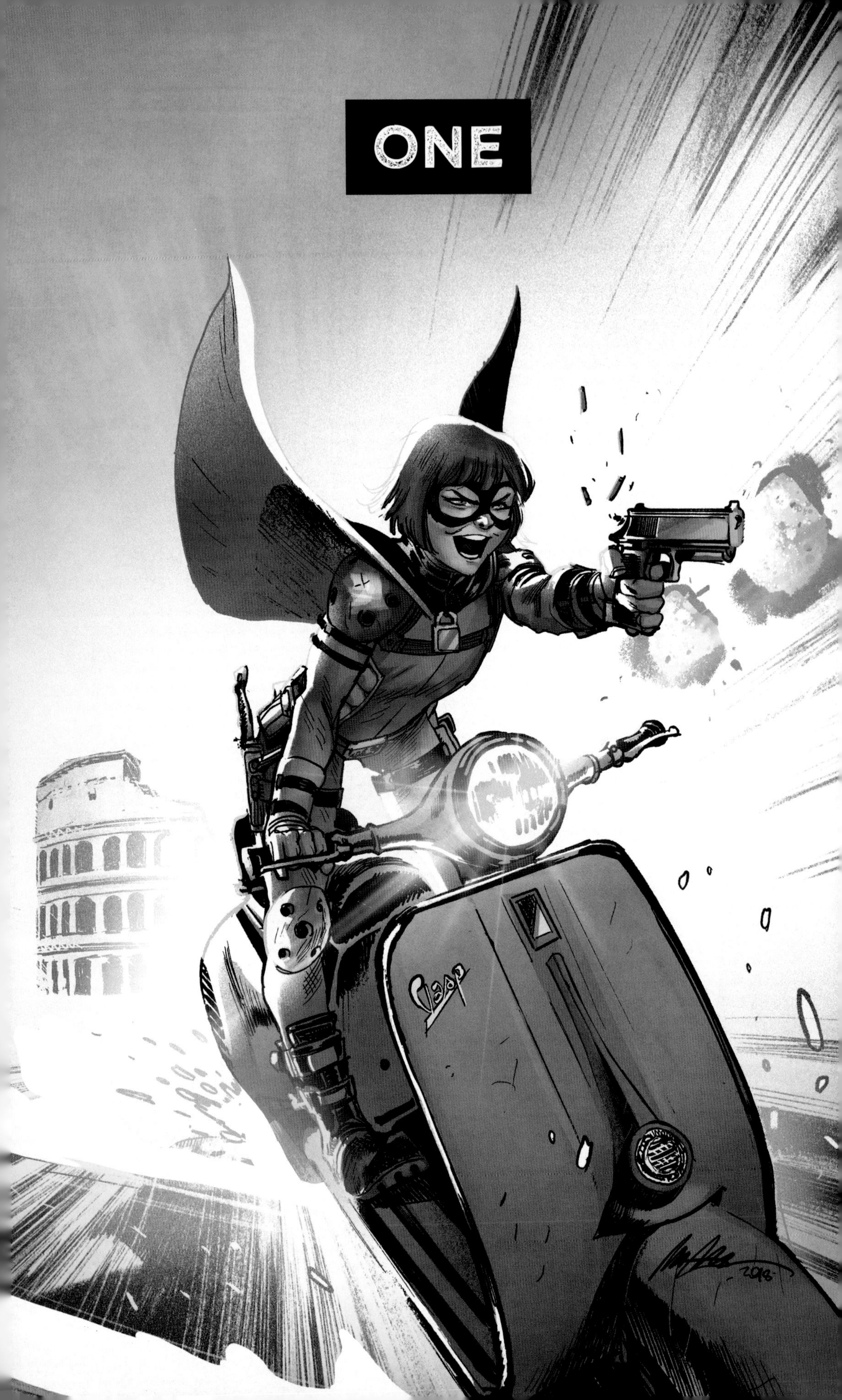

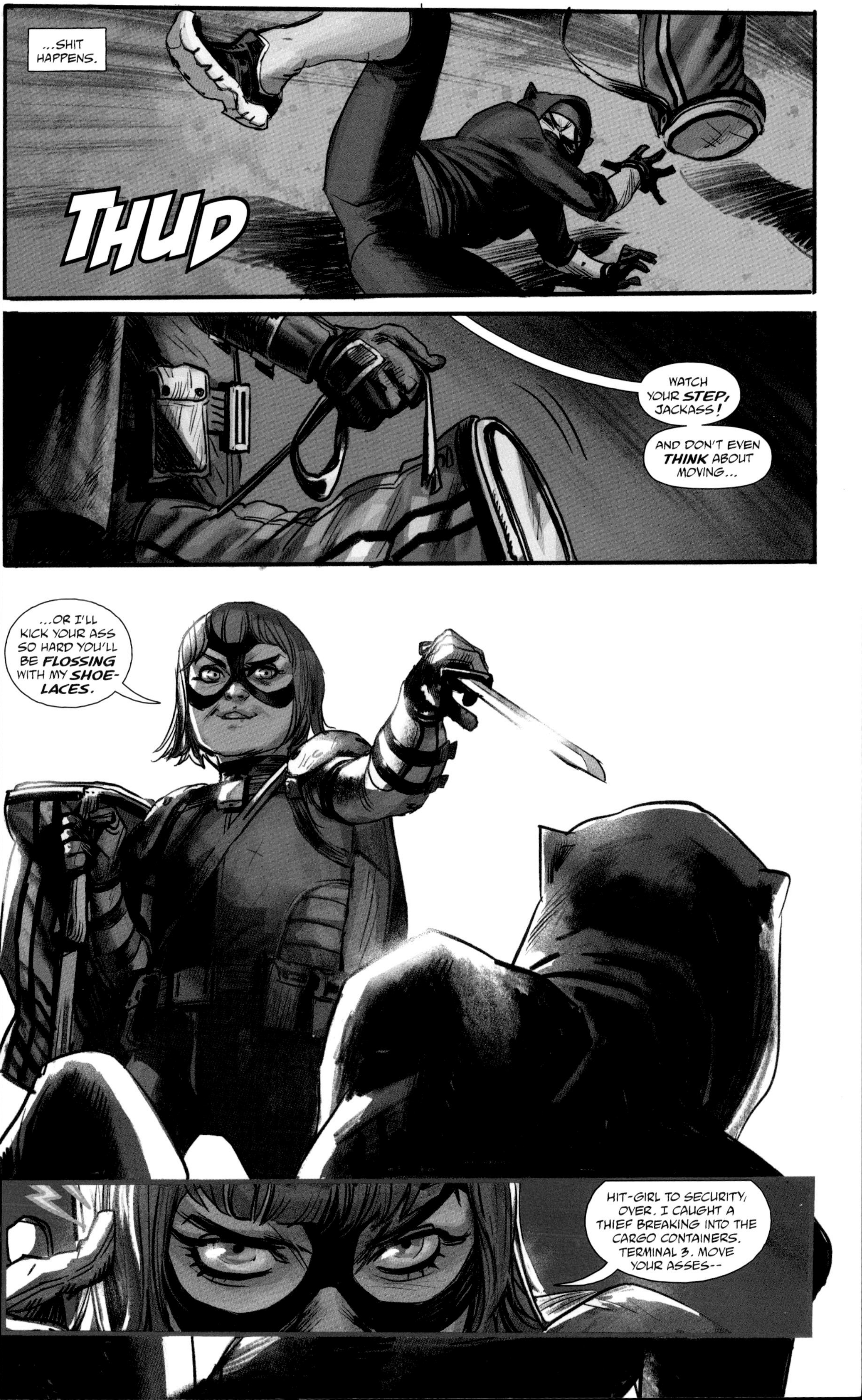
...SHIT HAPPENS.
THUD
WATCH YOUR STEP, JACKASS!
AND DON'T EVEN THINK ABOUT MOVING...
...OR I'LL KICK YOUR ASS SO HARD YOU'LL BE FLOSSING WITH MY SHOE-LACES.
HIT-GIRL TO SECURITY, OVER. I CAUGHT A THIEF BREAKING INTO THE CARGO CONTAINERS. TERMINAL 3. MOVE YOUR ASSES--

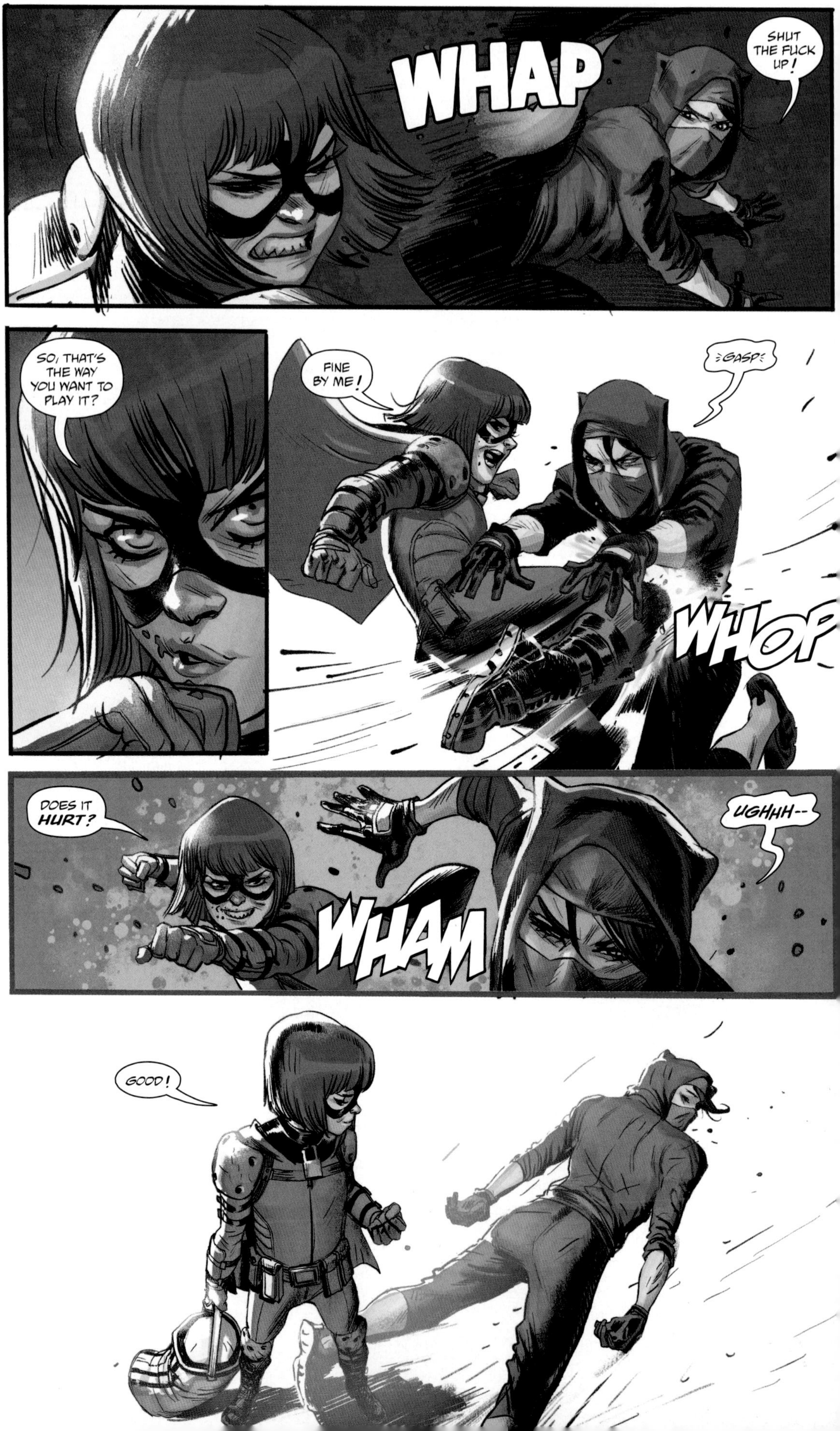
WHAP
SHUT THE FUCK UP!
SO, THAT'S THE WAY YOU WANT TO PLAY IT?
FINE BY ME!
GASP
WHOP
DOES IT HURT?
UGHHH--
WHAM
GOOD!

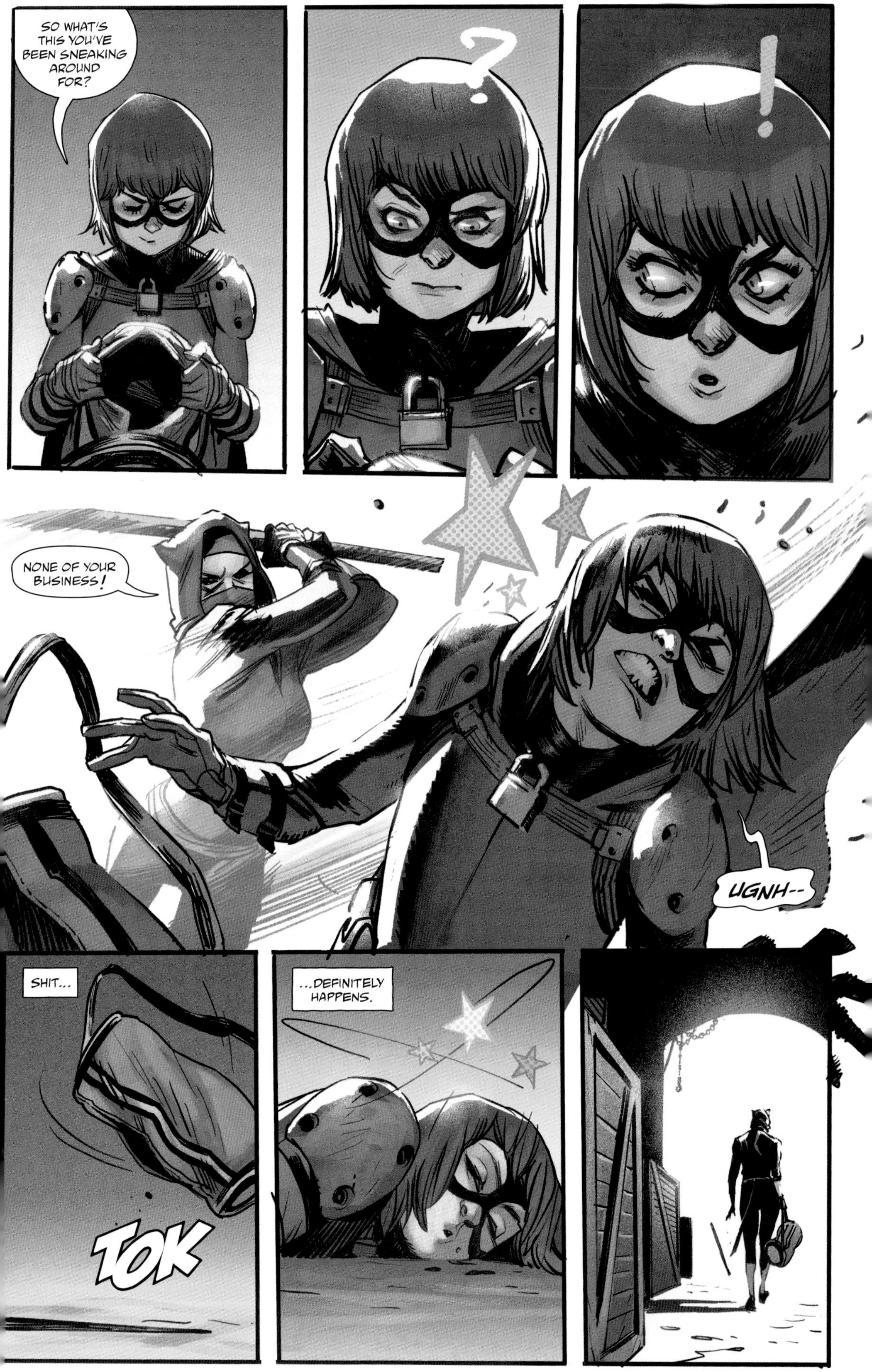
SO WHAT'S THIS YOU'VE BEEN SNEAKING AROUND FOR?
?
!
NONE OF YOUR BUSINESS!
UGNH--
SHIT...
TOK
...DEFINITELY HAPPENS.

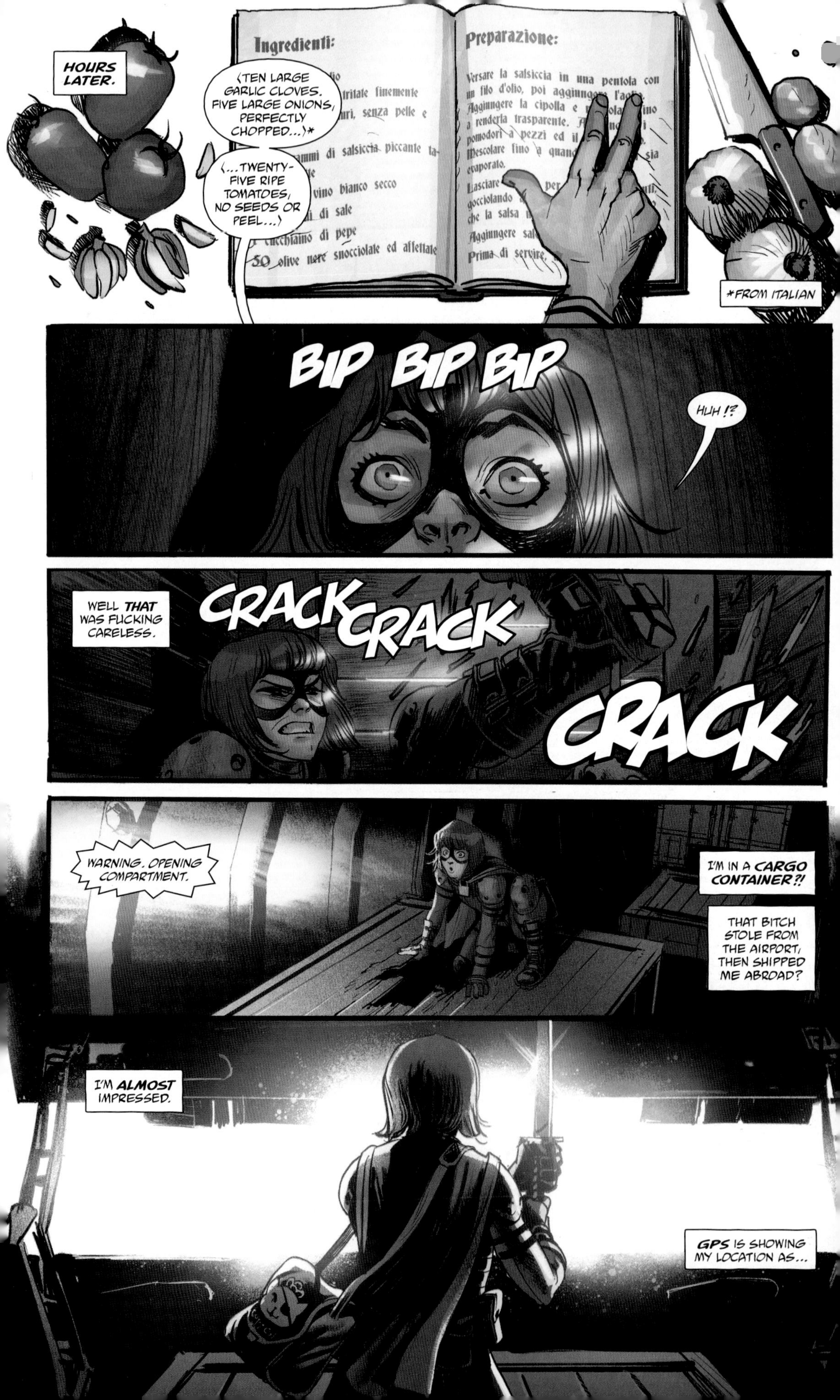

HOURS LATER.
Ingredienti:
Preparazione:
‹TEN LARGE GARLIC CLOVES. FIVE LARGE ONIONS, PERFECTLY CHOPPED...›*
‹...TWENTY-FIVE RIPE TOMATOES, NO SEEDS OR PEEL...›
*FROM ITALIAN
BIP BIP BIP
HUH !?
WELL THAT WAS FUCKING CARELESS.
CRACK CRACK
CRACK
WARNING. OPENING COMPARTMENT.
I'M IN A CARGO CONTAINER?!
THAT BITCH STOLE FROM THE AIRPORT, THEN SHIPPED ME ABROAD?
I'M ALMOST IMPRESSED.
GPS IS SHOWING MY LOCATION AS...

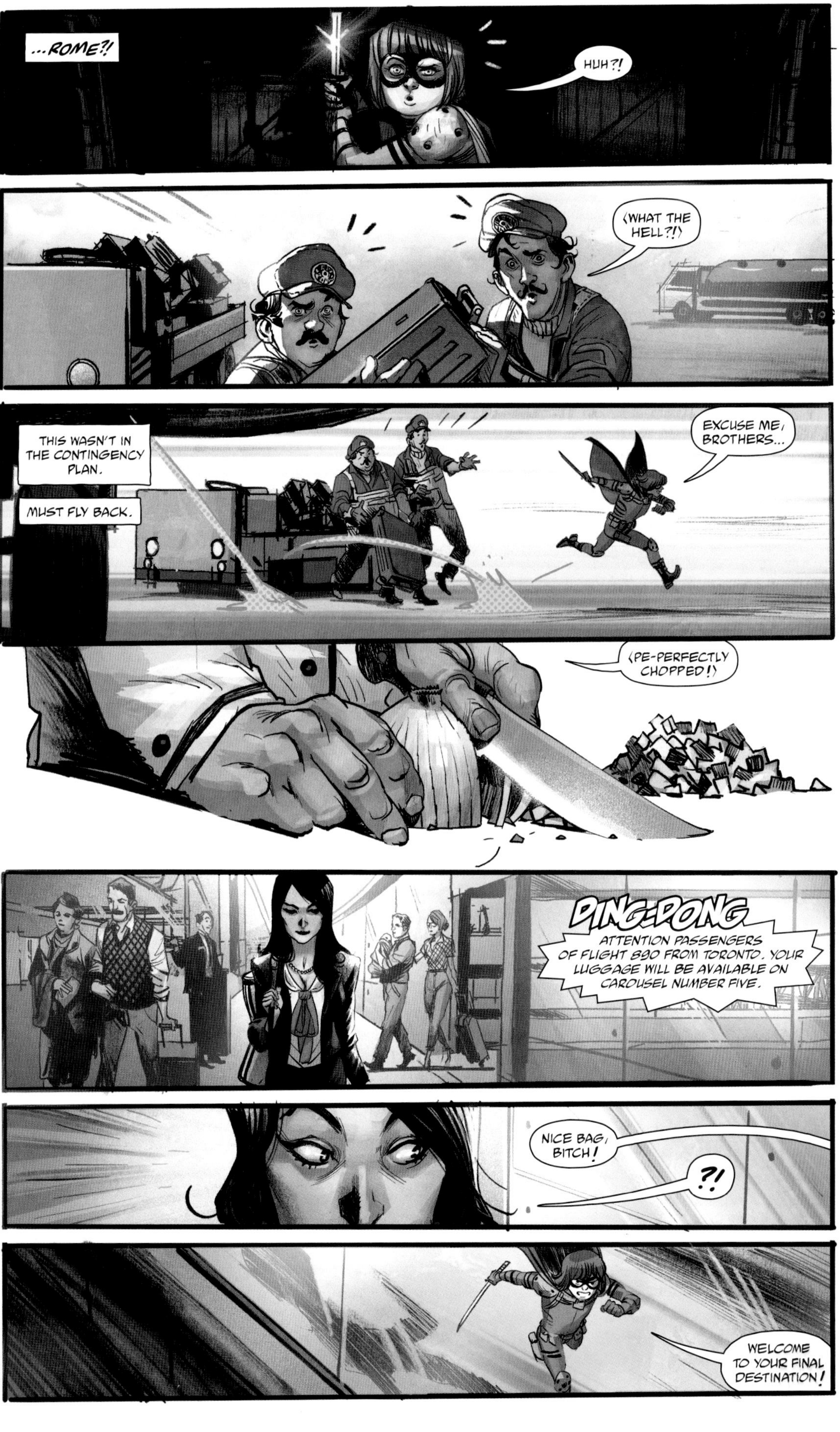

...ROME?!
HUH?!
⟨WHAT THE HELL?!⟩
THIS WASN'T IN THE CONTINGENCY PLAN.
MUST FLY BACK.
EXCUSE ME, BROTHERS...
⟨PE-PERFECTLY CHOPPED!⟩
DING-DONG
ATTENTION PASSENGERS OF FLIGHT 890 FROM TORONTO. YOUR LUGGAGE WILL BE AVAILABLE ON CAROUSEL NUMBER FIVE.
NICE BAG, BITCH!
?!
WELCOME TO YOUR FINAL DESTINATION!

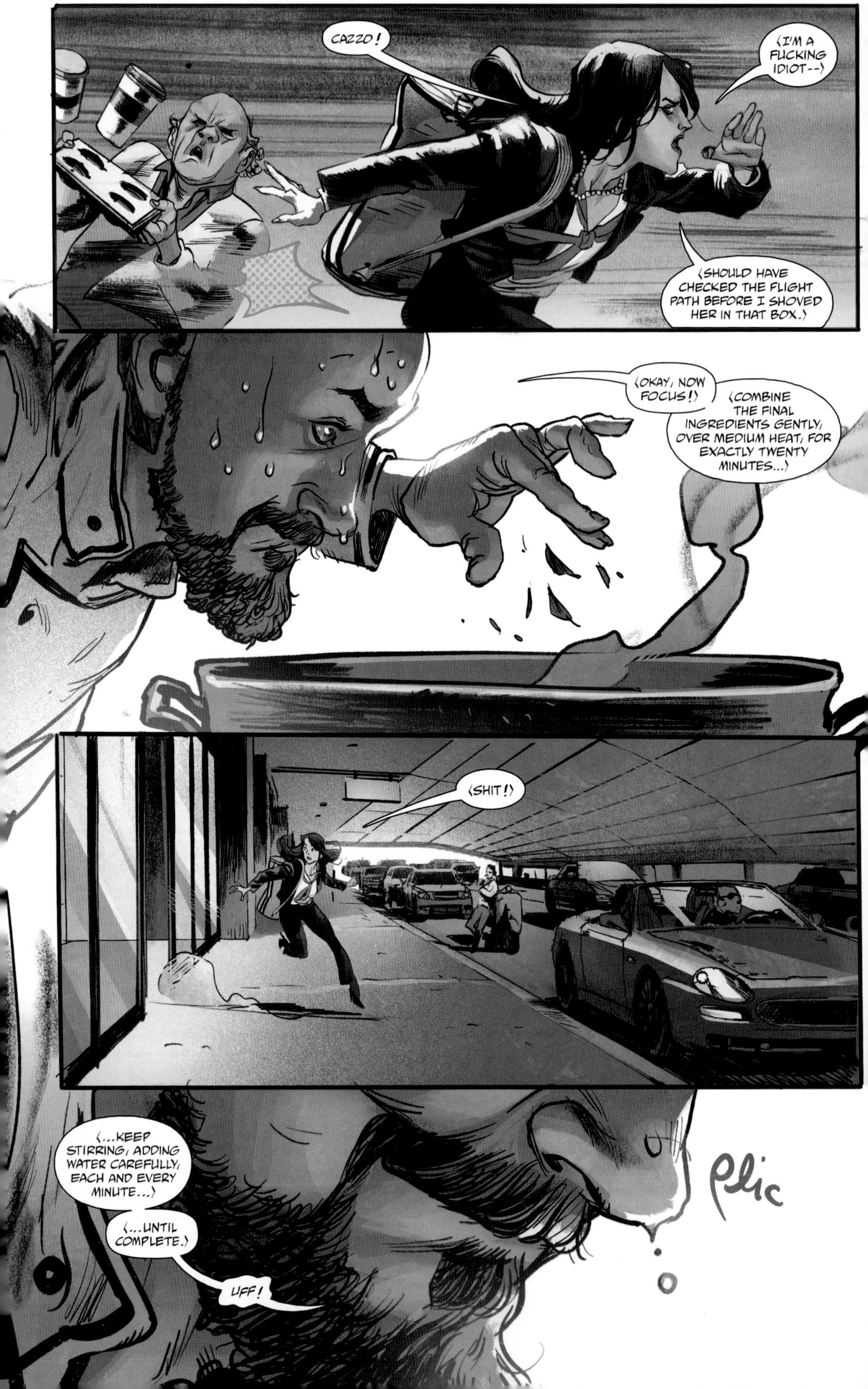
CAZZO!
⟨I'M A FUCKING IDIOT--⟩
⟨SHOULD HAVE CHECKED THE FLIGHT PATH BEFORE I SHOVED HER IN THAT BOX.⟩
⟨OKAY, NOW FOCUS!⟩
⟨COMBINE THE FINAL INGREDIENTS GENTLY, OVER MEDIUM HEAT, FOR EXACTLY TWENTY MINUTES...⟩
⟨SHIT!⟩
⟨...KEEP STIRRING, ADDING WATER CAREFULLY, EACH AND EVERY MINUTE...⟩
⟨...UNTIL COMPLETE.⟩
UFF!
Plic

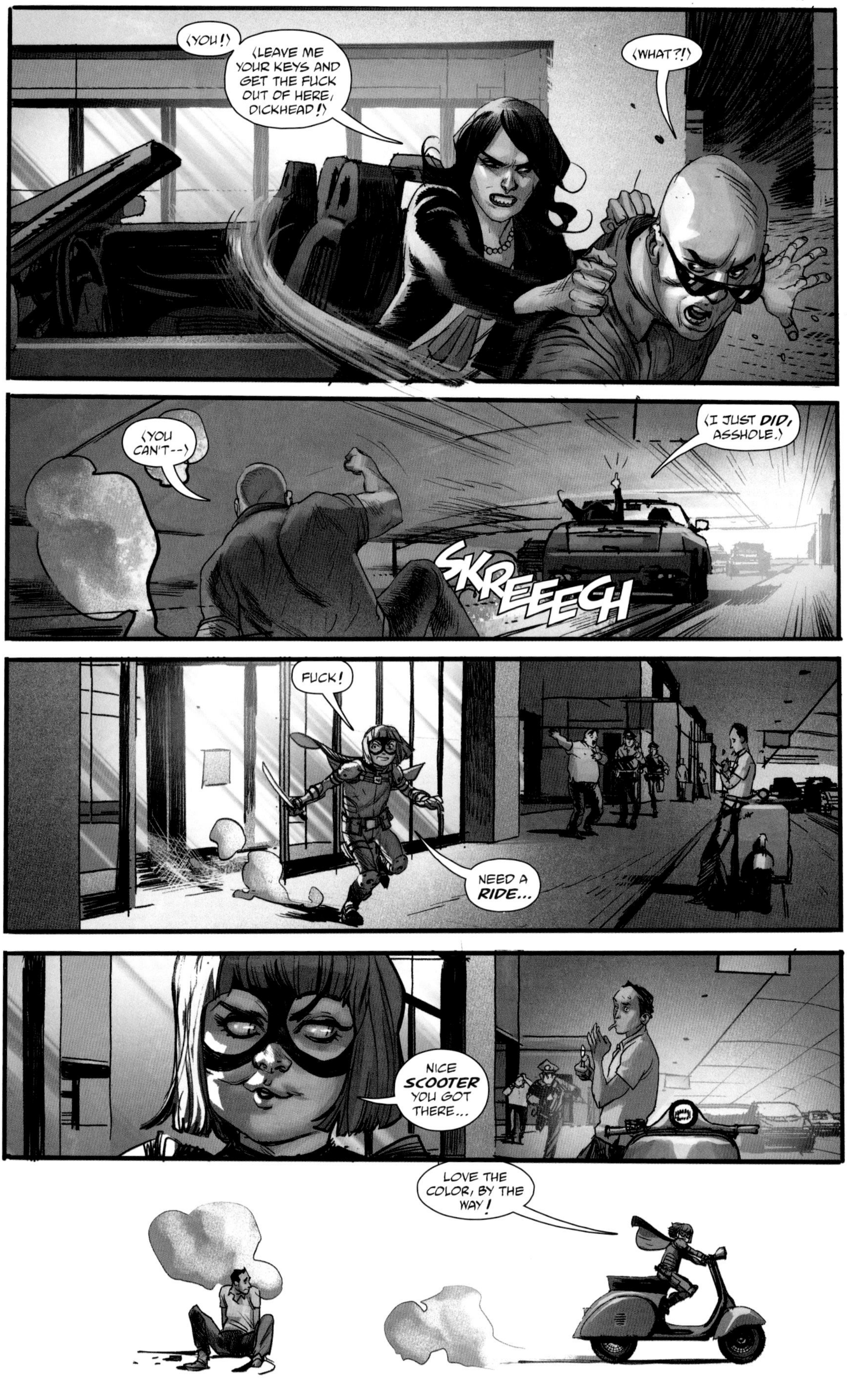

⟨YOU!⟩
⟨LEAVE ME YOUR KEYS AND GET THE FUCK OUT OF HERE, DICKHEAD!⟩
⟨WHAT?!⟩
⟨YOU CAN'T--⟩
⟨I JUST DID, ASSHOLE.⟩
SKREEEECH
FUCK!
NEED A RIDE...
NICE SCOOTER YOU GOT THERE...
LOVE THE COLOR, BY THE WAY!

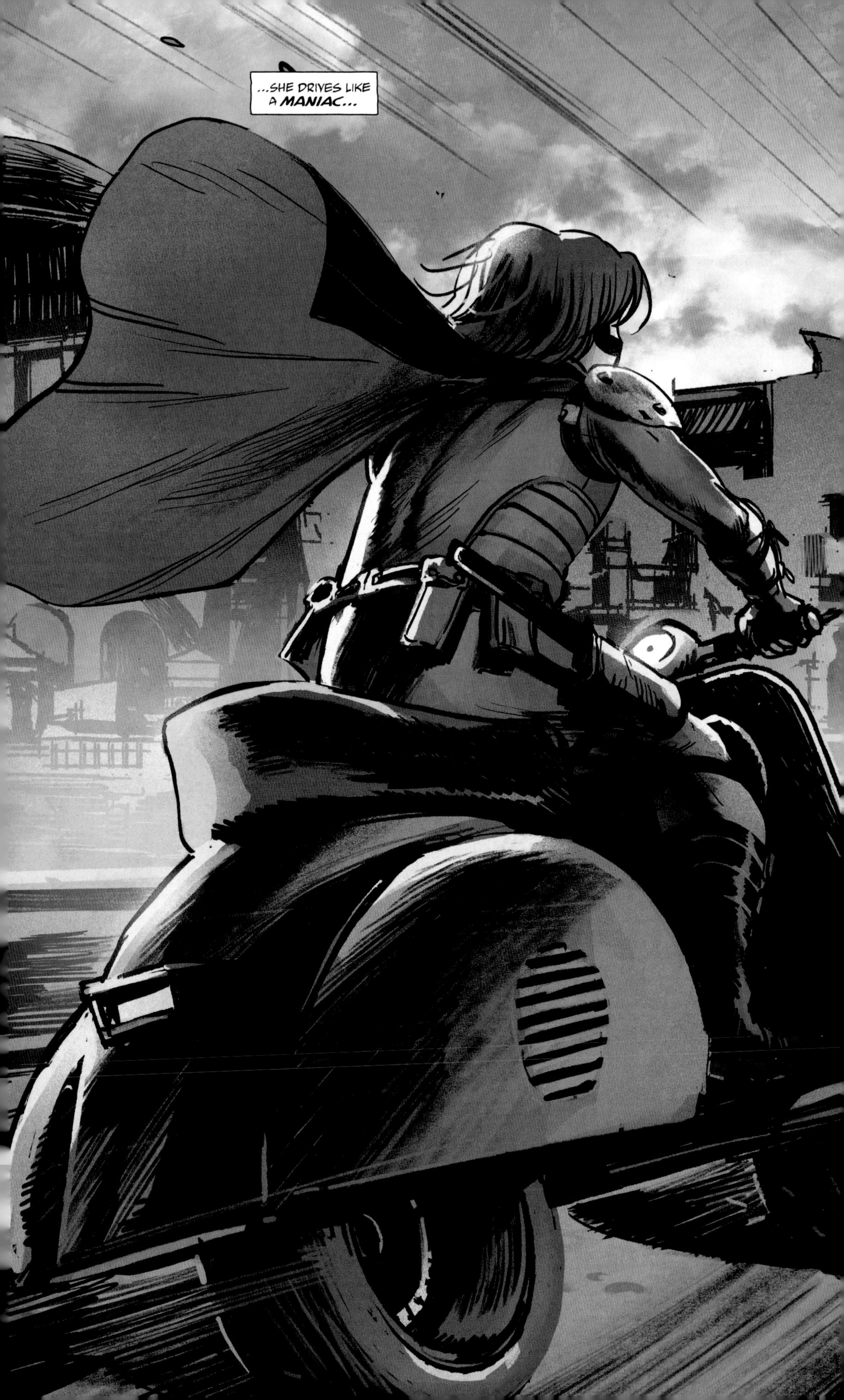
...SHE DRIVES LIKE A MANIAC...

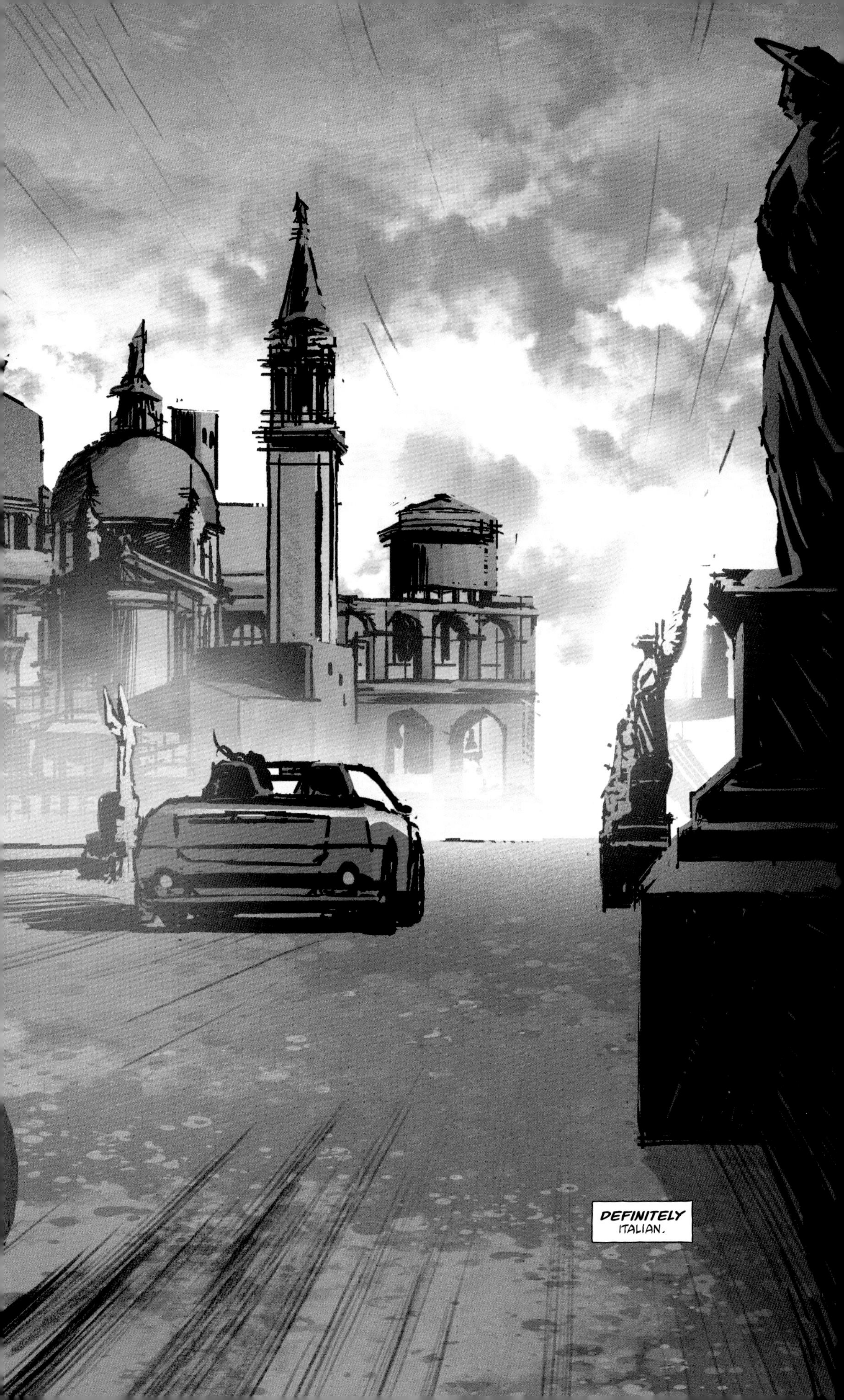
DEFINITELY ITALIAN.

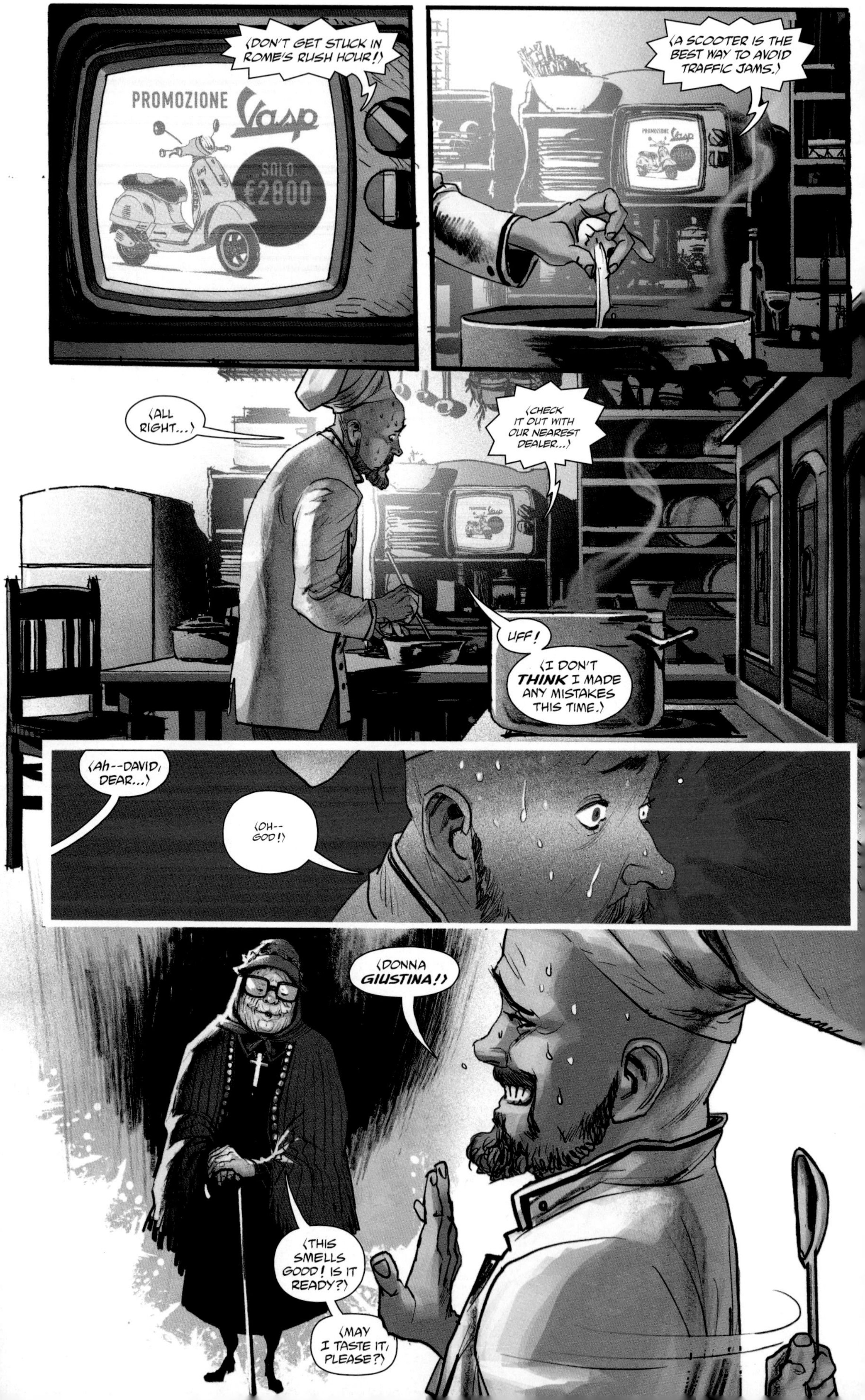
PROMOZIONE Vasp
SOLO €2800
‹DON'T GET STUCK IN ROME'S RUSH HOUR!›
‹A SCOOTER IS THE BEST WAY TO AVOID TRAFFIC JAMS.›
‹ALL RIGHT...›
‹CHECK IT OUT WITH OUR NEAREST DEALER...›
UFF!
‹I DON'T THINK I MADE ANY MISTAKES THIS TIME.›
‹Ah--DAVID, DEAR...›
‹OH--GOD!›
‹DONNA GIUSTINA!›
‹THIS SMELLS GOOD! IS IT READY?›
‹MAY I TASTE IT, PLEASE?›

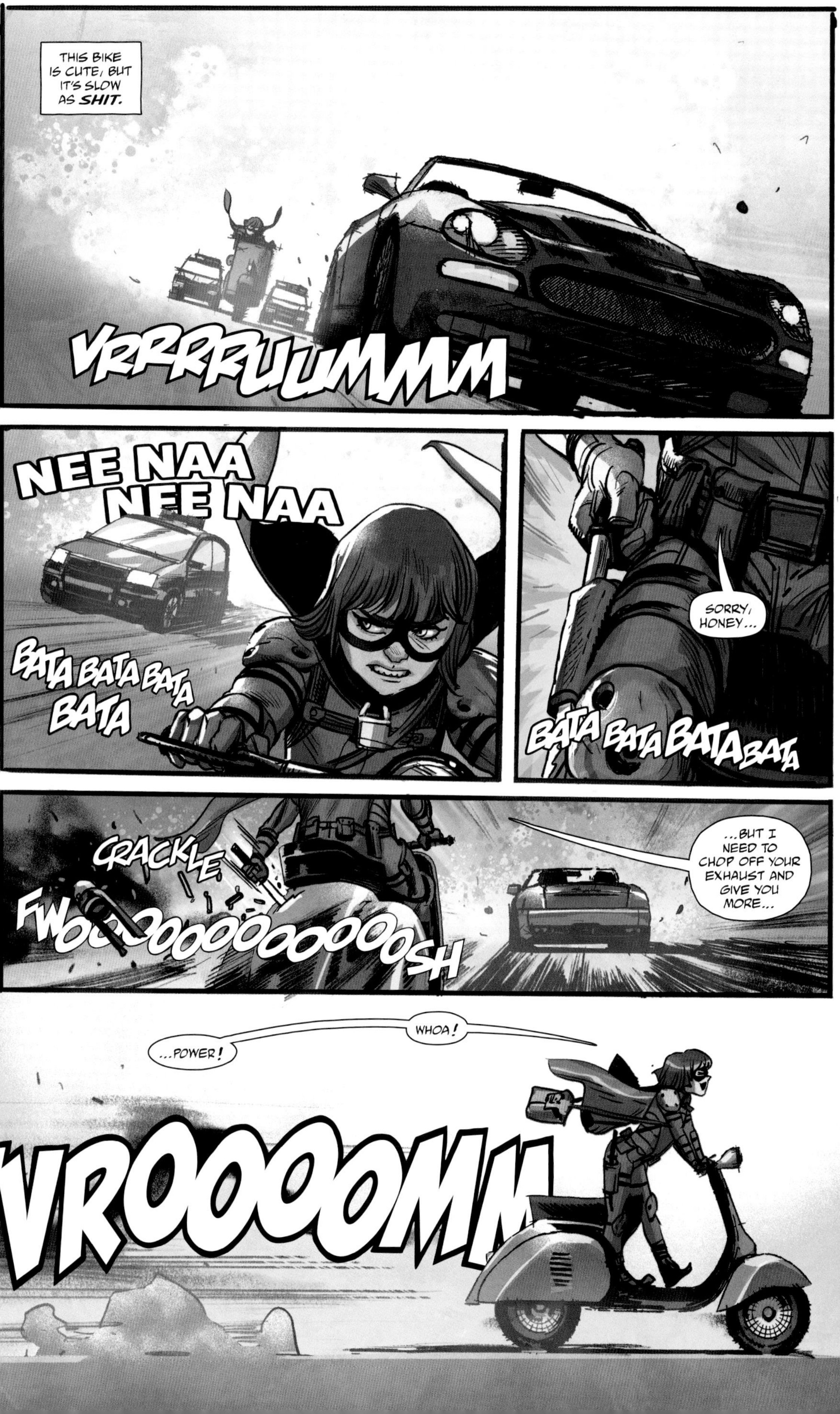

THIS BIKE IS CUTE, BUT IT'S SLOW AS SHIT.
VRRRRUUMMM
NEE NAA NEE NAA
BATA BATA BATA BATA BATA
SORRY, HONEY...
BATA BATA BATA BATA
CRACKLE
FWOOOOOOOOOOOOOSH
...BUT I NEED TO CHOP OFF YOUR EXHAUST AND GIVE YOU MORE...
...POWER!
WHOA!
VROOOOMM

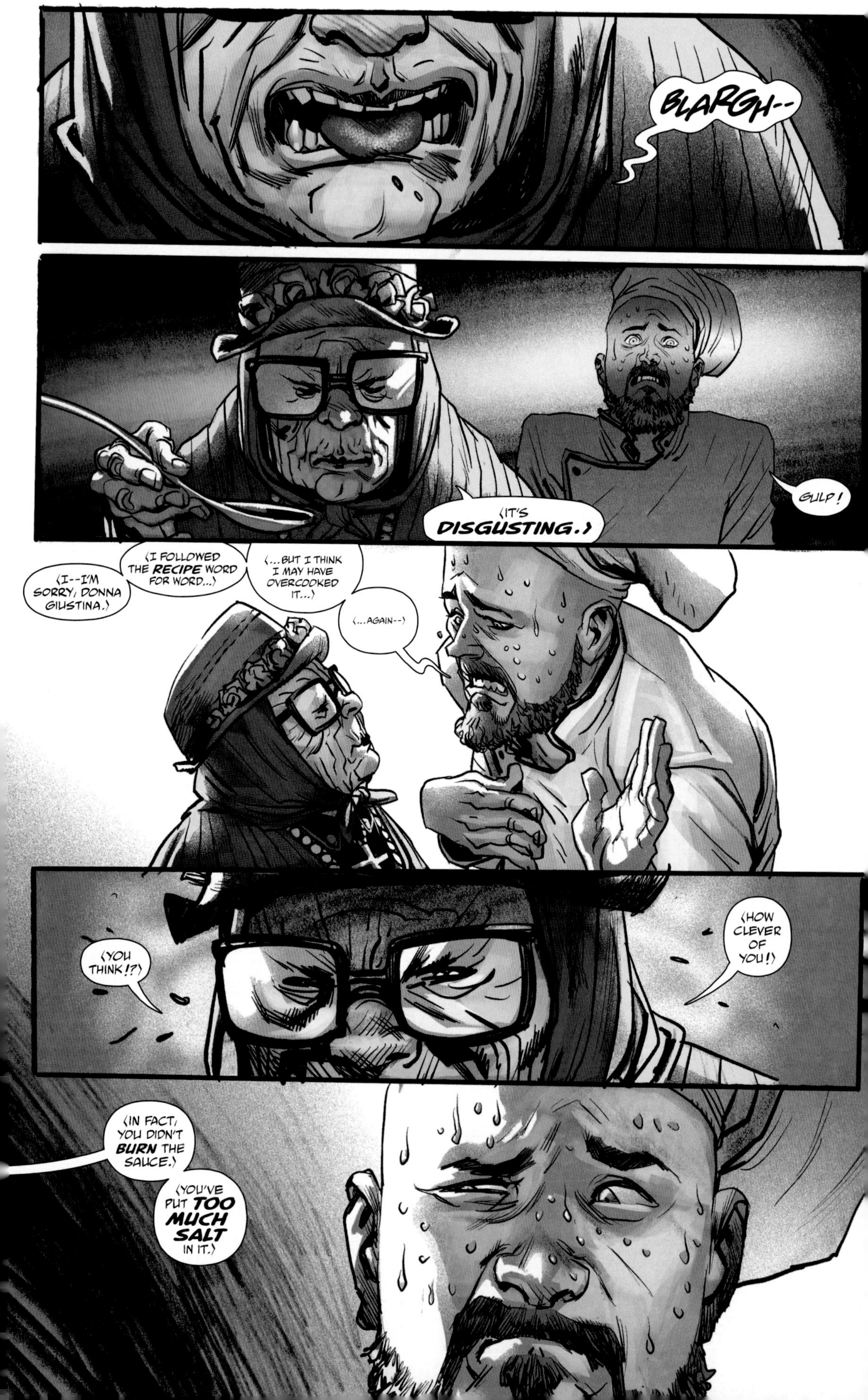
BLARGH--
GULP!
‹IT'S DISGUSTING.›
‹I--I'M SORRY, DONNA GIUSTINA.›
‹I FOLLOWED THE RECIPE WORD FOR WORD...›
‹...BUT I THINK I MAY HAVE OVERCOOKED IT...›
‹...AGAIN--›
‹YOU THINK!?›
‹HOW CLEVER OF YOU!›
‹IN FACT, YOU DIDN'T BURN THE SAUCE.›
‹YOU'VE PUT TOO MUCH SALT IN IT.›

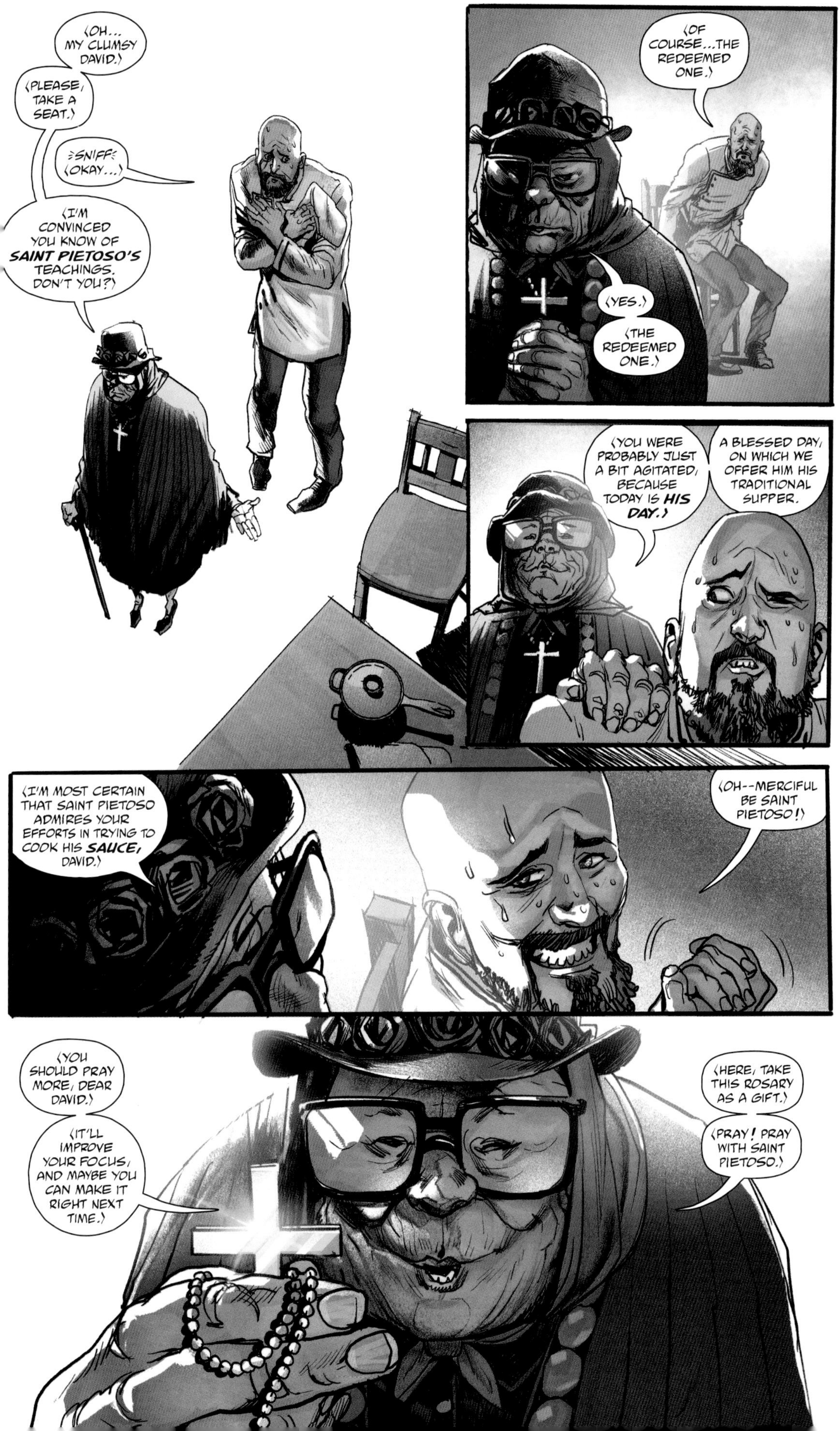
‹OH... MY CLUMSY DAVID.›
‹PLEASE, TAKE A SEAT.›
≈SNIFF≈ ‹OKAY...›
‹I'M CONVINCED YOU KNOW OF SAINT PIETOSO'S TEACHINGS. DON'T YOU?›
‹OF COURSE...THE REDEEMED ONE.›
‹YES.›
‹THE REDEEMED ONE.›
‹YOU WERE PROBABLY JUST A BIT AGITATED, BECAUSE TODAY IS HIS DAY.›
A BLESSED DAY, ON WHICH WE OFFER HIM HIS TRADITIONAL SUPPER.
‹I'M MOST CERTAIN THAT SAINT PIETOSO ADMIRES YOUR EFFORTS IN TRYING TO COOK HIS SAUCE, DAVID.›
‹OH--MERCIFUL BE SAINT PIETOSO!›
‹YOU SHOULD PRAY MORE, DEAR DAVID.›
‹IT'LL IMPROVE YOUR FOCUS, AND MAYBE YOU CAN MAKE IT RIGHT NEXT TIME.›
‹HERE, TAKE THIS ROSARY AS A GIFT.›
‹PRAY! PRAY WITH SAINT PIETOSO.›

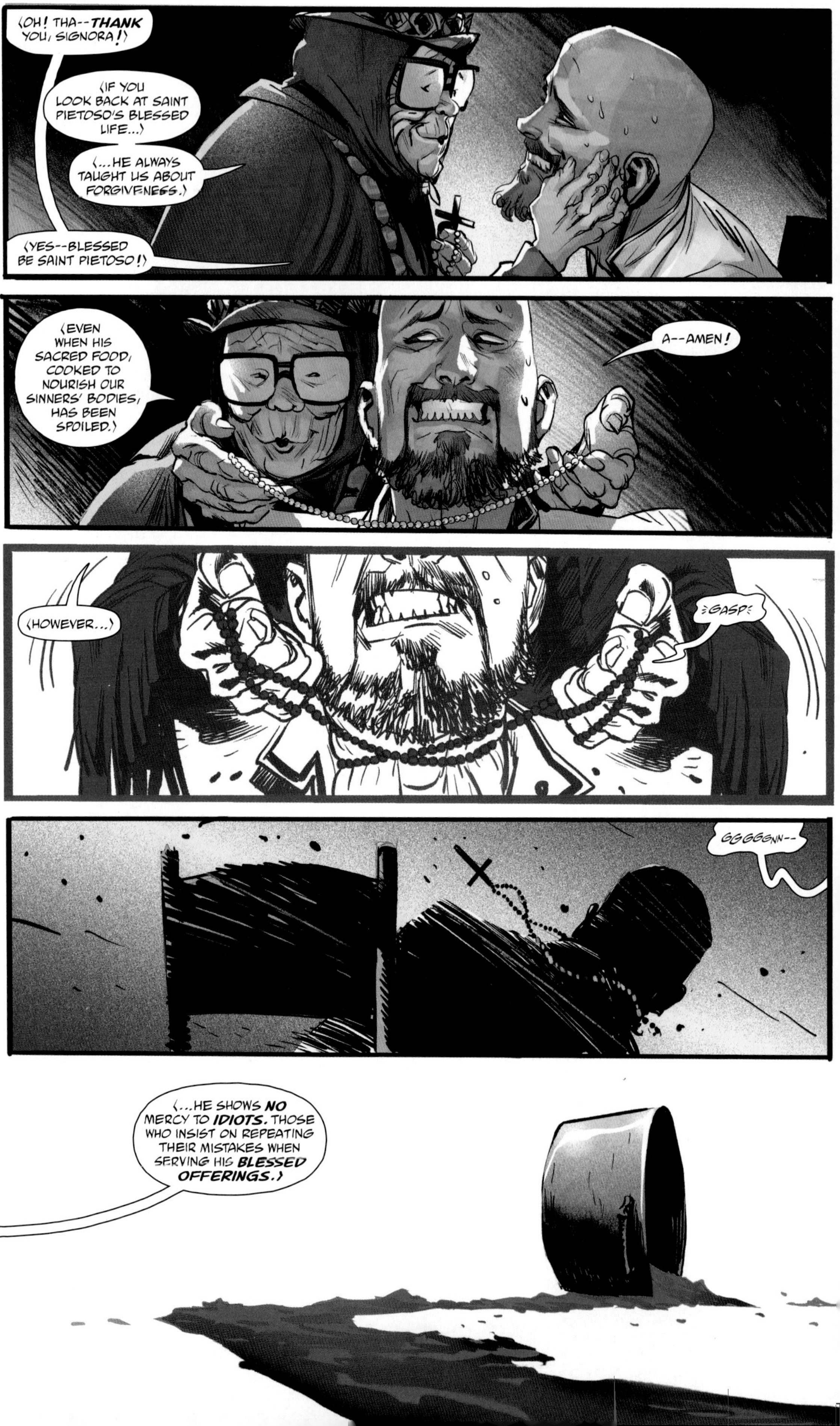
‹OH! THA--THANK YOU, SIGNORA!›
‹IF YOU LOOK BACK AT SAINT PIETOSO'S BLESSED LIFE...›
‹...HE ALWAYS TAUGHT US ABOUT FORGIVENESS.›
‹YES--BLESSED BE SAINT PIETOSO!›
‹EVEN WHEN HIS SACRED FOOD, COOKED TO NOURISH OUR SINNERS' BODIES, HAS BEEN SPOILED.›
A--AMEN!
‹HOWEVER...›
GASP
GGGGGNN--
‹...HE SHOWS NO MERCY TO IDIOTS. THOSE WHO INSIST ON REPEATING THEIR MISTAKES WHEN SERVING HIS BLESSED OFFERINGS.›

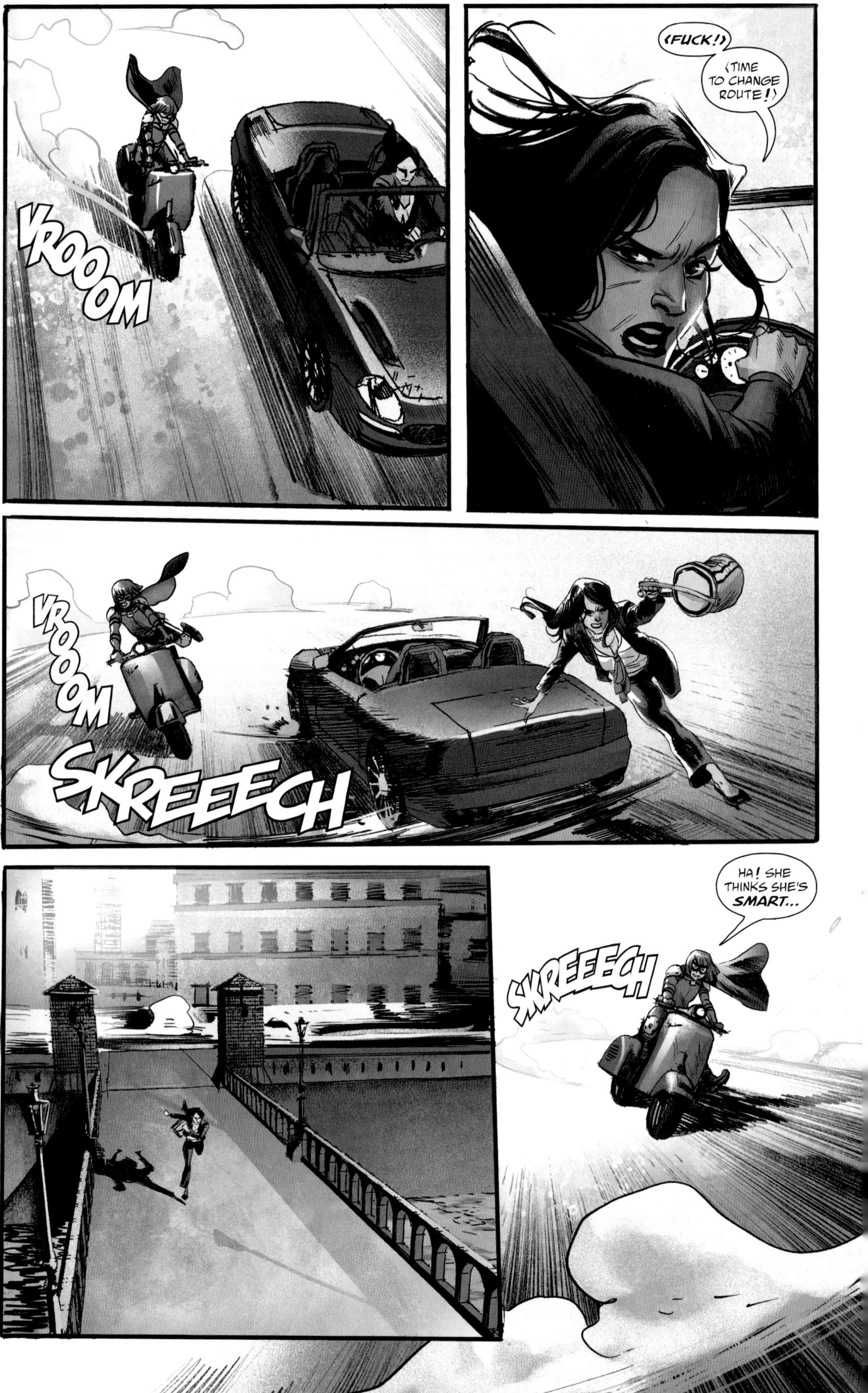
VROOOM
‹FUCK!›
‹TIME TO CHANGE ROUTE!›
VROOOM
SKREEECH
HA! SHE THINKS SHE'S SMART...
SKREEECH

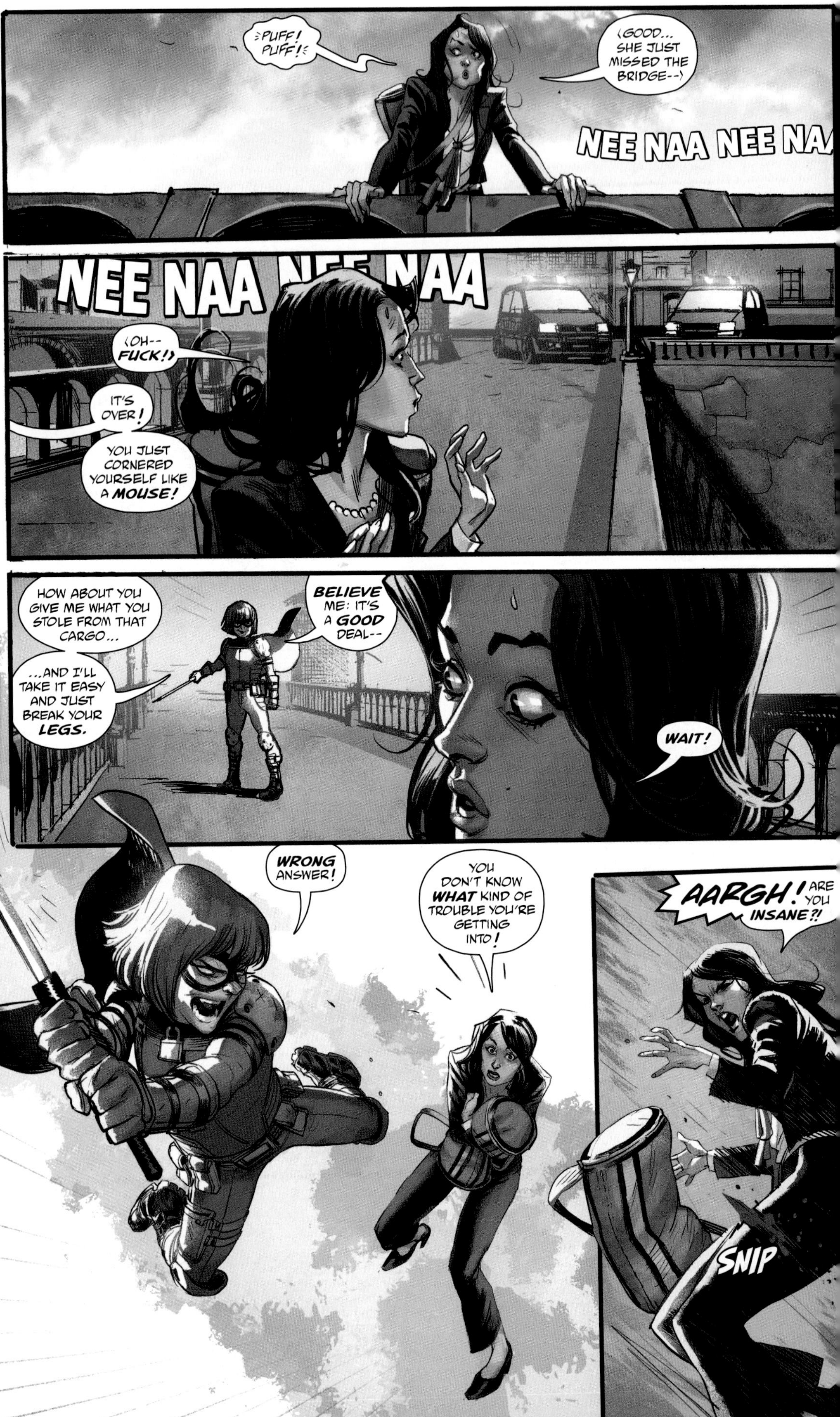

PUFF! PUFF!
(GOOD... SHE JUST MISSED THE BRIDGE--)
NEE NAA NEE NAA
NEE NAA NEE NAA
(OH-- FUCK!)
IT'S OVER!
YOU JUST CORNERED YOURSELF LIKE A MOUSE!
HOW ABOUT YOU GIVE ME WHAT YOU STOLE FROM THAT CARGO...
...AND I'LL TAKE IT EASY AND JUST BREAK YOUR LEGS.
BELIEVE ME: IT'S A GOOD DEAL--
WAIT!
WRONG ANSWER!
YOU DON'T KNOW WHAT KIND OF TROUBLE YOU'RE GETTING INTO!
AARGH!
ARE YOU INSANE?!
SNIP

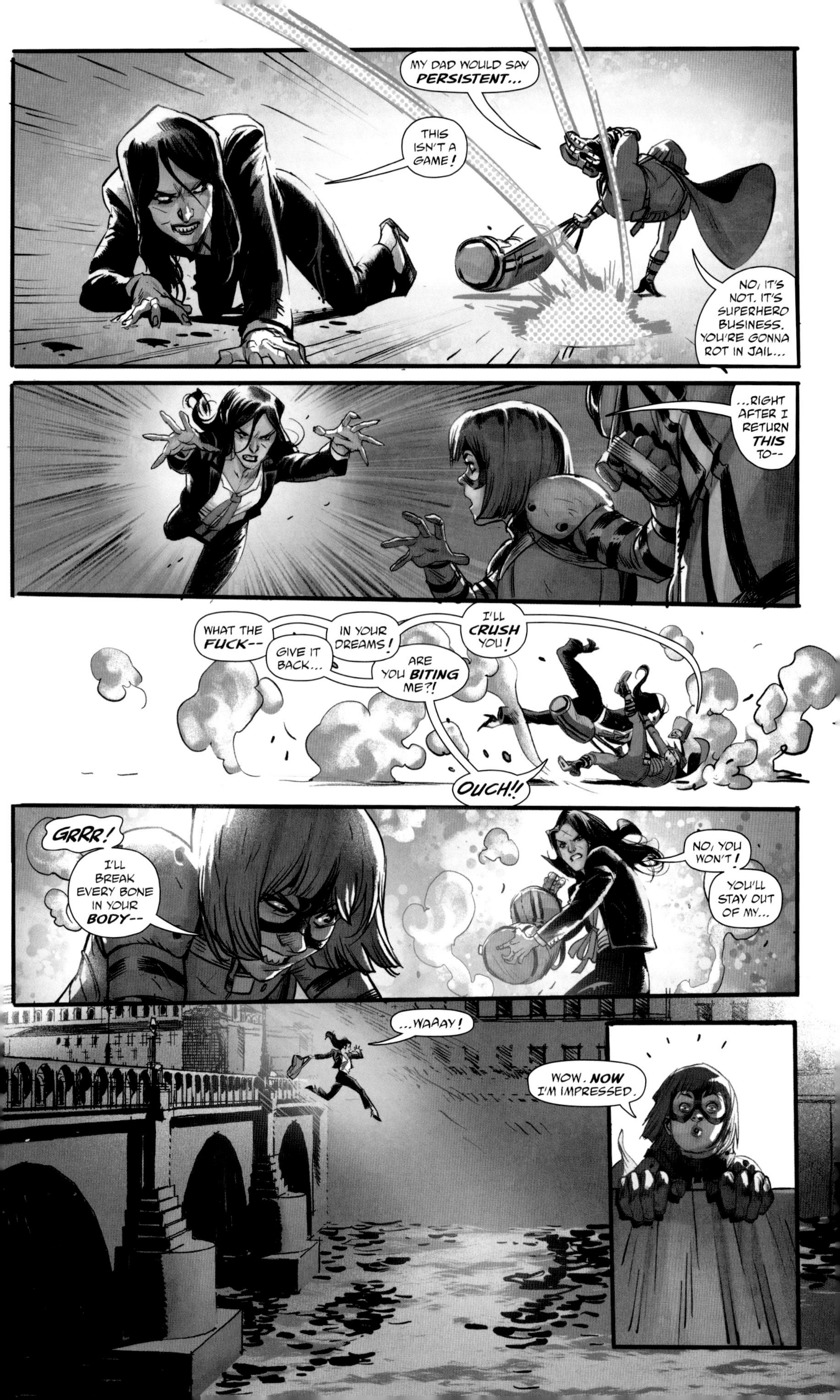
MY DAD WOULD SAY PERSISTENT...
THIS ISN'T A GAME!
NO, IT'S NOT. IT'S SUPERHERO BUSINESS. YOU'RE GONNA ROT IN JAIL...
...RIGHT AFTER I RETURN THIS TO--
WHAT THE FUCK--
GIVE IT BACK...
IN YOUR DREAMS!
ARE YOU BITING ME?!
I'LL CRUSH YOU!
OUCH!!
GRRR!
I'LL BREAK EVERY BONE IN YOUR BODY--
NO, YOU WON'T!
YOU'LL STAY OUT OF MY...
...WAAAY!
WOW. NOW I'M IMPRESSED.

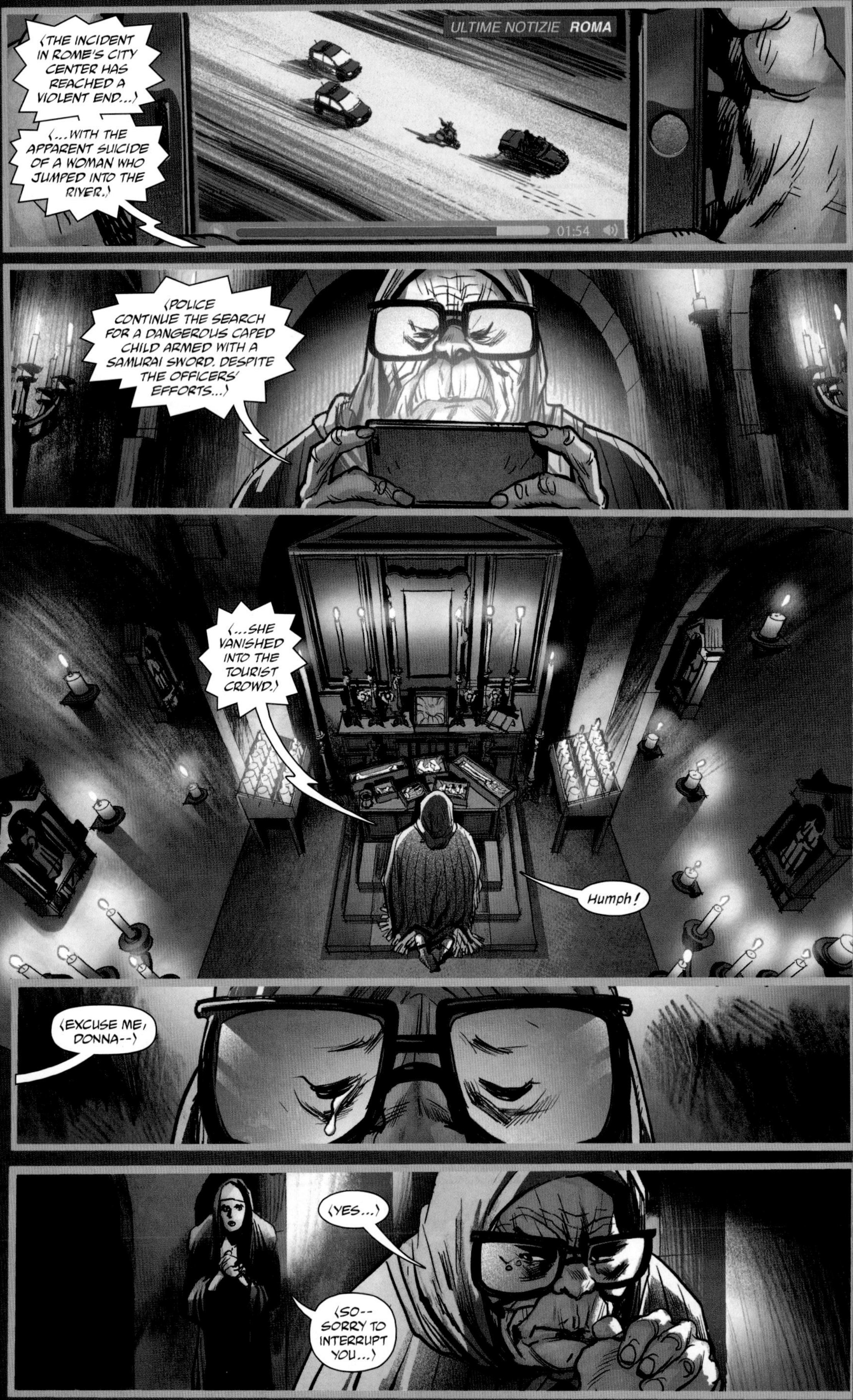
ULTIME NOTIZIE ROMA
01:54
⟨THE INCIDENT IN ROME'S CITY CENTER HAS REACHED A VIOLENT END...⟩
⟨...WITH THE APPARENT SUICIDE OF A WOMAN WHO JUMPED INTO THE RIVER.⟩
⟨POLICE CONTINUE THE SEARCH FOR A DANGEROUS CAPED CHILD ARMED WITH A SAMURAI SWORD. DESPITE THE OFFICERS' EFFORTS...⟩
⟨...SHE VANISHED INTO THE TOURIST CROWD.⟩
Humph!
⟨EXCUSE ME, DONNA--⟩
⟨YES...⟩
⟨SO-- SORRY TO INTERRUPT YOU...⟩

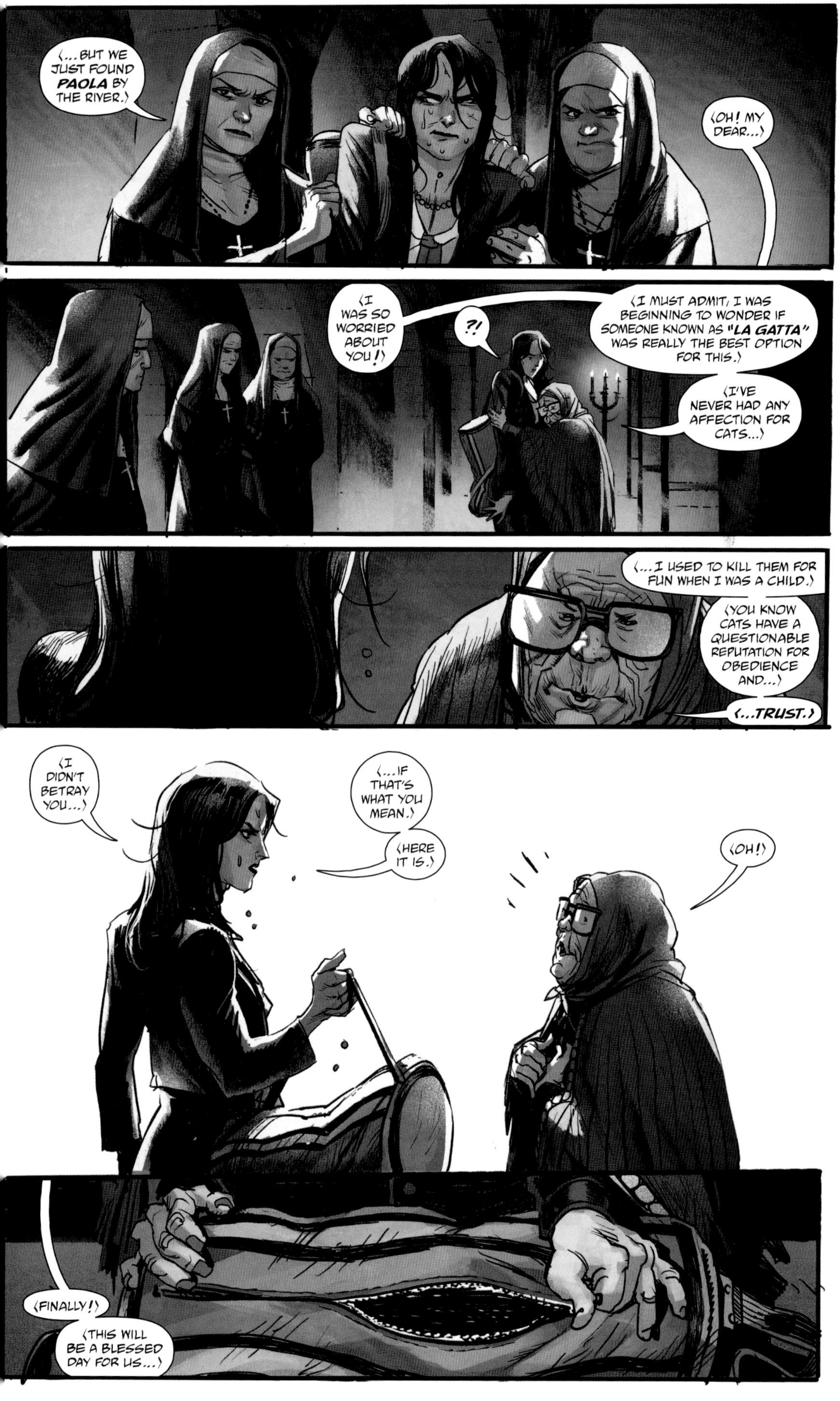

⟨...BUT WE JUST FOUND PAOLA BY THE RIVER.⟩
⟨OH! MY DEAR...⟩
⟨I WAS SO WORRIED ABOUT YOU!⟩
?!
⟨I MUST ADMIT, I WAS BEGINNING TO WONDER IF SOMEONE KNOWN AS "LA GATTA" WAS REALLY THE BEST OPTION FOR THIS.⟩
⟨I'VE NEVER HAD ANY AFFECTION FOR CATS...⟩
⟨...I USED TO KILL THEM FOR FUN WHEN I WAS A CHILD.⟩
⟨YOU KNOW CATS HAVE A QUESTIONABLE REPUTATION FOR OBEDIENCE AND...⟩
⟨...TRUST.⟩
⟨I DIDN'T BETRAY YOU...⟩
⟨...IF THAT'S WHAT YOU MEAN.⟩
⟨HERE IT IS.⟩
⟨OH!⟩
⟨FINALLY!⟩
⟨THIS WILL BE A BLESSED DAY FOR US...⟩

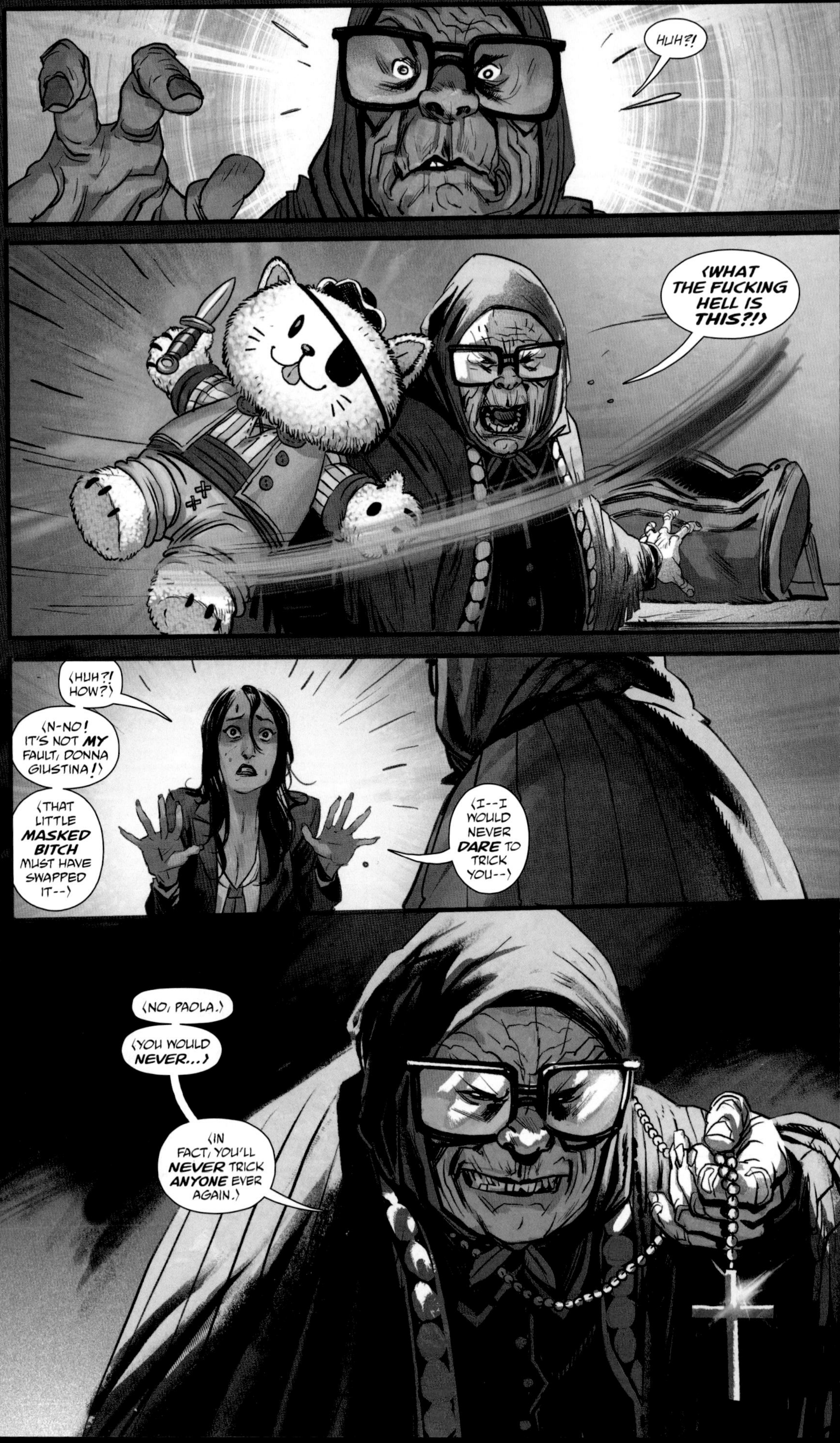
HUH?!
‹WHAT THE FUCKING HELL IS THIS?!›
‹HUH?! HOW?›
‹N-NO! IT'S NOT MY FAULT, DONNA GIUSTINA!›
‹THAT LITTLE MASKED BITCH MUST HAVE SWAPPED IT--›
‹I--I WOULD NEVER DARE TO TRICK YOU--›
‹NO, PAOLA.›
‹YOU WOULD NEVER...›
‹IN FACT, YOU'LL NEVER TRICK ANYONE EVER AGAIN.›

TWO

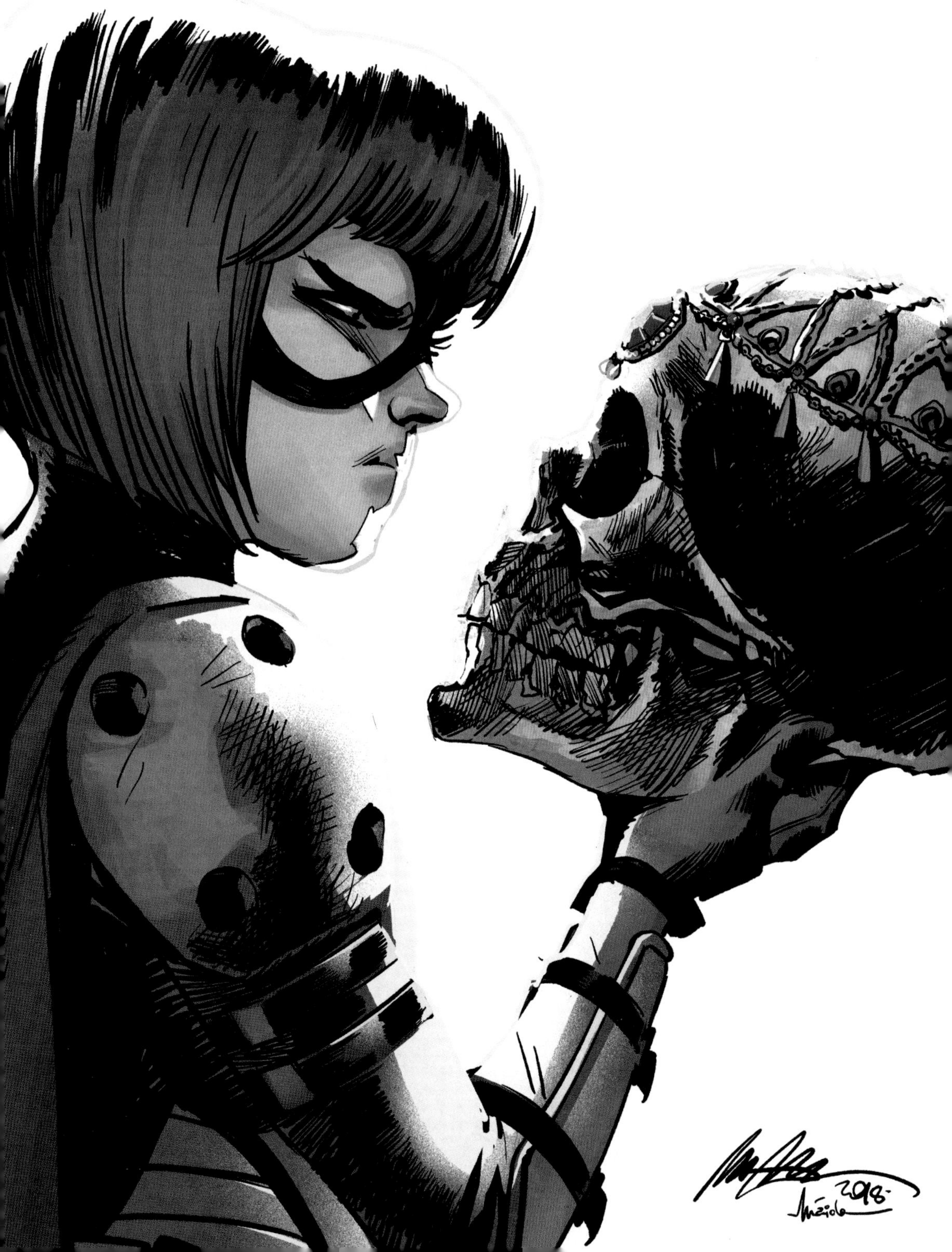

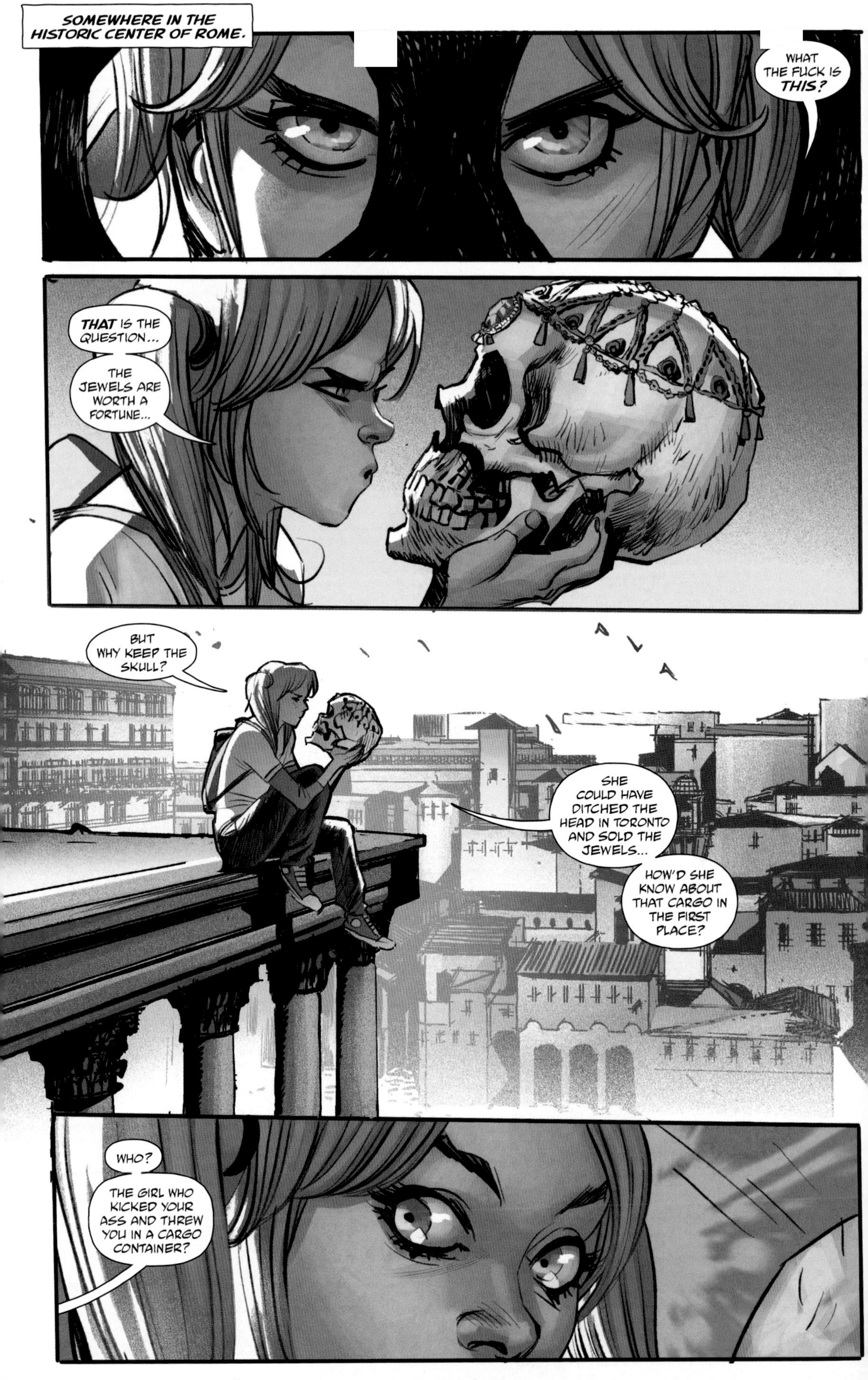
SOMEWHERE IN THE HISTORIC CENTER OF ROME.
WHAT THE FUCK IS THIS?
THAT IS THE QUESTION...
THE JEWELS ARE WORTH A FORTUNE...
BUT WHY KEEP THE SKULL?
SHE COULD HAVE DITCHED THE HEAD IN TORONTO AND SOLD THE JEWELS...
HOW'D SHE KNOW ABOUT THAT CARGO IN THE FIRST PLACE?
WHO?
THE GIRL WHO KICKED YOUR ASS AND THREW YOU IN A CARGO CONTAINER?

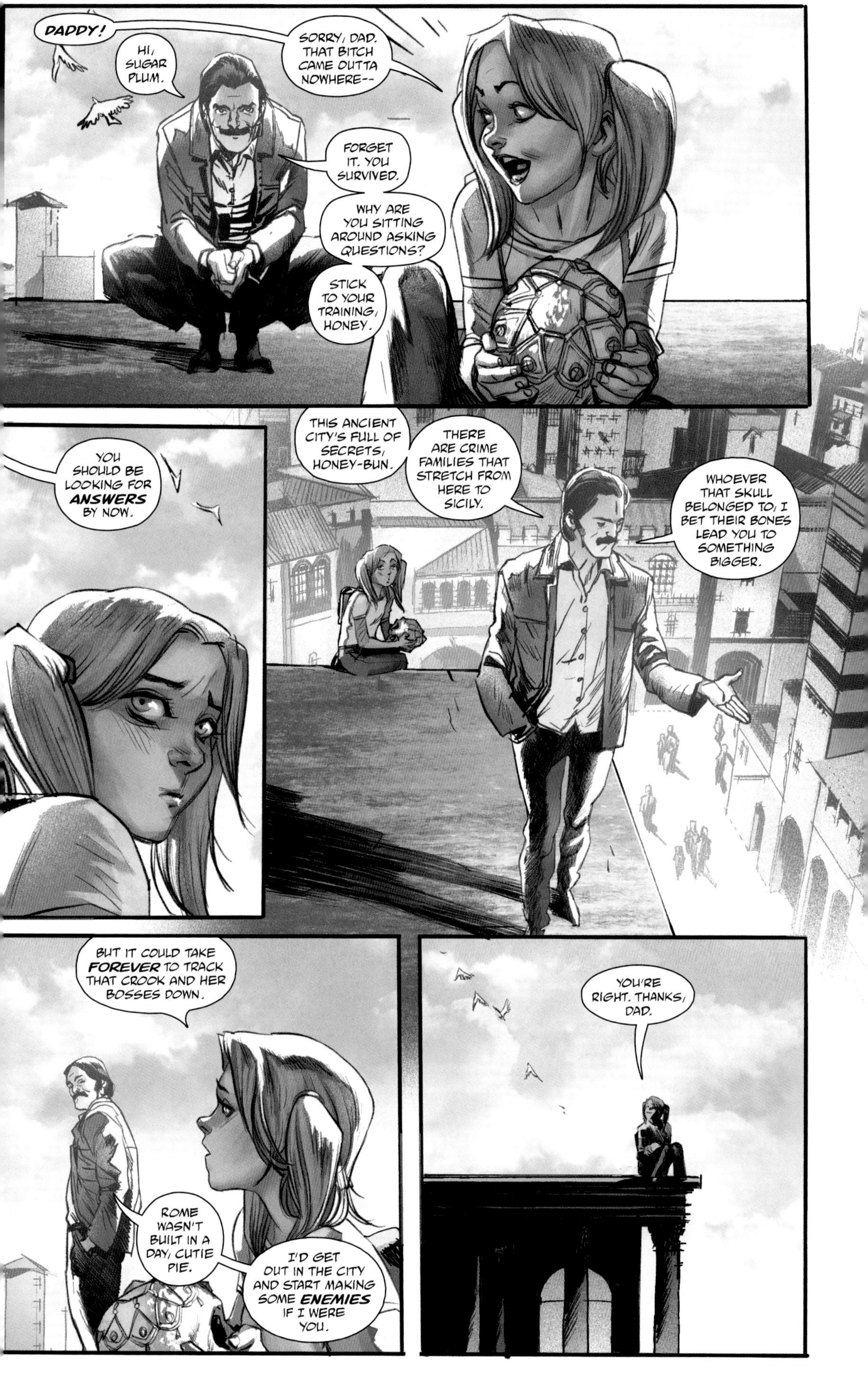
DADDY!
HI, SUGAR PLUM.
SORRY, DAD. THAT BITCH CAME OUTTA NOWHERE--
FORGET IT. YOU SURVIVED.
WHY ARE YOU SITTING AROUND ASKING QUESTIONS?
STICK TO YOUR TRAINING, HONEY.
YOU SHOULD BE LOOKING FOR **ANSWERS** BY NOW.
THIS ANCIENT CITY'S FULL OF SECRETS, HONEY-BUN.
THERE ARE CRIME FAMILIES THAT STRETCH FROM HERE TO SICILY.
WHOEVER THAT SKULL BELONGED TO, I BET THEIR BONES LEAD YOU TO SOMETHING BIGGER.
BUT IT COULD TAKE **FOREVER** TO TRACK THAT CROOK AND HER BOSSES DOWN.
ROME WASN'T BUILT IN A DAY, CUTIE PIE.
I'D GET OUT IN THE CITY AND START MAKING SOME **ENEMIES** IF I WERE YOU.
YOU'RE RIGHT. THANKS, DAD.

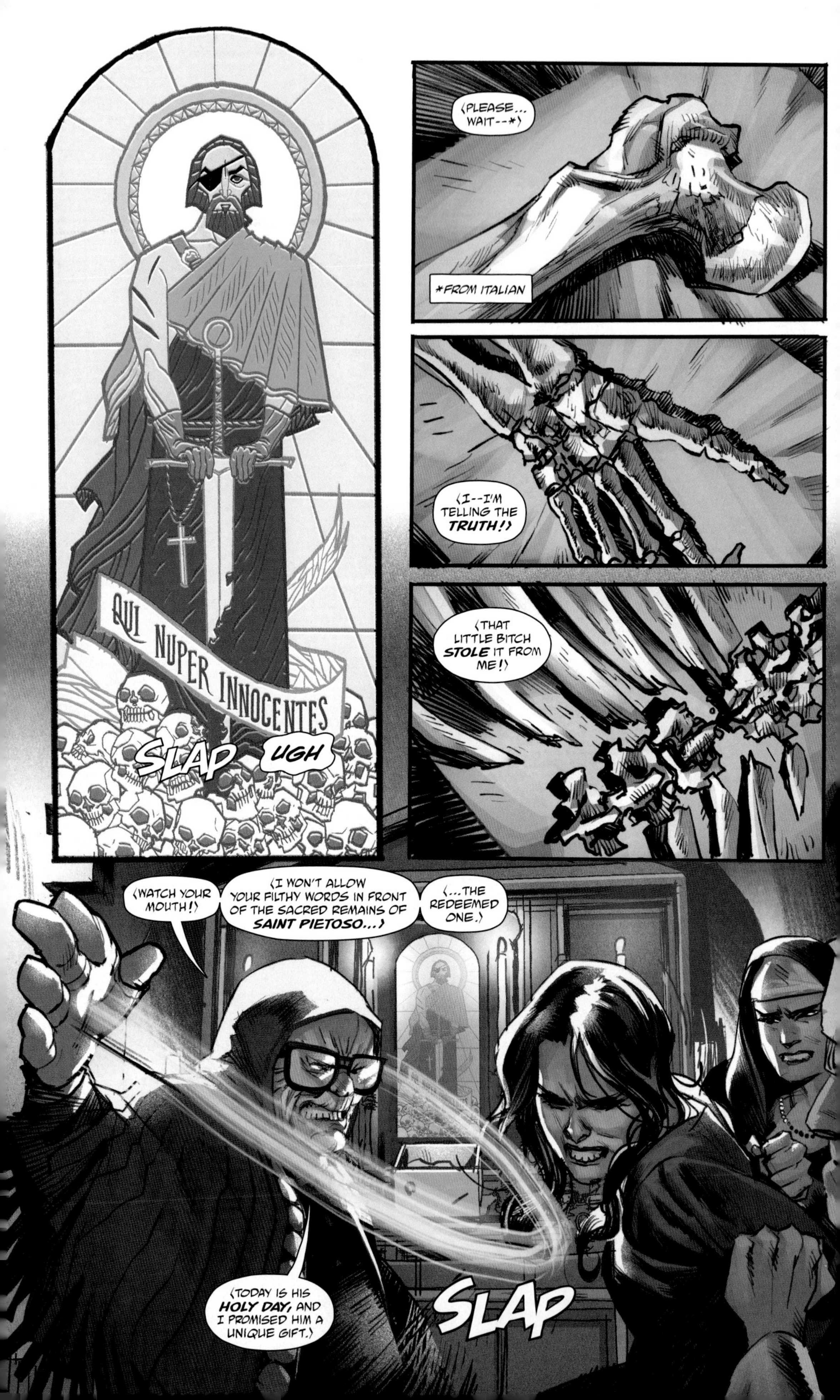
QUI NUPER INNOCENTES
SLAP
UGH
‹PLEASE... WAIT--*›
*FROM ITALIAN
‹I--I'M TELLING THE TRUTH!›
‹THAT LITTLE BITCH STOLE IT FROM ME!›
‹WATCH YOUR MOUTH!›
‹I WON'T ALLOW YOUR FILTHY WORDS IN FRONT OF THE SACRED REMAINS OF SAINT PIETOSO...›
‹...THE REDEEMED ONE.›
‹TODAY IS HIS HOLY DAY, AND I PROMISED HIM A UNIQUE GIFT.›
SLAP

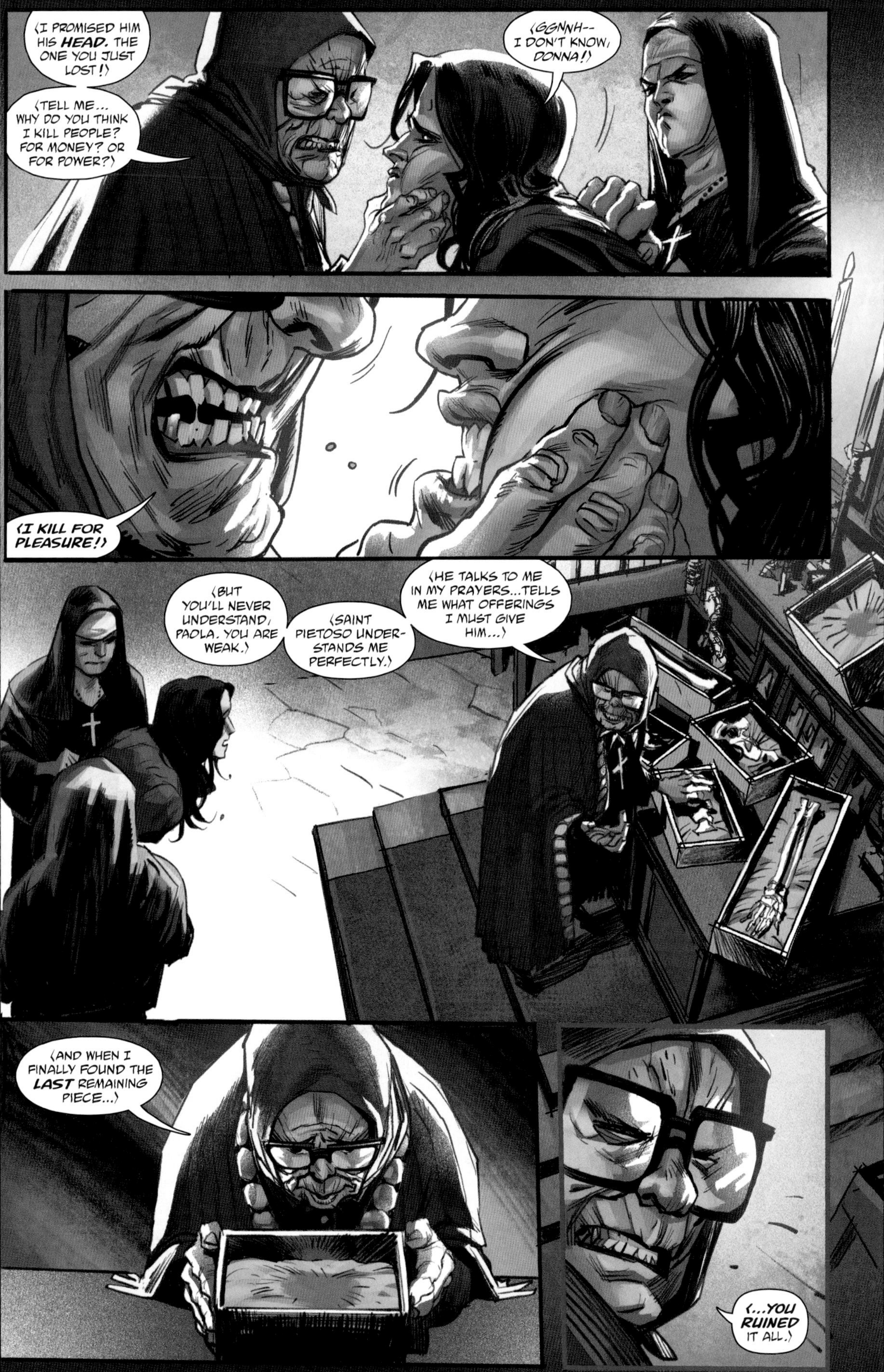
〈I PROMISED HIM HIS HEAD. THE ONE YOU JUST LOST!〉
〈TELL ME... WHY DO YOU THINK I KILL PEOPLE? FOR MONEY? OR FOR POWER?〉
〈GGNNH-- I DON'T KNOW, DONNA!〉
〈I KILL FOR PLEASURE!〉
〈BUT YOU'LL NEVER UNDERSTAND, PAOLA. YOU ARE WEAK.〉
〈SAINT PIETOSO UNDERSTANDS ME PERFECTLY.〉
〈HE TALKS TO ME IN MY PRAYERS...TELLS ME WHAT OFFERINGS I MUST GIVE HIM...〉
〈AND WHEN I FINALLY FOUND THE LAST REMAINING PIECE...〉
〈...YOU RUINED IT ALL.〉

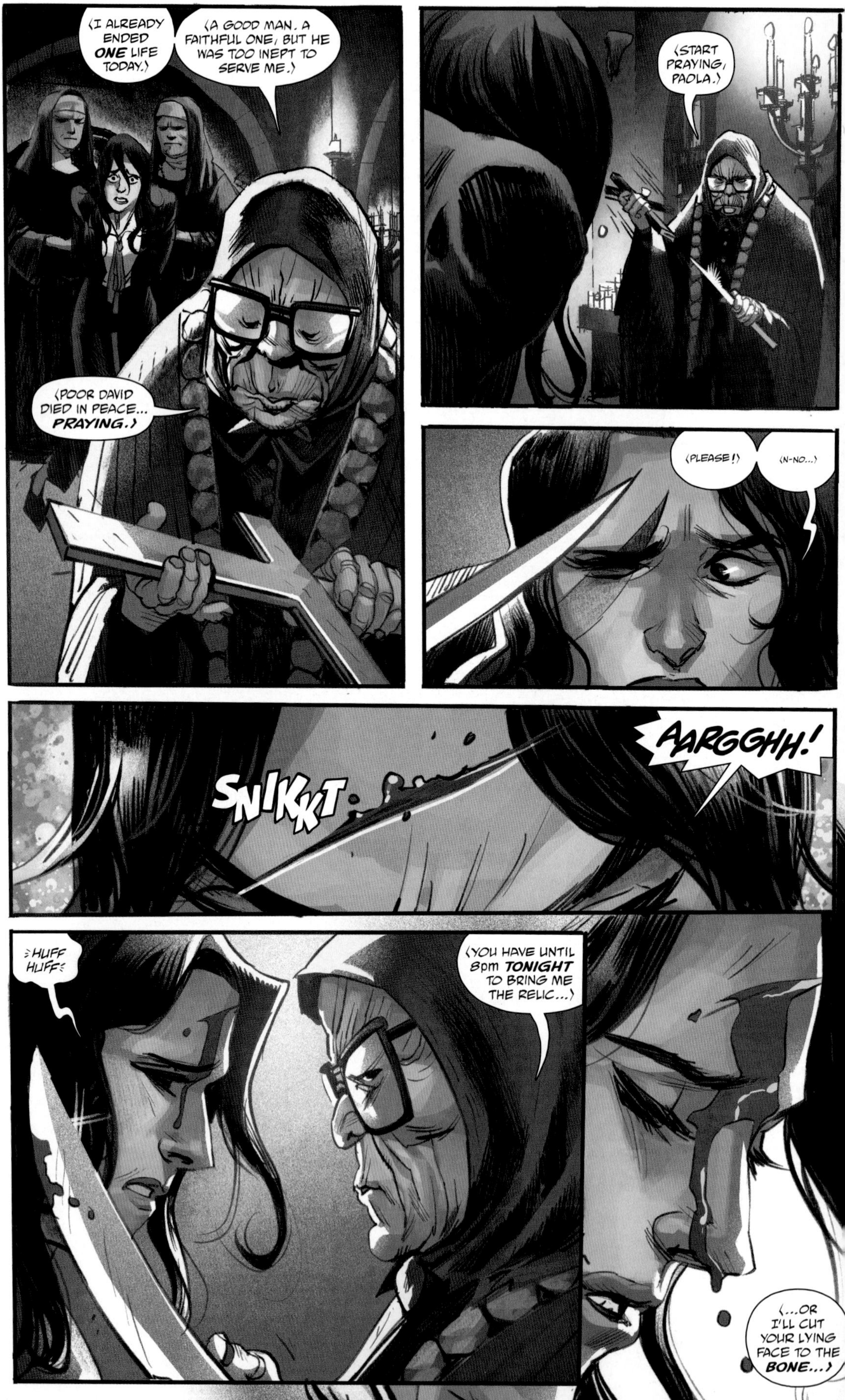
‹I ALREADY ENDED ONE LIFE TODAY.›
‹A GOOD MAN. A FAITHFUL ONE, BUT HE WAS TOO INEPT TO SERVE ME.›
‹POOR DAVID DIED IN PEACE... PRAYING.›
‹START PRAYING, PAOLA.›
‹PLEASE!›
‹N-NO...›
SNIKKT
AARGGHH!
HUFF HUFF
‹YOU HAVE UNTIL 8pm TONIGHT TO BRING ME THE RELIC...›
‹...OR I'LL CUT YOUR LYING FACE TO THE BONE...›

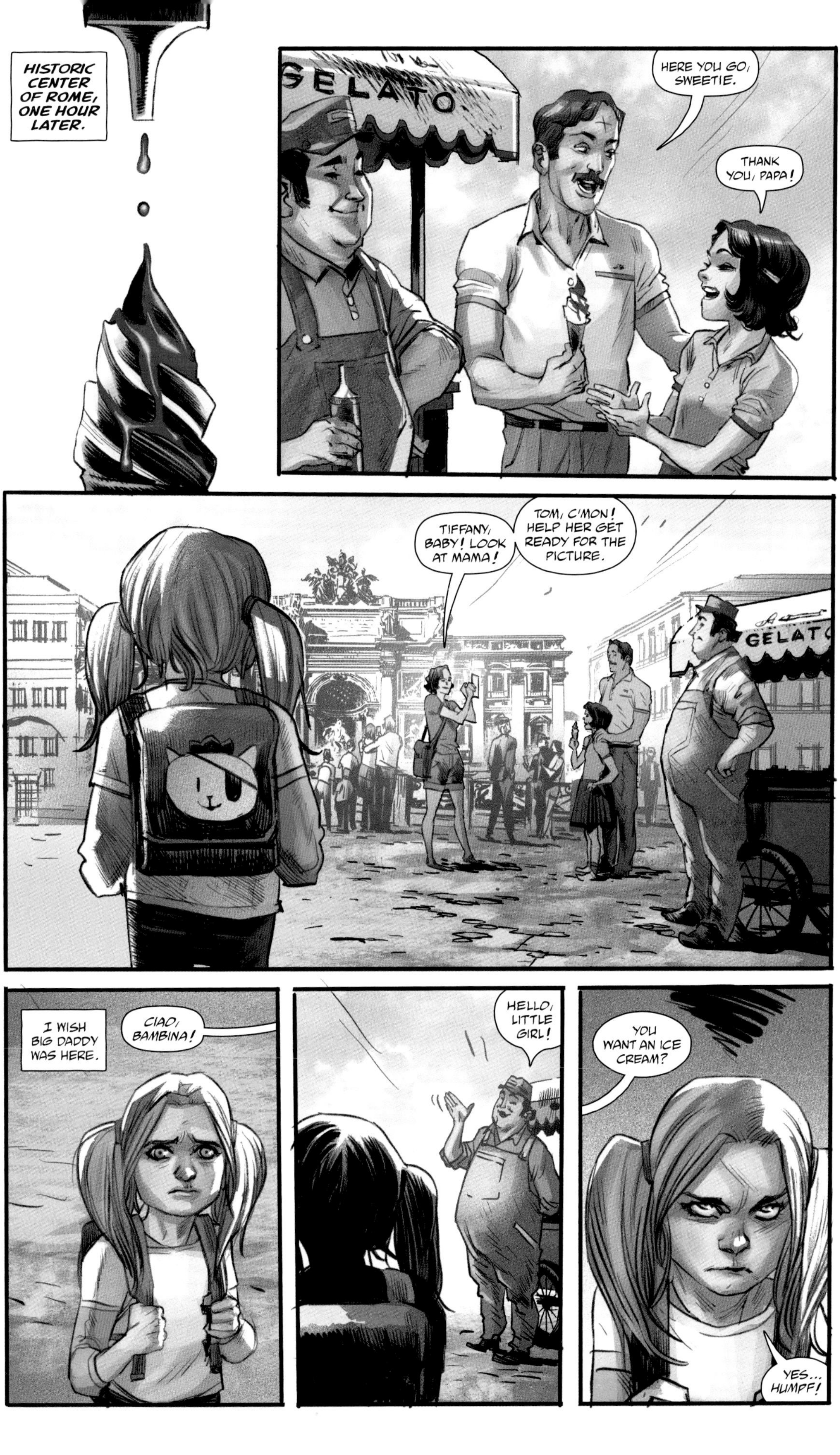
HISTORIC CENTER OF ROME, ONE HOUR LATER.
HERE YOU GO, SWEETIE.
THANK YOU, PAPA!
TIFFANY, BABY! LOOK AT MAMA!
TOM, C'MON! HELP HER GET READY FOR THE PICTURE.
GELATO
I WISH BIG DADDY WAS HERE.
CIAO, BAMBINA!
HELLO, LITTLE GIRL!
YOU WANT AN ICE CREAM?
YES... HUMPF!

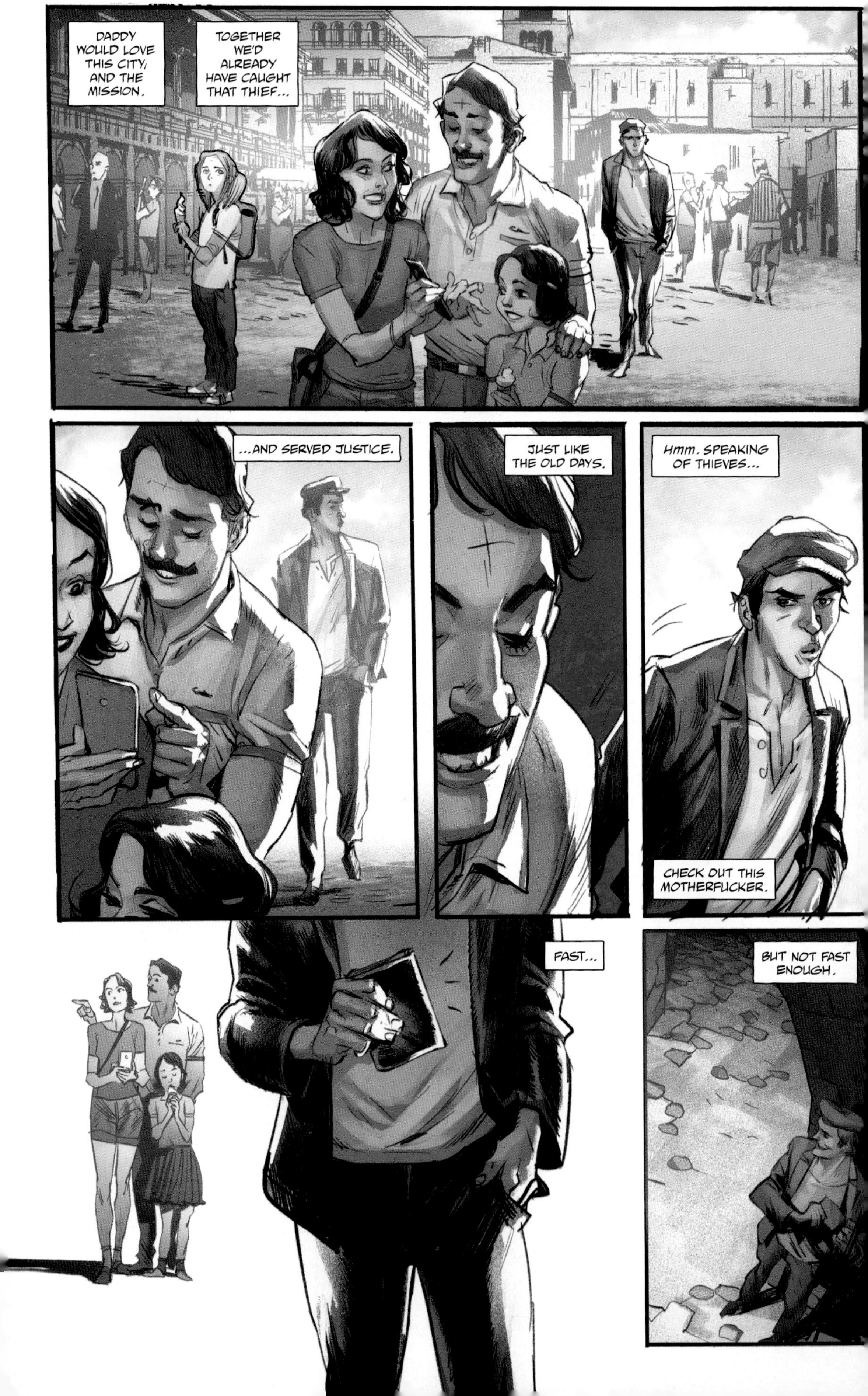
DADDY WOULD LOVE THIS CITY, AND THE MISSION.
TOGETHER WE'D ALREADY HAVE CAUGHT THAT THIEF...
...AND SERVED JUSTICE.
JUST LIKE THE OLD DAYS.
Hmm. SPEAKING OF THIEVES...
CHECK OUT THIS MOTHERFUCKER.
FAST...
BUT NOT FAST ENOUGH.

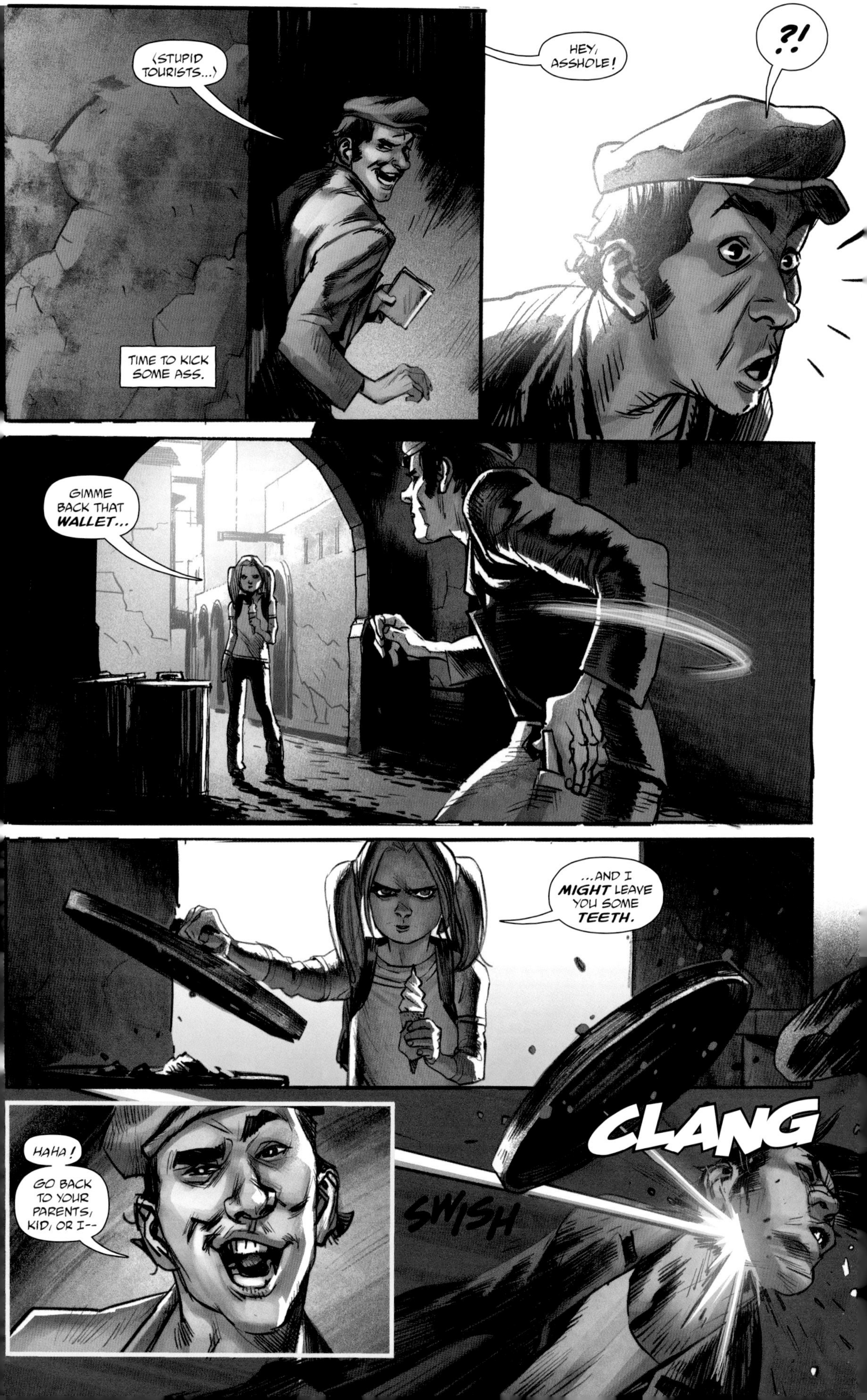
(STUPID TOURISTS...)
TIME TO KICK SOME ASS.
HEY, ASSHOLE!
?!
GIMME BACK THAT **WALLET...**
...AND I **MIGHT** LEAVE YOU SOME **TEETH.**
HAHA!
GO BACK TO YOUR PARENTS, KID, OR I--
SWISH
CLANG

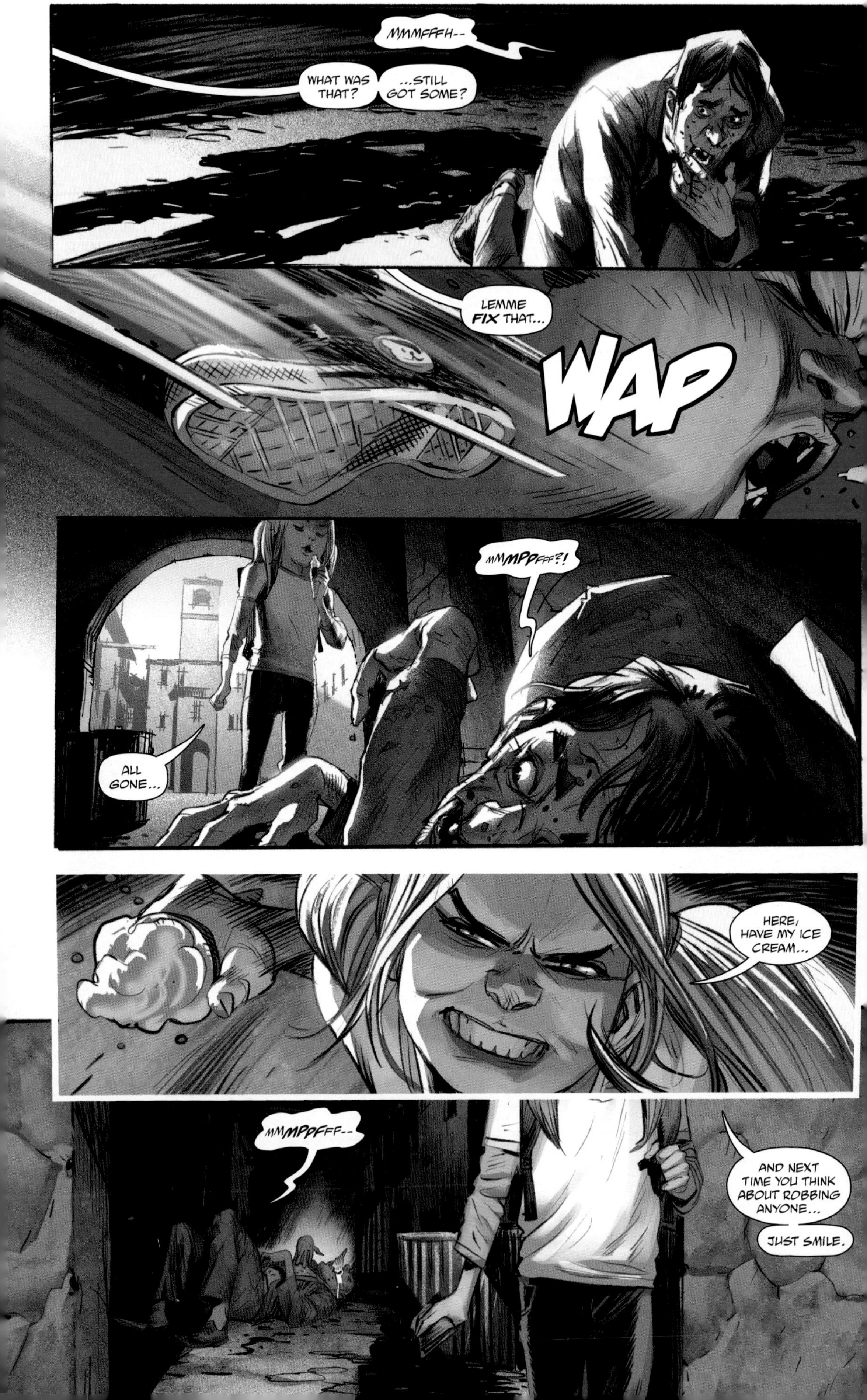
MMMFFFH--
WHAT WAS THAT?
...STILL GOT SOME?
LEMME FIX THAT...
WAP
MMMPPFFF?!
ALL GONE...
HERE, HAVE MY ICE CREAM...
MMMPPFFF--
AND NEXT TIME YOU THINK ABOUT ROBBING ANYONE...
JUST SMILE.

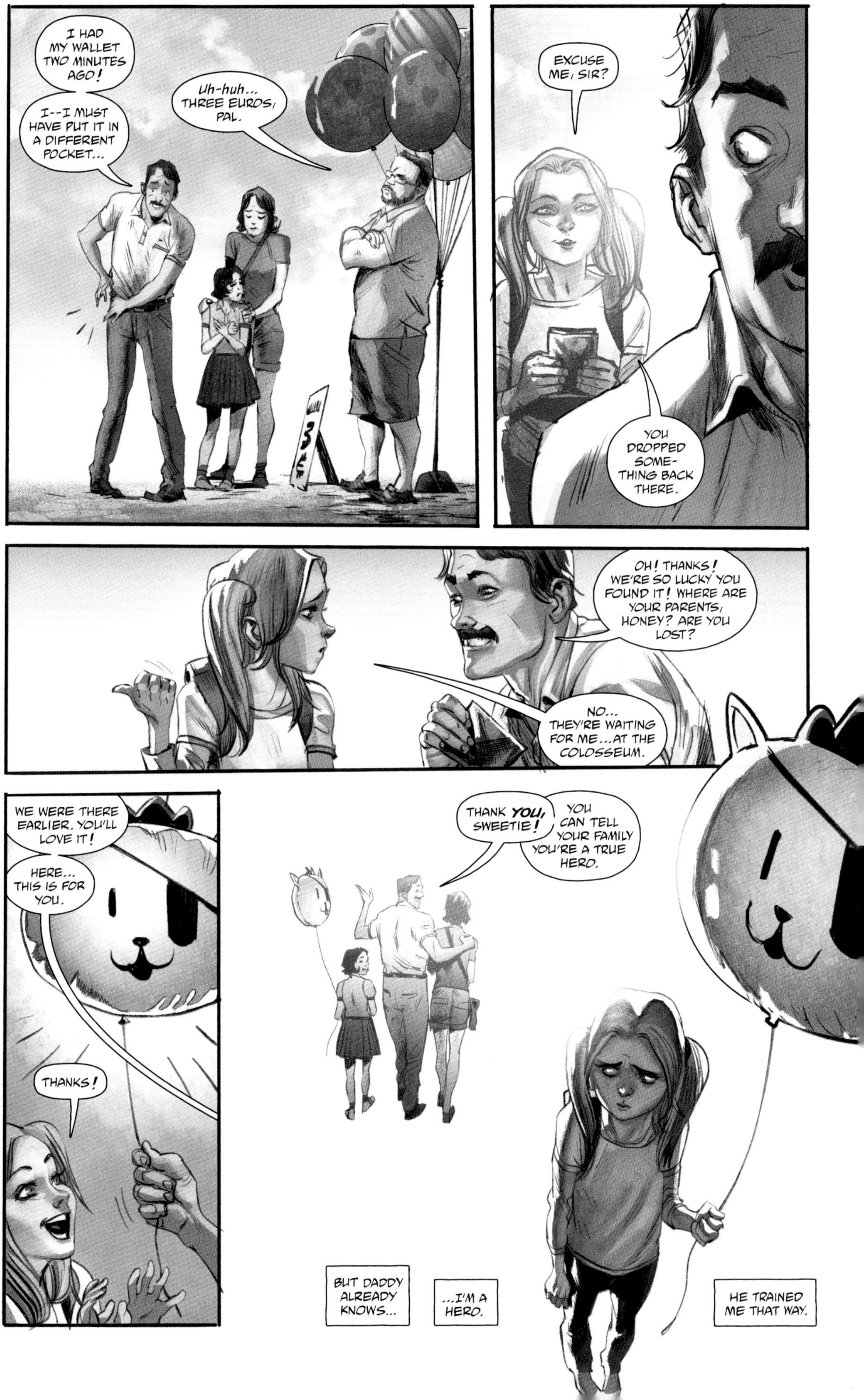
I HAD MY WALLET TWO MINUTES AGO!
I--I MUST HAVE PUT IT IN A DIFFERENT POCKET...
Uh-huh... THREE EUROS, PAL.
3€
EXCUSE ME, SIR?
YOU DROPPED SOME-THING BACK THERE.
OH! THANKS! WE'RE SO LUCKY YOU FOUND IT! WHERE ARE YOUR PARENTS, HONEY? ARE YOU LOST?
NO... THEY'RE WAITING FOR ME... AT THE COLOSSEUM.
WE WERE THERE EARLIER. YOU'LL LOVE IT!
HERE... THIS IS FOR YOU.
THANKS!
THANK YOU, SWEETIE!
YOU CAN TELL YOUR FAMILY YOU'RE A TRUE HERO.
BUT DADDY ALREADY KNOWS...
...I'M A HERO.
HE TRAINED ME THAT WAY.

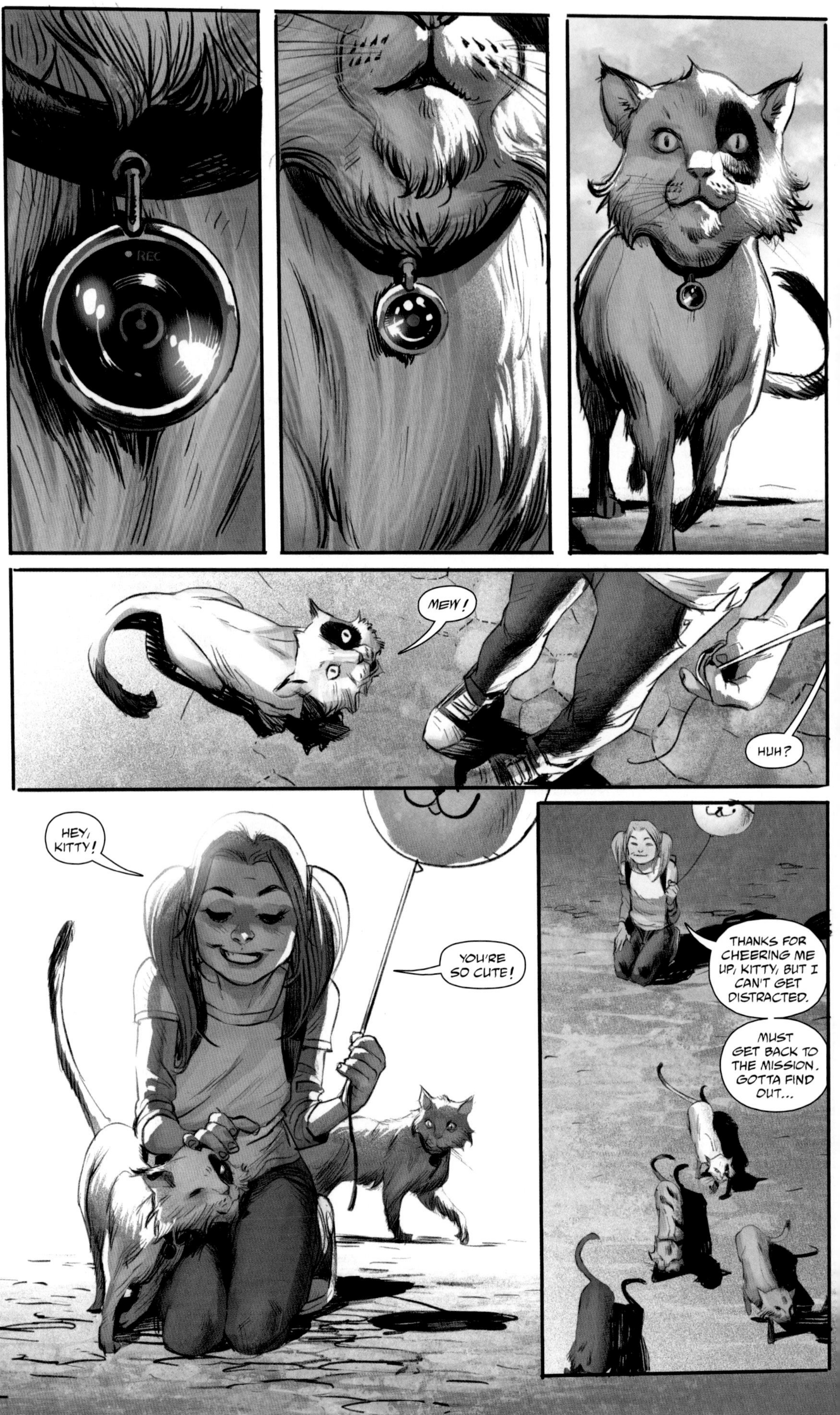

REC
MEW!
HUH?
HEY, KITTY!
YOU'RE SO CUTE!
THANKS FOR CHEERING ME UP, KITTY, BUT I CAN'T GET DISTRACTED.
MUST GET BACK TO THE MISSION. GOTTA FIND OUT...

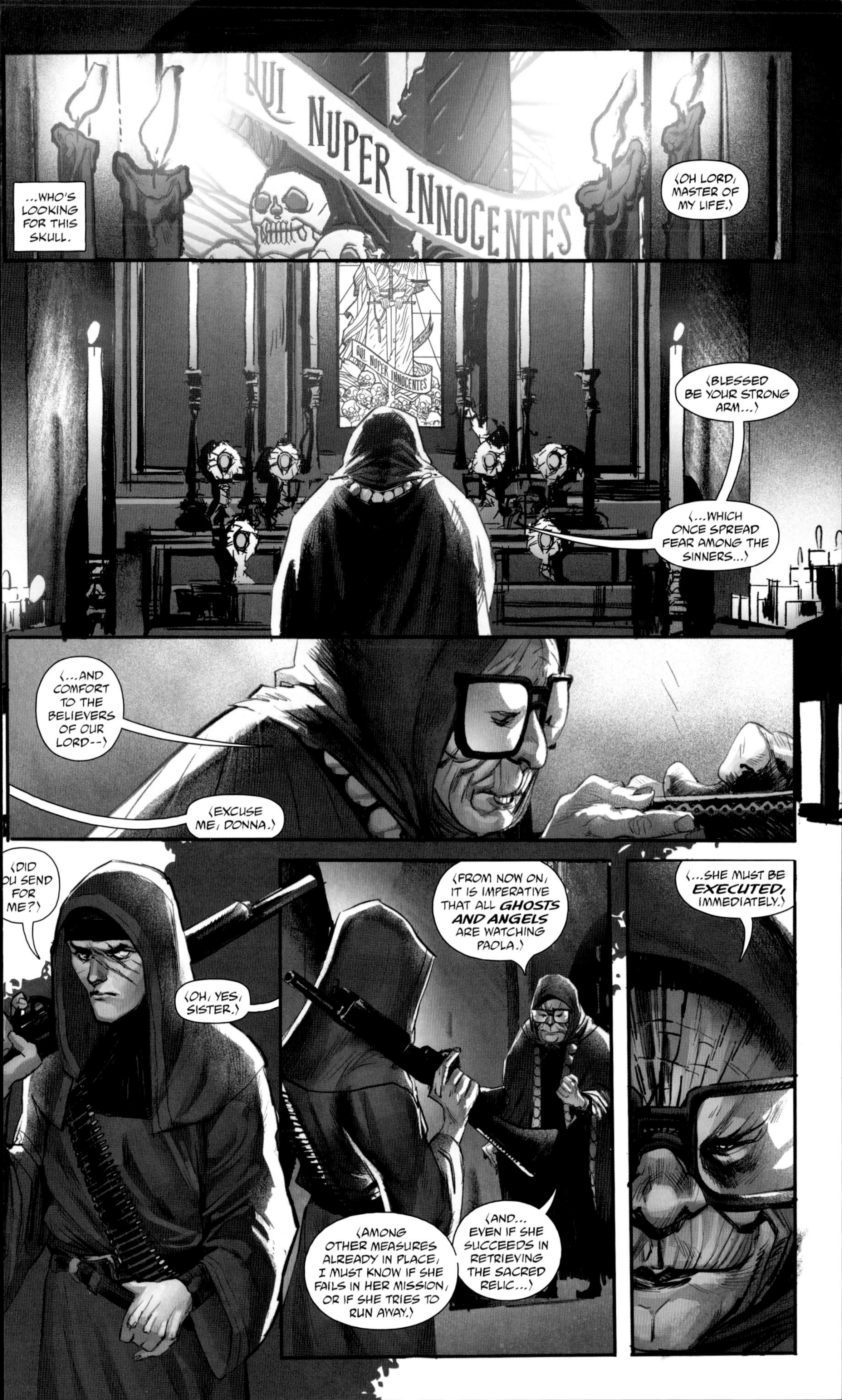
QUI NUPER INNOCENTES
...WHO'S LOOKING FOR THIS SKULL.
(OH LORD, MASTER OF MY LIFE.)
QUI NUPER INNOCENTES
(BLESSED BE YOUR STRONG ARM...)
(...WHICH ONCE SPREAD FEAR AMONG THE SINNERS...)
(...AND COMFORT TO THE BELIEVERS OF OUR LORD--)
(EXCUSE ME, DONNA.)
(DID OU SEND FOR ME?)
(OH, YES, SISTER.)
(FROM NOW ON, IT IS IMPERATIVE THAT ALL GHOSTS AND ANGELS ARE WATCHING PAOLA.)
(AMONG OTHER MEASURES ALREADY IN PLACE, I MUST KNOW IF SHE FAILS IN HER MISSION, OR IF SHE TRIES TO RUN AWAY.)
(AND... EVEN IF SHE SUCCEEDS IN RETRIEVING THE SACRED RELIC...)
(...SHE MUST BE EXECUTED, IMMEDIATELY.)

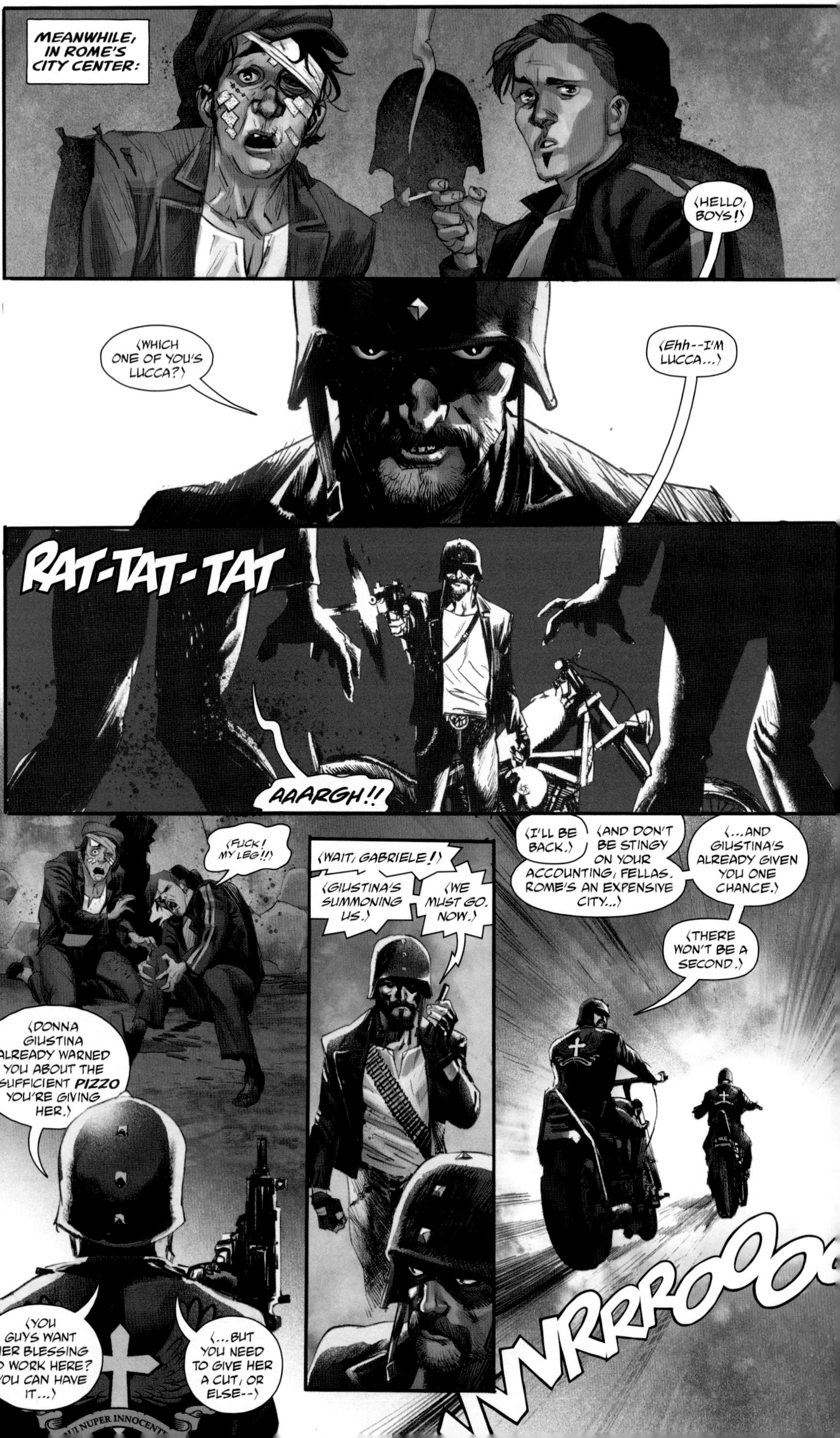
MEANWHILE, IN ROME'S CITY CENTER:
⟨HELLO, BOYS!⟩
⟨WHICH ONE OF YOU'S LUCCA?⟩
⟨Ehh--I'M LUCCA...⟩
RAT-TAT-TAT
AAARGH!!
⟨FUCK! MY LEG!!⟩
⟨DONNA GIUSTINA ALREADY WARNED YOU ABOUT THE INSUFFICIENT PIZZO YOU'RE GIVING HER.⟩
⟨YOU GUYS WANT HER BLESSING TO WORK HERE? YOU CAN HAVE IT...⟩
⟨...BUT YOU NEED TO GIVE HER A CUT, OR ELSE--⟩
⟨WAIT, GABRIELE!⟩
⟨GIUSTINA'S SUMMONING US.⟩
⟨WE MUST GO. NOW.⟩
⟨I'LL BE BACK.⟩
⟨AND DON'T BE STINGY ON YOUR ACCOUNTING, FELLAS. ROME'S AN EXPENSIVE CITY...⟩
⟨...AND GIUSTINA'S ALREADY GIVEN YOU ONE CHANCE.⟩
⟨THERE WON'T BE A SECOND.⟩
VVVRRROOOOO

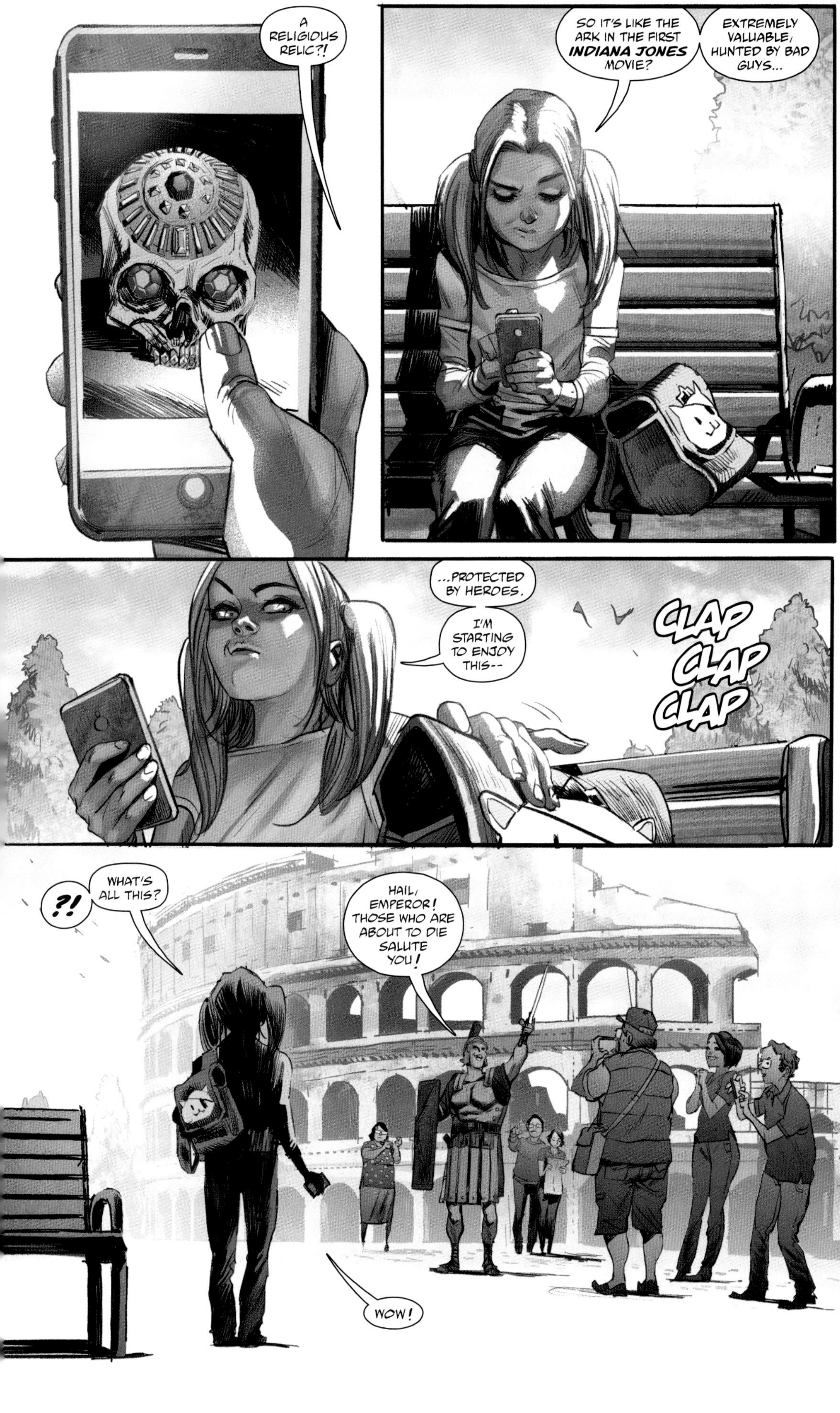
A RELIGIOUS RELIC?!
SO IT'S LIKE THE ARK IN THE FIRST INDIANA JONES MOVIE?
EXTREMELY VALUABLE, HUNTED BY BAD GUYS...
...PROTECTED BY HEROES.
I'M STARTING TO ENJOY THIS--
CLAP CLAP CLAP
?!
WHAT'S ALL THIS?
HAIL, EMPEROR! THOSE WHO ARE ABOUT TO DIE SALUTE YOU!
WOW!

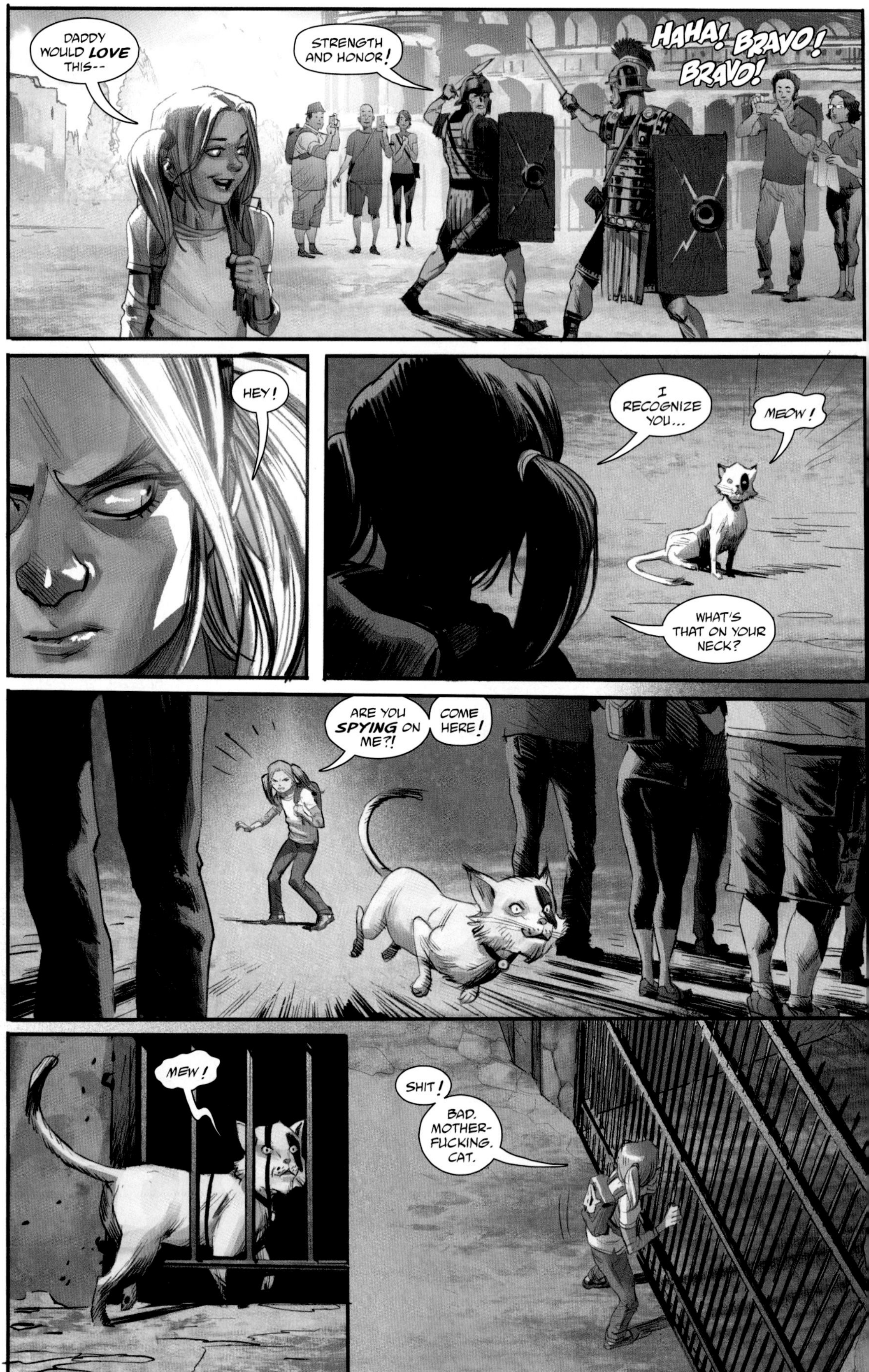
DADDY WOULD LOVE THIS--
STRENGTH AND HONOR!
HAHA! BRAVO! BRAVO!
HEY!
I RECOGNIZE YOU...
MEOW!
WHAT'S THAT ON YOUR NECK?
ARE YOU SPYING ON ME?!
COME HERE!
MEW!
SHIT!
BAD. MOTHER-FUCKING. CAT.

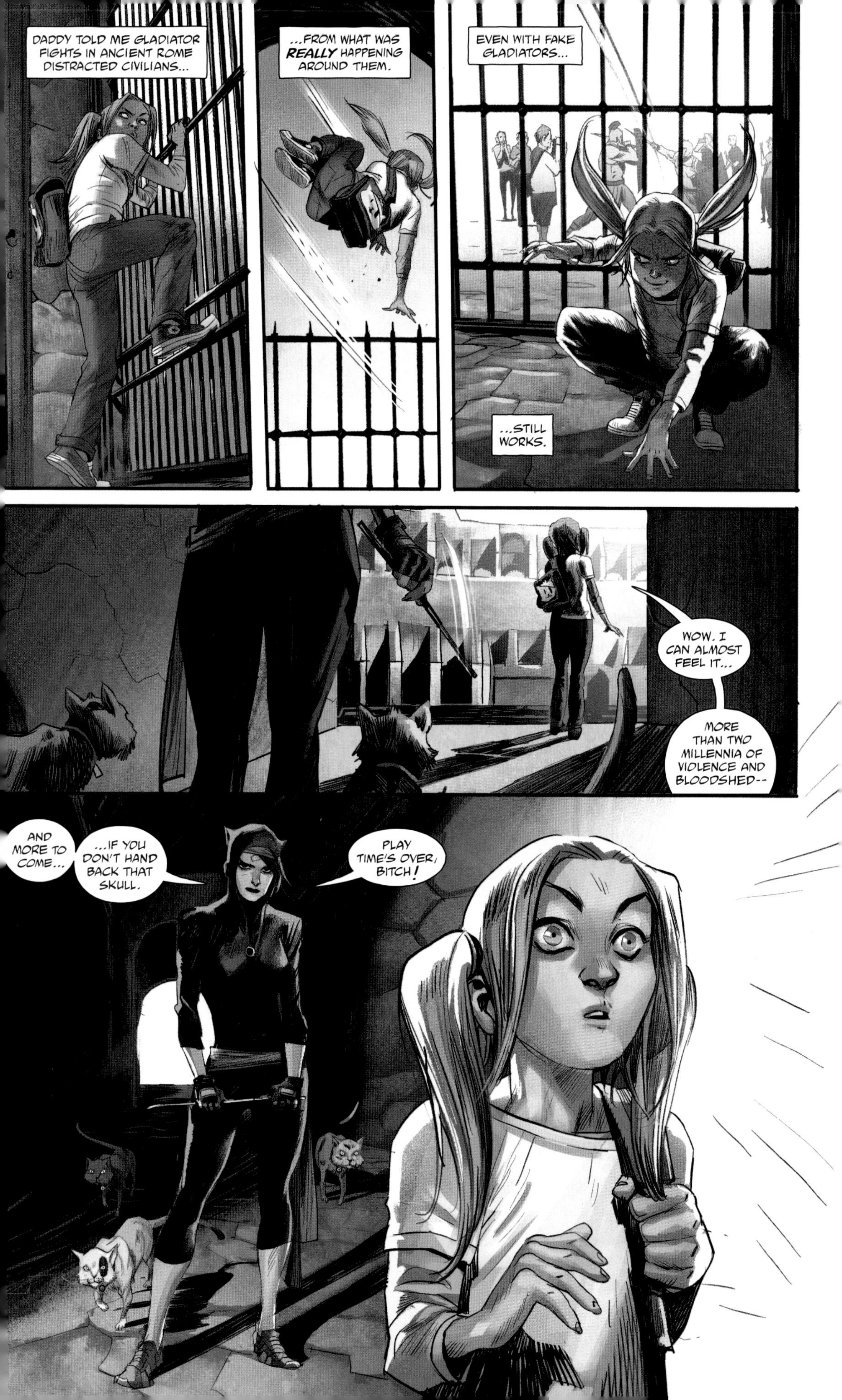

DADDY TOLD ME GLADIATOR FIGHTS IN ANCIENT ROME DISTRACTED CIVILIANS...
...FROM WHAT WAS REALLY HAPPENING AROUND THEM.
EVEN WITH FAKE GLADIATORS...
...STILL WORKS.
WOW. I CAN ALMOST FEEL IT...
MORE THAN TWO MILLENNIA OF VIOLENCE AND BLOODSHED--
AND MORE TO COME...
...IF YOU DON'T HAND BACK THAT SKULL.
PLAY TIME'S OVER, BITCH!

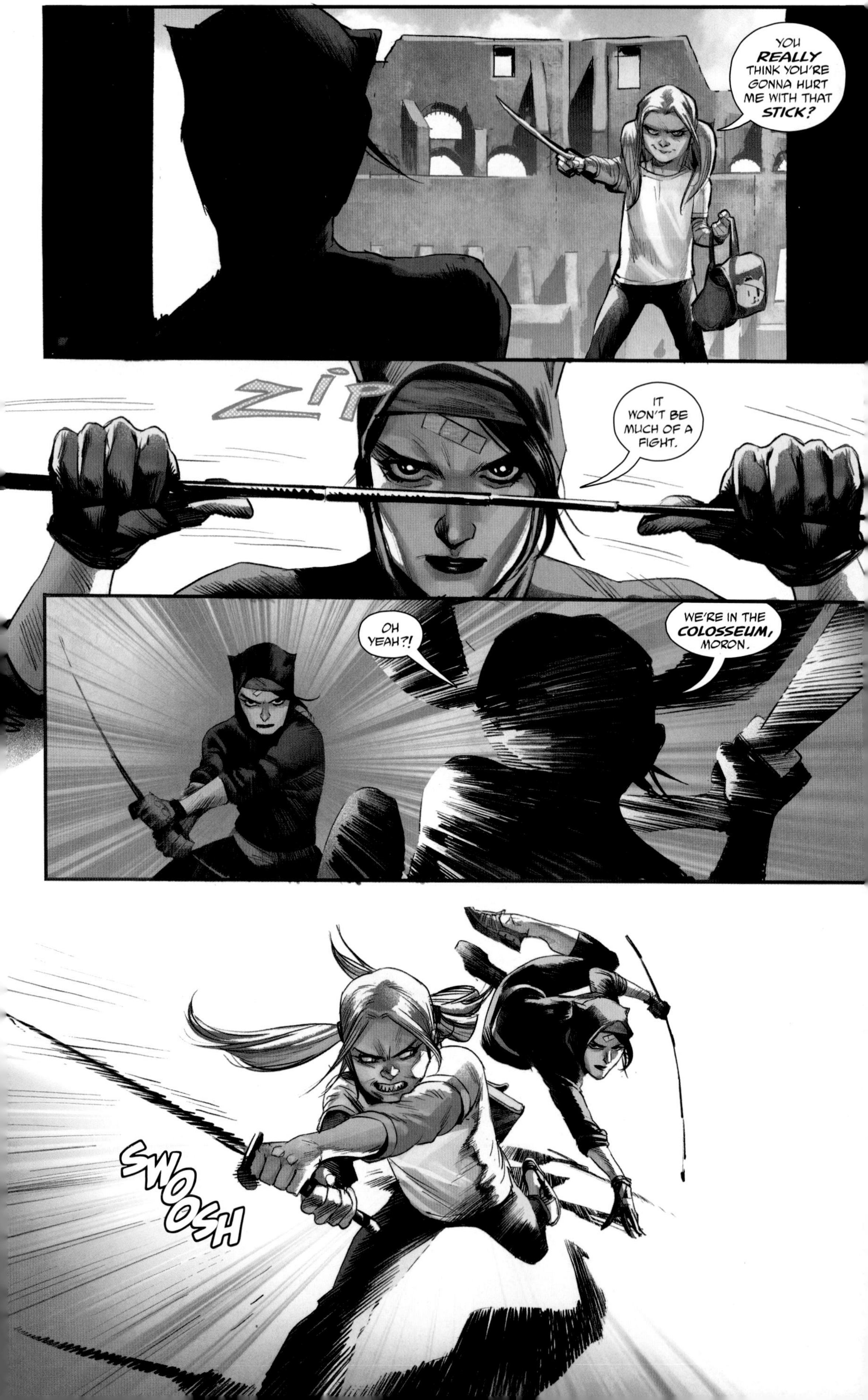
YOU REALLY THINK YOU'RE GONNA HURT ME WITH THAT STICK?
ZIP
IT WON'T BE MUCH OF A FIGHT.
OH YEAH?!
WE'RE IN THE COLOSSEUM, MORON.
SWOOSH

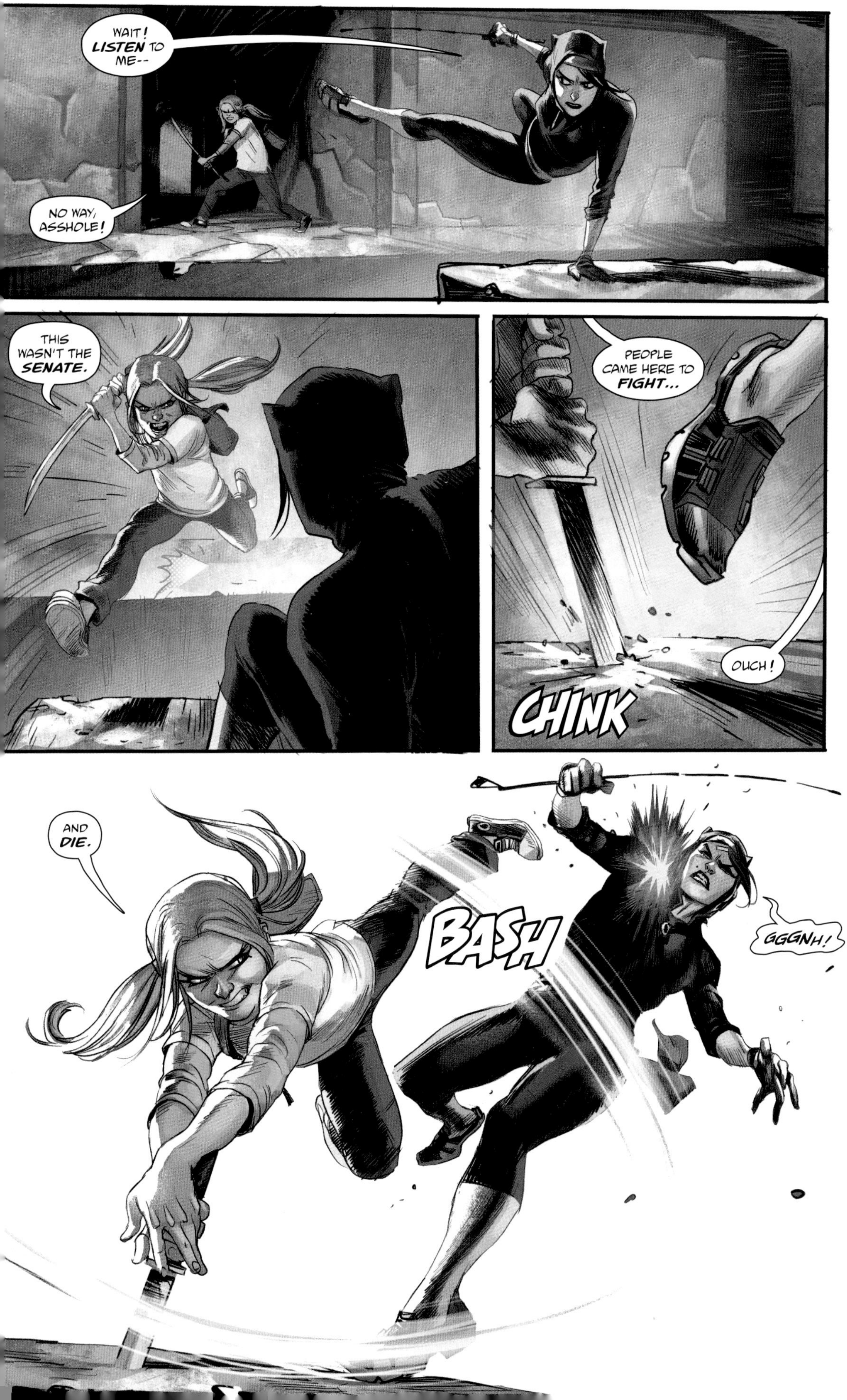

WAIT! LISTEN TO ME--
NO WAY, ASSHOLE!
THIS WASN'T THE SENATE.
PEOPLE CAME HERE TO FIGHT...
OUCH!
CHINK
AND DIE.
BASH
GGGNH!

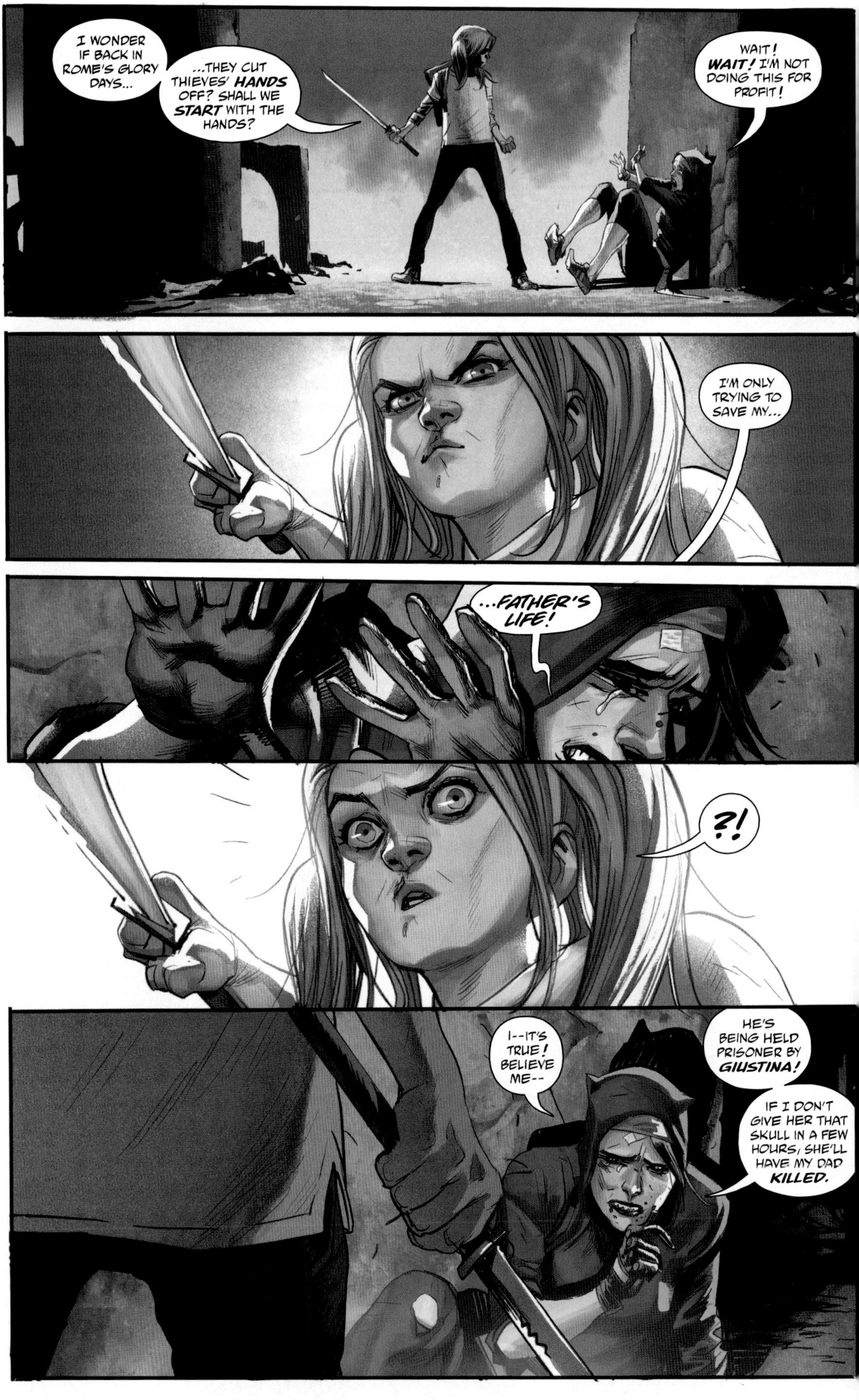
I WONDER IF BACK IN ROME'S GLORY DAYS...
...THEY CUT THIEVES' HANDS OFF? SHALL WE START WITH THE HANDS?
WAIT! WAIT! I'M NOT DOING THIS FOR PROFIT!
I'M ONLY TRYING TO SAVE MY...
...FATHER'S LIFE!
?!
I--IT'S TRUE! BELIEVE ME--
HE'S BEING HELD PRISONER BY GIUSTINA!
IF I DON'T GIVE HER THAT SKULL IN A FEW HOURS, SHE'LL HAVE MY DAD KILLED.

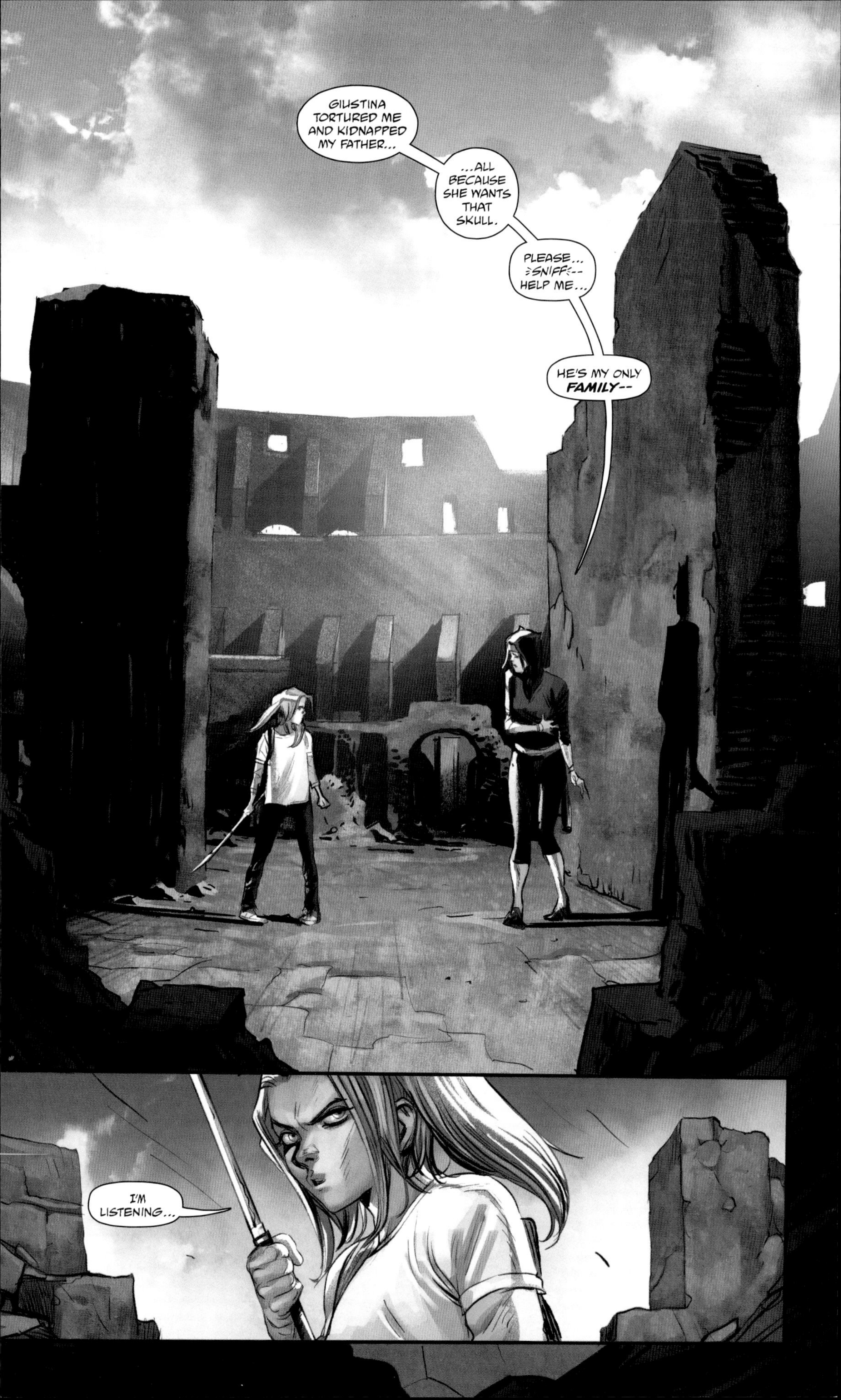
GIUSTINA TORTURED ME AND KIDNAPPED MY FATHER...
...ALL BECAUSE SHE WANTS THAT SKULL.
PLEASE... SNIFF-- HELP ME...
HE'S MY ONLY **FAMILY**--
I'M LISTENING...

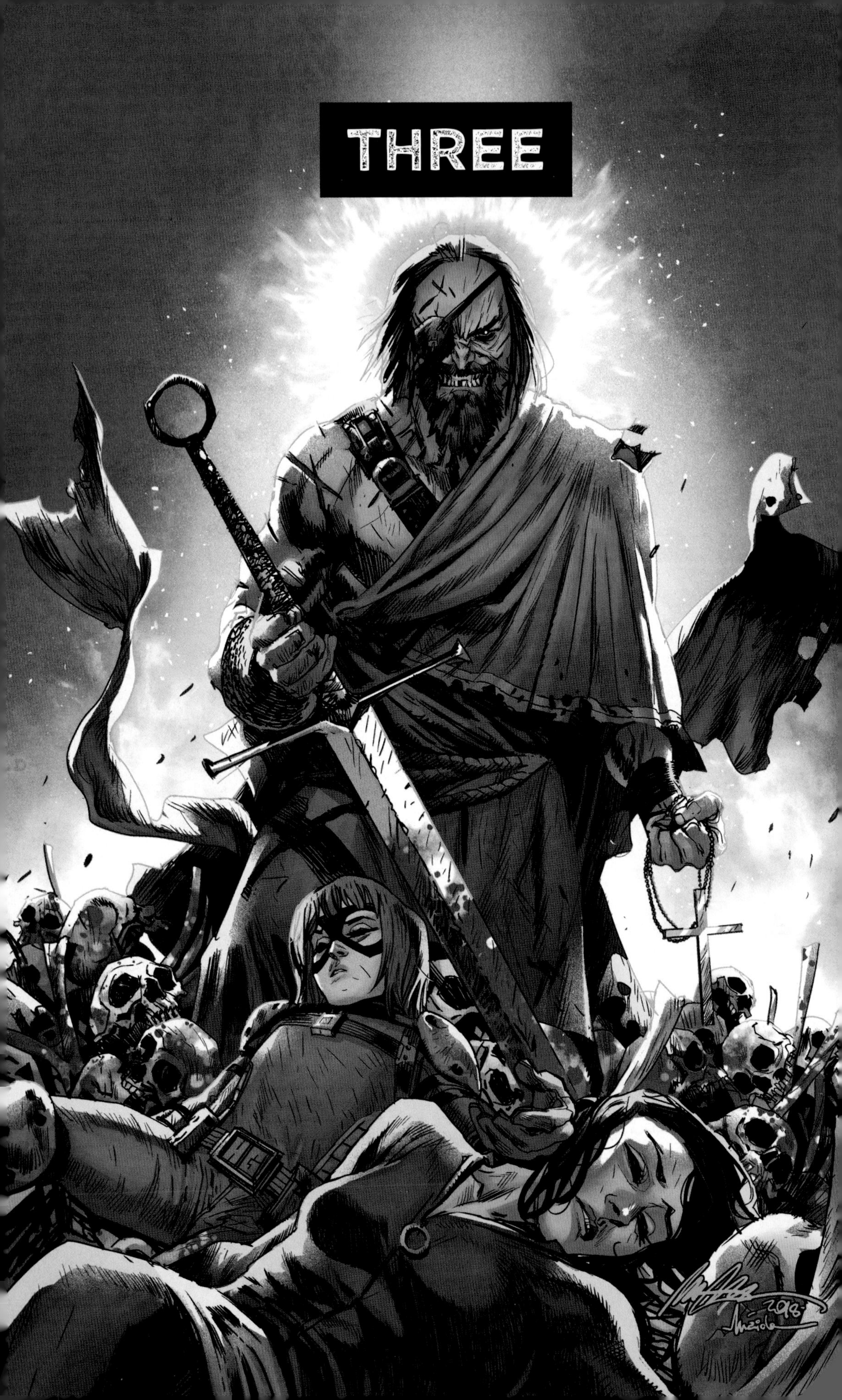
THREE

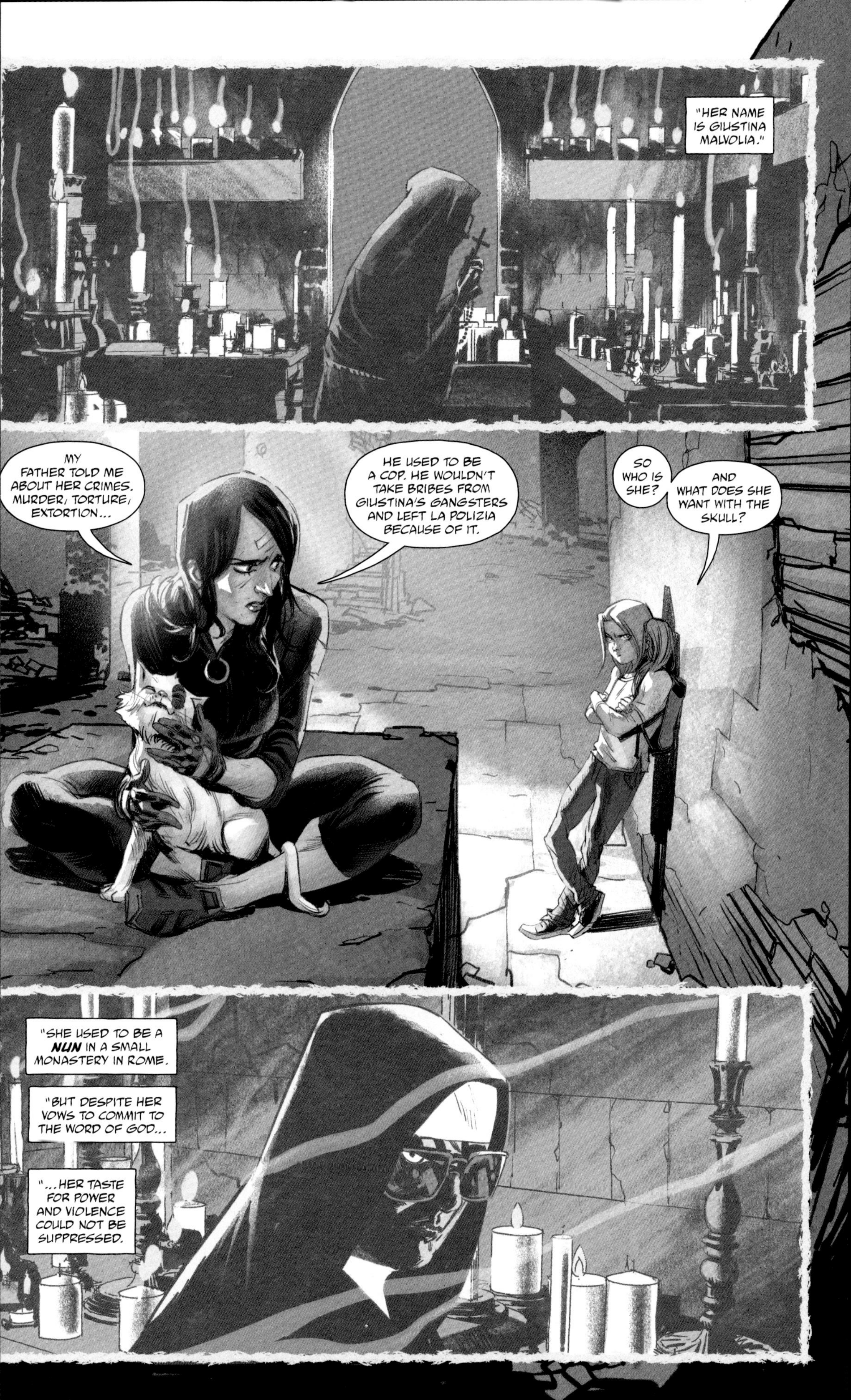
"HER NAME IS GIUSTINA MALVOLIA."
MY FATHER TOLD ME ABOUT HER CRIMES. MURDER, TORTURE, EXTORTION...
HE USED TO BE A COP. HE WOULDN'T TAKE BRIBES FROM GIUSTINA'S GANGSTERS AND LEFT LA POLIZIA BECAUSE OF IT.
SO WHO IS SHE?
AND WHAT DOES SHE WANT WITH THE SKULL?
"SHE USED TO BE A NUN IN A SMALL MONASTERY IN ROME.
"BUT DESPITE HER VOWS TO COMMIT TO THE WORD OF GOD...
"...HER TASTE FOR POWER AND VIOLENCE COULD NOT BE SUPPRESSED.

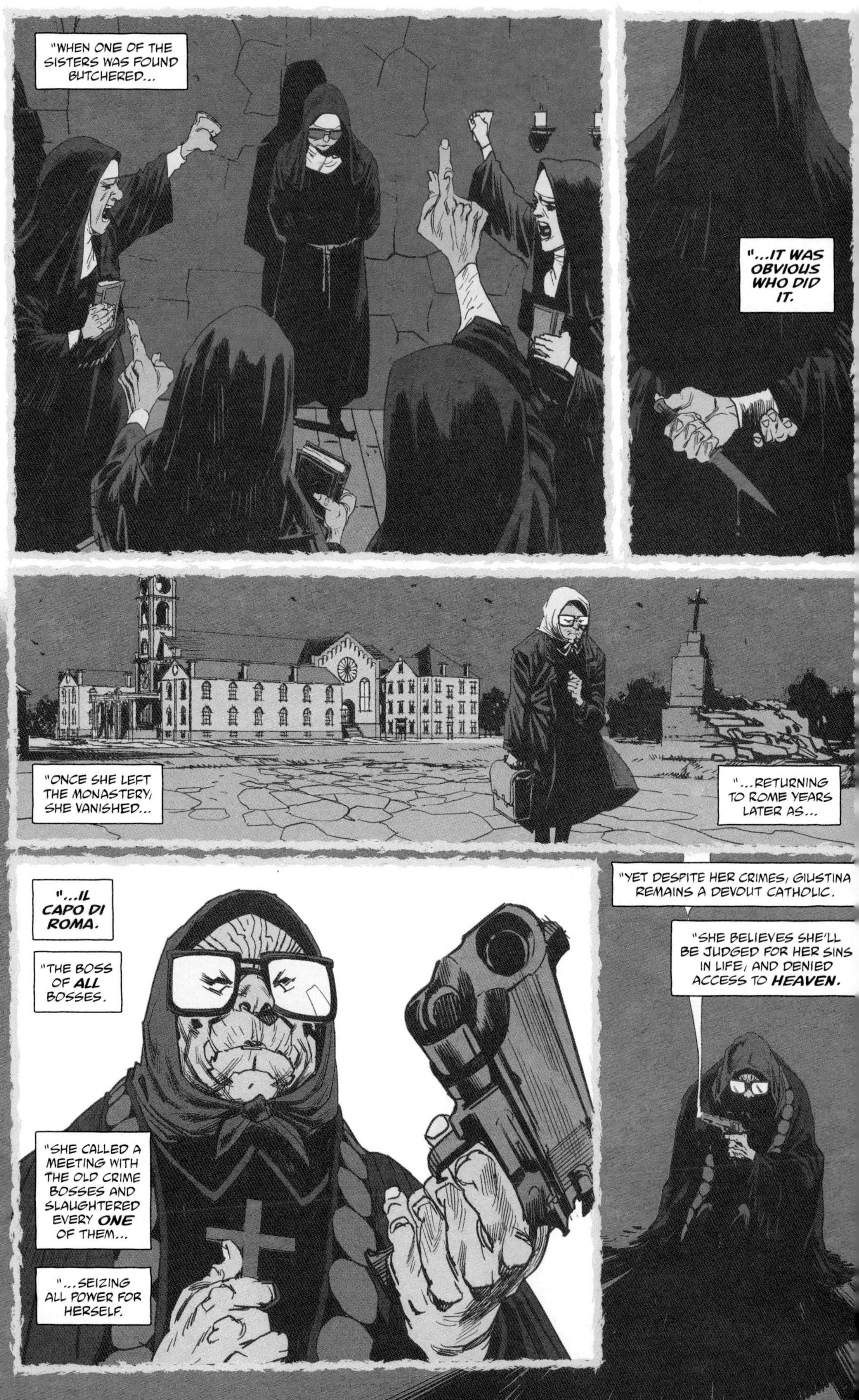
"WHEN ONE OF THE SISTERS WAS FOUND BUTCHERED...
"...IT WAS OBVIOUS WHO DID IT.
"ONCE SHE LEFT THE MONASTERY, SHE VANISHED...
"...RETURNING TO ROME YEARS LATER AS...
"...IL CAPO DI ROMA.
"THE BOSS OF ALL BOSSES.
"SHE CALLED A MEETING WITH THE OLD CRIME BOSSES AND SLAUGHTERED EVERY ONE OF THEM...
"...SEIZING ALL POWER FOR HERSELF.
"YET DESPITE HER CRIMES, GIUSTINA REMAINS A DEVOUT CATHOLIC.
"SHE BELIEVES SHE'LL BE JUDGED FOR HER SINS IN LIFE, AND DENIED ACCESS TO HEAVEN.

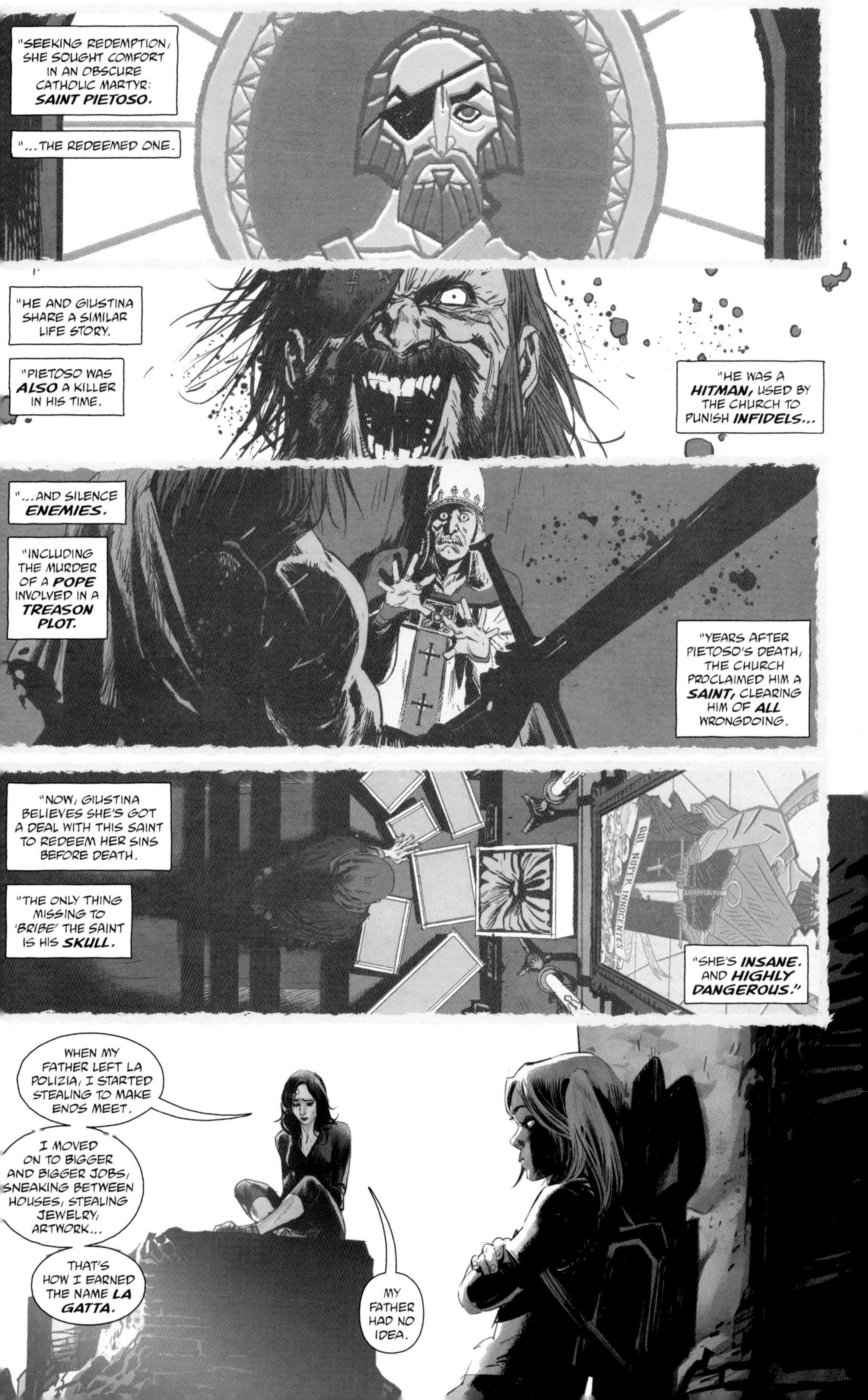
"SEEKING REDEMPTION, SHE SOUGHT COMFORT IN AN OBSCURE CATHOLIC MARTYR: SAINT PIETOSO.
"...THE REDEEMED ONE.
"HE AND GIUSTINA SHARE A SIMILAR LIFE STORY.
"PIETOSO WAS ALSO A KILLER IN HIS TIME.
"HE WAS A HITMAN, USED BY THE CHURCH TO PUNISH INFIDELS...
"...AND SILENCE ENEMIES.
"INCLUDING THE MURDER OF A POPE INVOLVED IN A TREASON PLOT.
"YEARS AFTER PIETOSO'S DEATH, THE CHURCH PROCLAIMED HIM A SAINT, CLEARING HIM OF ALL WRONGDOING.
"NOW, GIUSTINA BELIEVES SHE'S GOT A DEAL WITH THIS SAINT TO REDEEM HER SINS BEFORE DEATH.
"THE ONLY THING MISSING TO 'BRIBE' THE SAINT IS HIS SKULL.
QUI NUPER INNOCENTES
"SHE'S INSANE. AND HIGHLY DANGEROUS."
WHEN MY FATHER LEFT LA POLIZIA, I STARTED STEALING TO MAKE ENDS MEET.
I MOVED ON TO BIGGER AND BIGGER JOBS, SNEAKING BETWEEN HOUSES, STEALING JEWELRY, ARTWORK...
THAT'S HOW I EARNED THE NAME LA GATTA.
MY FATHER HAD NO IDEA.

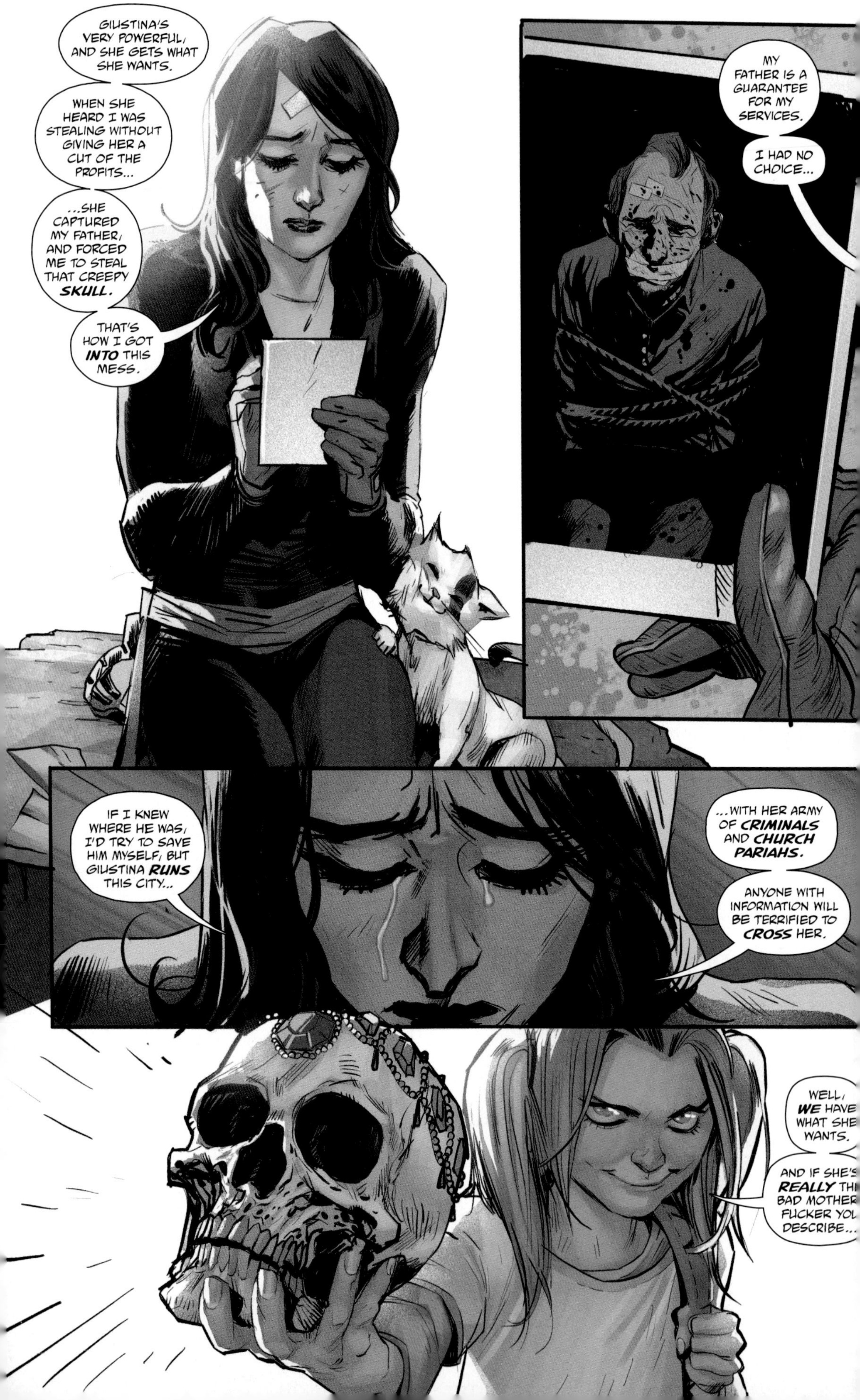
GIUSTINA'S VERY POWERFUL, AND SHE GETS WHAT SHE WANTS.
WHEN SHE HEARD I WAS STEALING WITHOUT GIVING HER A CUT OF THE PROFITS...
...SHE CAPTURED MY FATHER, AND FORCED ME TO STEAL THAT CREEPY **SKULL.**
THAT'S HOW I GOT **INTO** THIS MESS.
MY FATHER IS A GUARANTEE FOR MY SERVICES.
I HAD NO CHOICE...
IF I KNEW WHERE HE WAS, I'D TRY TO SAVE HIM MYSELF, BUT GIUSTINA **RUNS** THIS CITY...
...WITH HER ARMY OF **CRIMINALS** AND **CHURCH PARIAHS.**
ANYONE WITH INFORMATION WILL BE TERRIFIED TO **CROSS** HER.
WELL, **WE** HAVE WHAT SHE WANTS.
AND IF SHE'S **REALLY** TH BAD MOTHER FUCKER YOU DESCRIBE...

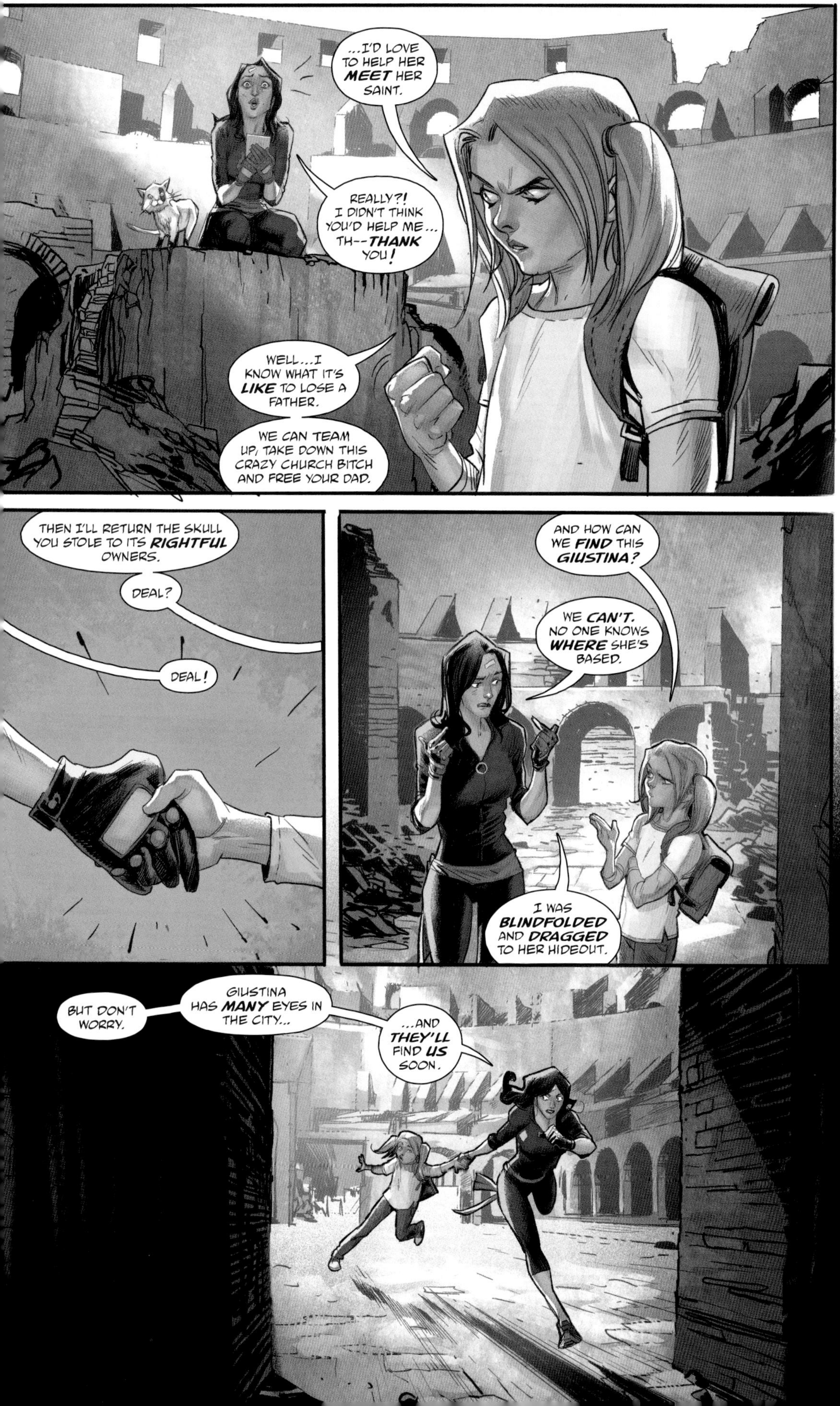
...I'D LOVE TO HELP HER MEET HER SAINT.
REALLY?! I DIDN'T THINK YOU'D HELP ME... TH--THANK YOU!
WELL...I KNOW WHAT IT'S LIKE TO LOSE A FATHER.
WE CAN TEAM UP, TAKE DOWN THIS CRAZY CHURCH BITCH AND FREE YOUR DAD.
THEN I'LL RETURN THE SKULL YOU STOLE TO ITS RIGHTFUL OWNERS.
DEAL?
DEAL!
AND HOW CAN WE FIND THIS GIUSTINA?
WE CAN'T. NO ONE KNOWS WHERE SHE'S BASED.
I WAS BLINDFOLDED AND DRAGGED TO HER HIDEOUT.
BUT DON'T WORRY.
GIUSTINA HAS MANY EYES IN THE CITY...
...AND THEY'LL FIND US SOON.

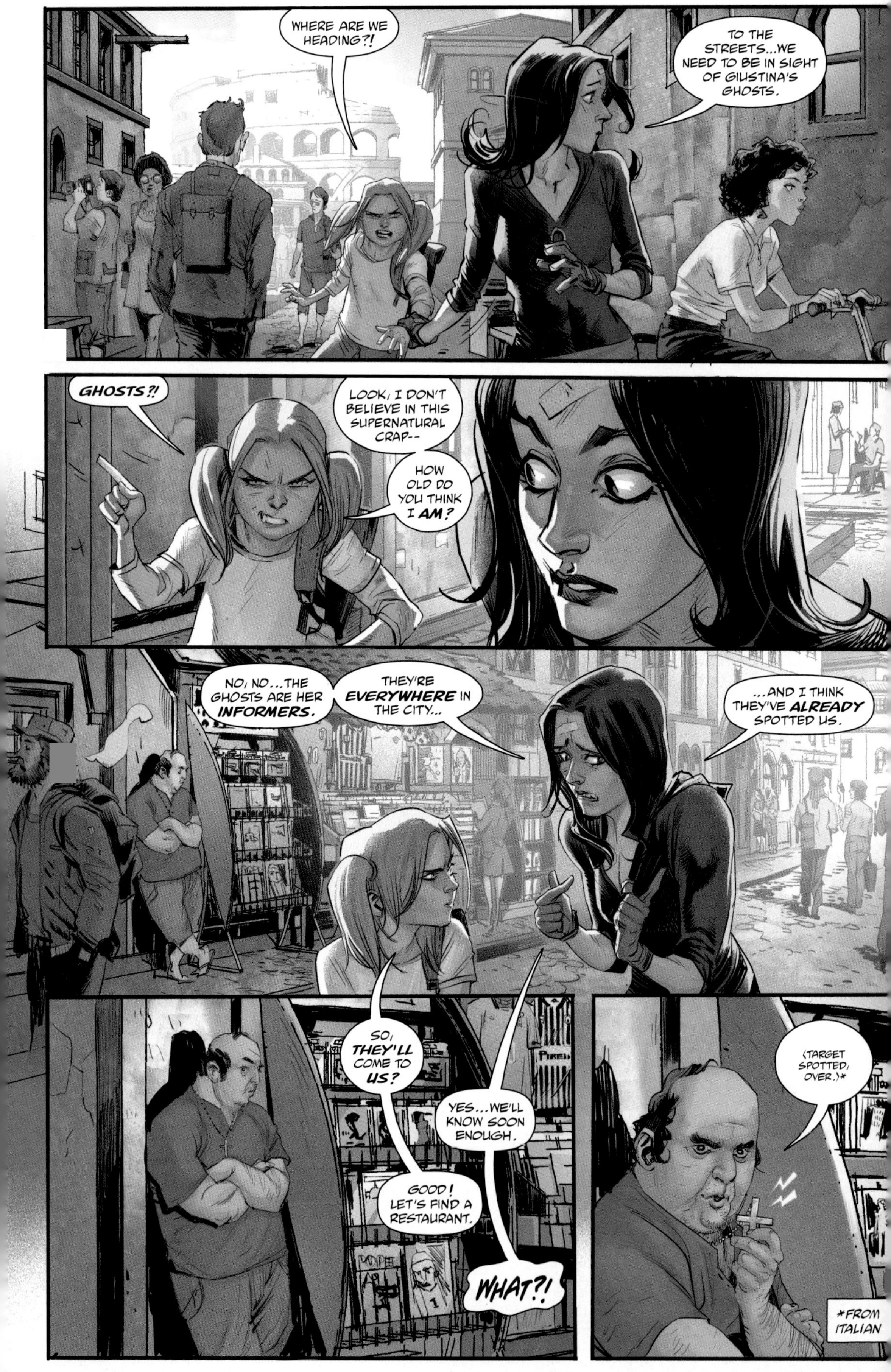
WHERE ARE WE HEADING?!
TO THE STREETS...WE NEED TO BE IN SIGHT OF GIUSTINA'S GHOSTS.
GHOSTS?!
LOOK, I DON'T BELIEVE IN THIS SUPERNATURAL CRAP--
HOW OLD DO YOU THINK I AM?
NO, NO...THE GHOSTS ARE HER INFORMERS.
THEY'RE EVERYWHERE IN THE CITY...
...AND I THINK THEY'VE ALREADY SPOTTED US.
SO, THEY'LL COME TO US?
YES...WE'LL KNOW SOON ENOUGH.
GOOD! LET'S FIND A RESTAURANT.
WHAT?!
(TARGET SPOTTED, OVER.)*
*FROM ITALIAN

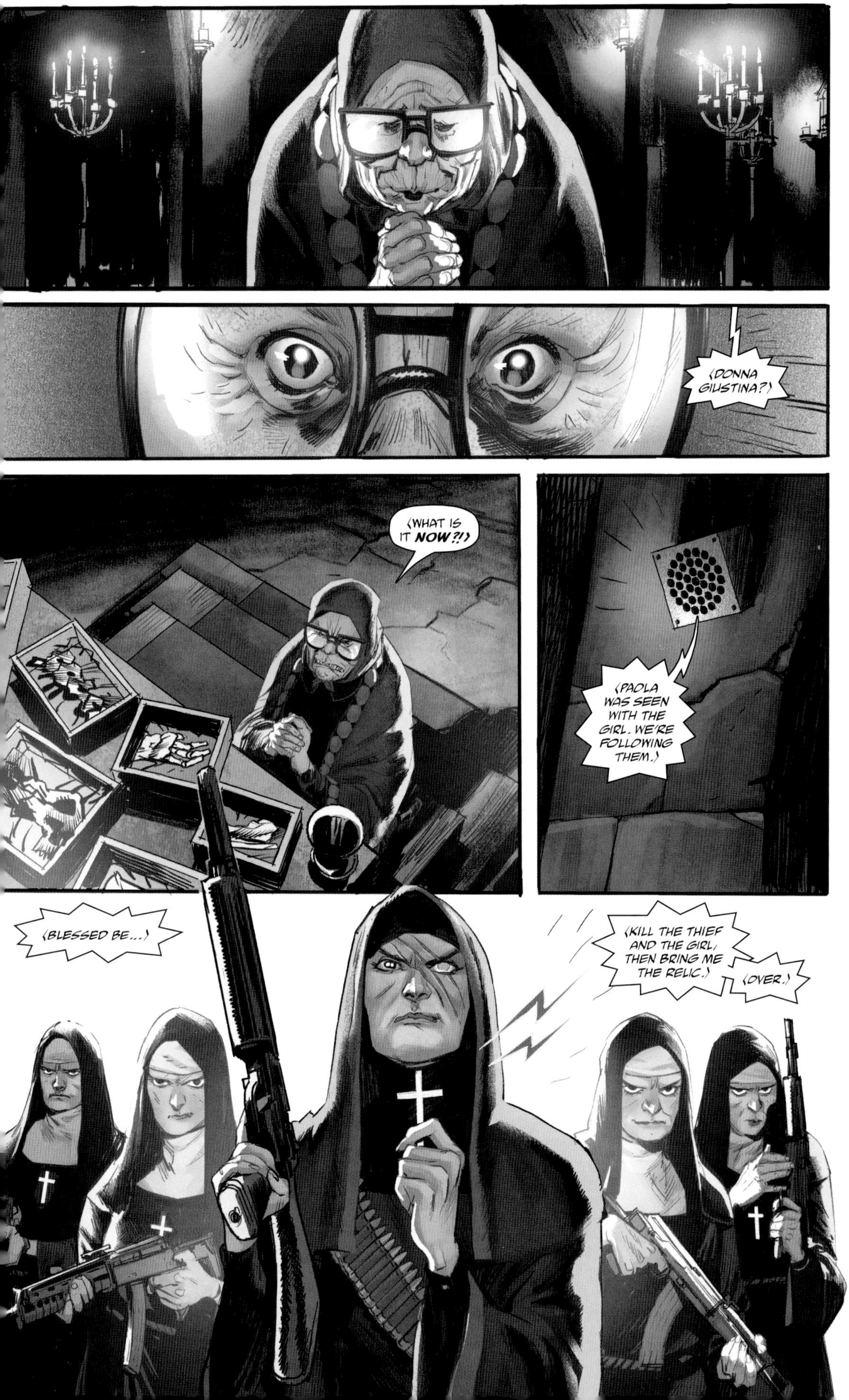

‹DONNA GIUSTINA?›
‹WHAT IS IT **NOW?!**›
‹PAOLA WAS SEEN WITH THE GIRL. WE'RE FOLLOWING THEM.›
‹BLESSED BE...›
‹KILL THE THIEF AND THE GIRL, THEN BRING ME THE RELIC.›
‹OVER.›

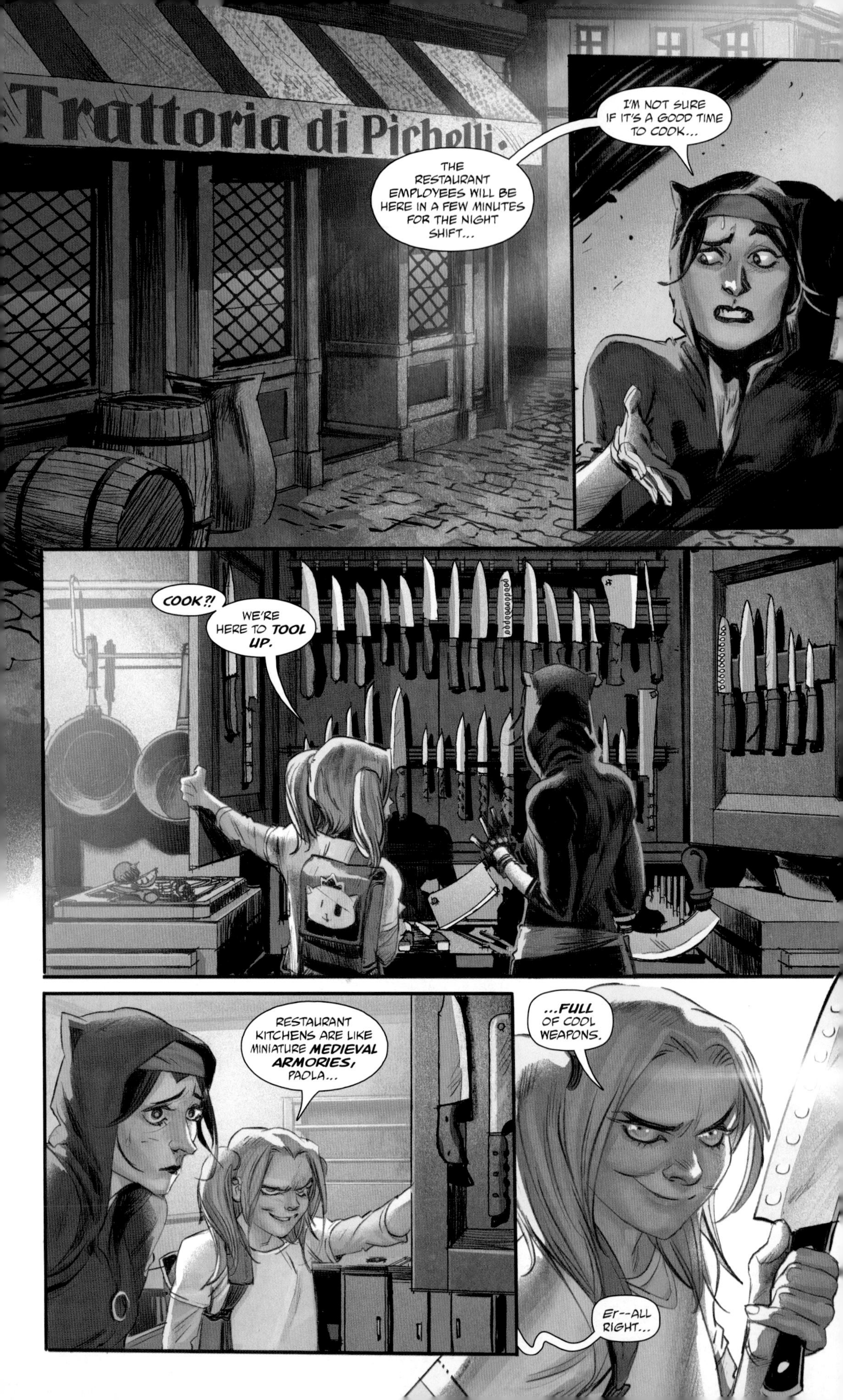
Trattoria di Pichelli.
THE RESTAURANT EMPLOYEES WILL BE HERE IN A FEW MINUTES FOR THE NIGHT SHIFT...
I'M NOT SURE IF IT'S A GOOD TIME TO COOK...
COOK?!
WE'RE HERE TO TOOL UP.
RESTAURANT KITCHENS ARE LIKE MINIATURE MEDIEVAL ARMORIES, PAOLA...
...FULL OF COOL WEAPONS.
Er--ALL RIGHT...

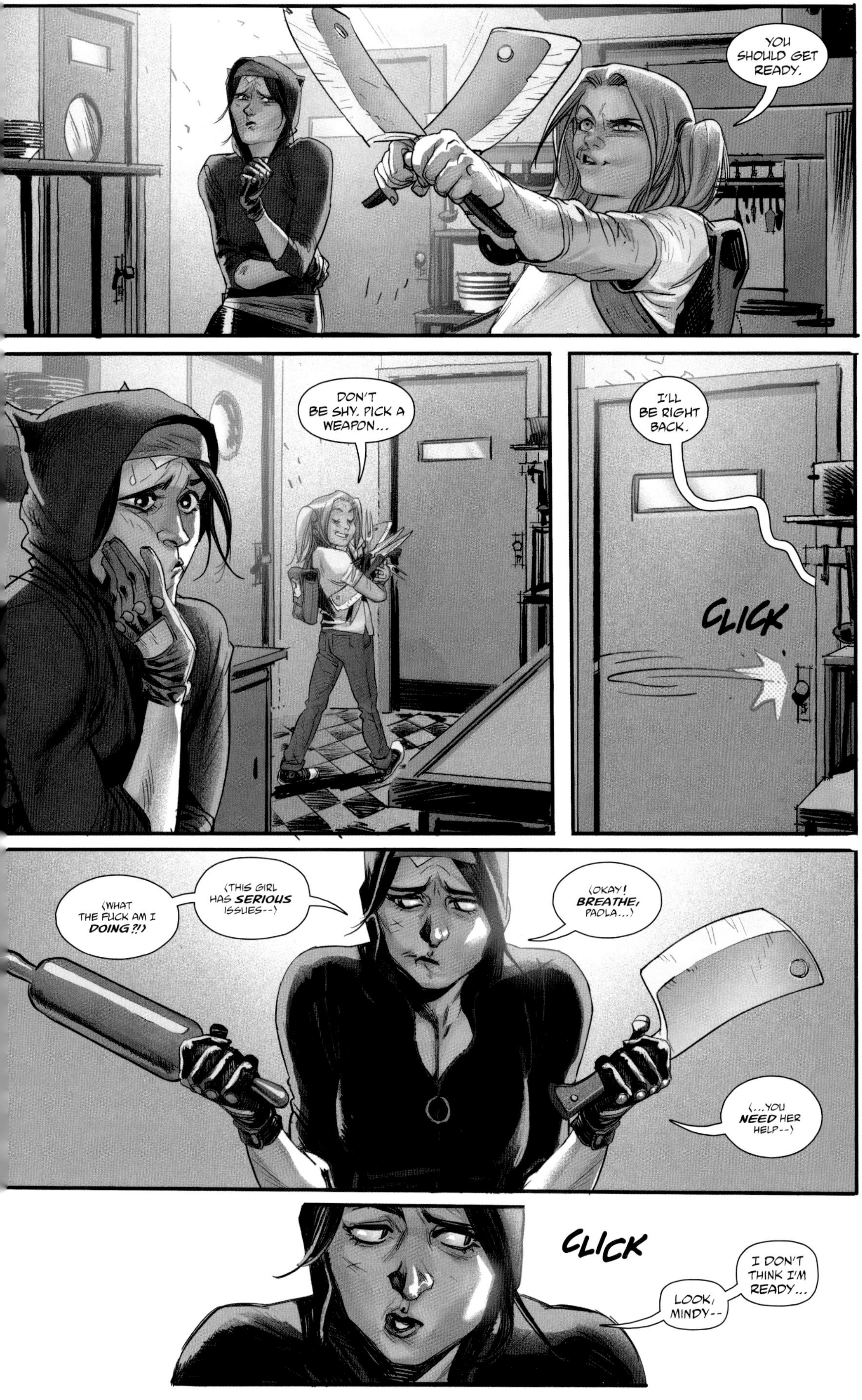

YOU SHOULD GET READY.
DON'T BE SHY. PICK A WEAPON...
I'LL BE RIGHT BACK.
CLICK
‹WHAT THE FUCK AM I *DOING?!*›
‹THIS GIRL HAS *SERIOUS* ISSUES--›
‹OKAY! *BREATHE,* PAOLA...›
‹...YOU *NEED* HER HELP--›
CLICK
LOOK, MINDY--
I DON'T THINK I'M READY...

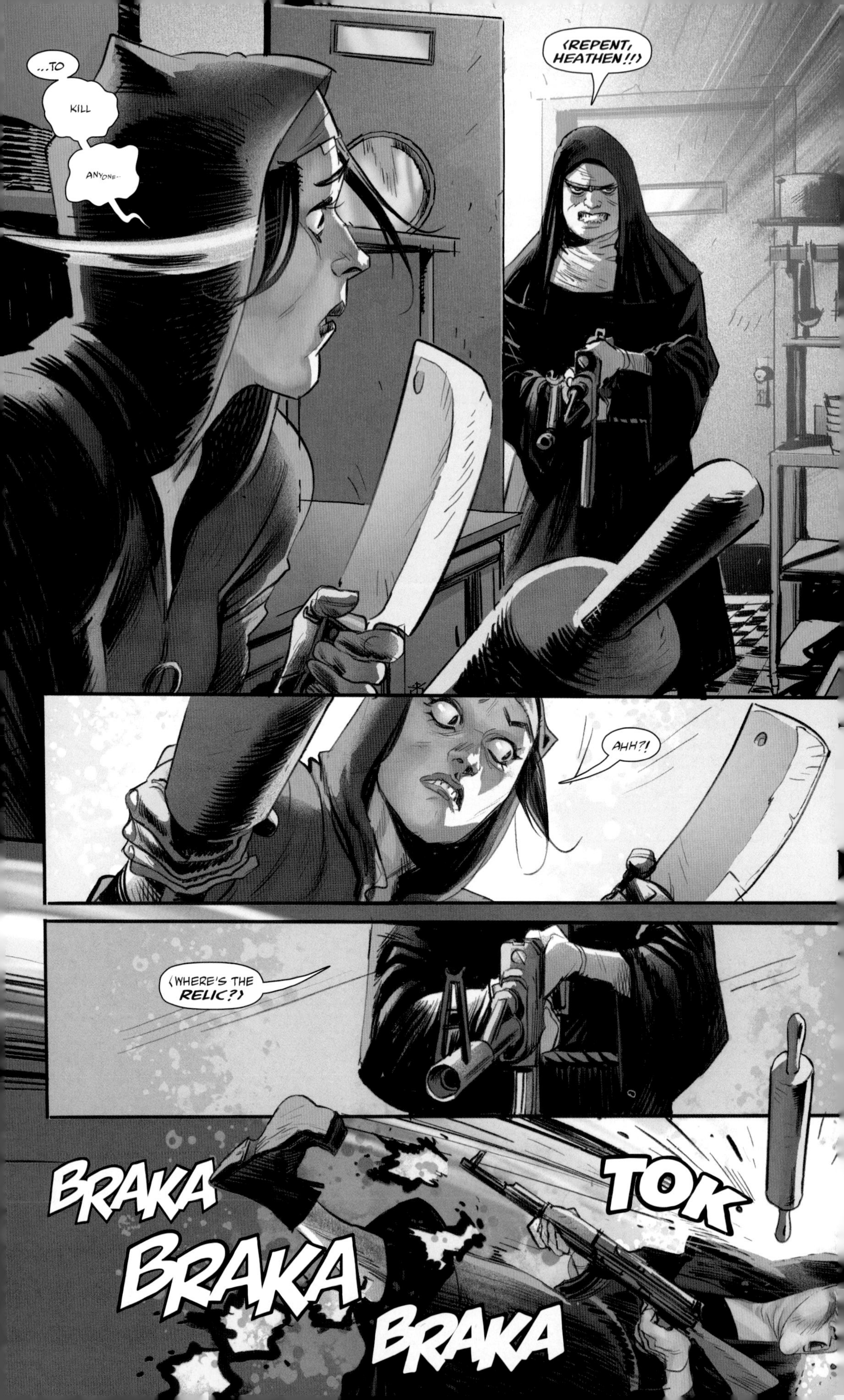
...TO
KILL
ANYONE...
‹REPENT, HEATHEN!!›
AHH?!
‹WHERE'S THE RELIC?›
BRAKA
BRAKA
BRAKA
TOK

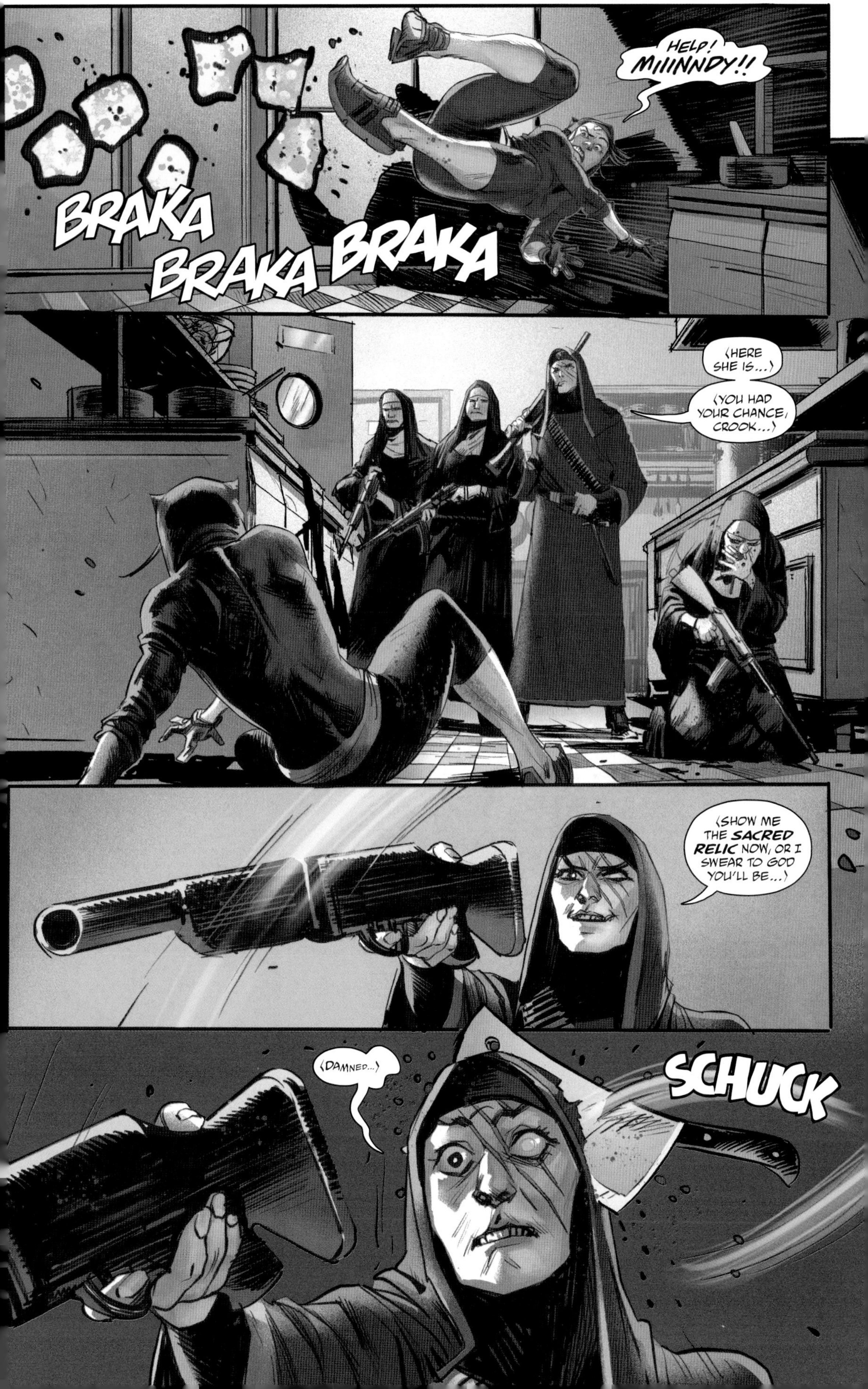
HELP! MIIINNDY!!
BRAKA
BRAKA BRAKA BRAKA
⟨HERE SHE IS...⟩
⟨YOU HAD YOUR CHANCE, CROOK...⟩
⟨SHOW ME THE SACRED RELIC NOW, OR I SWEAR TO GOD YOU'LL BE...⟩
⟨DAMNED...⟩
SCHUCK

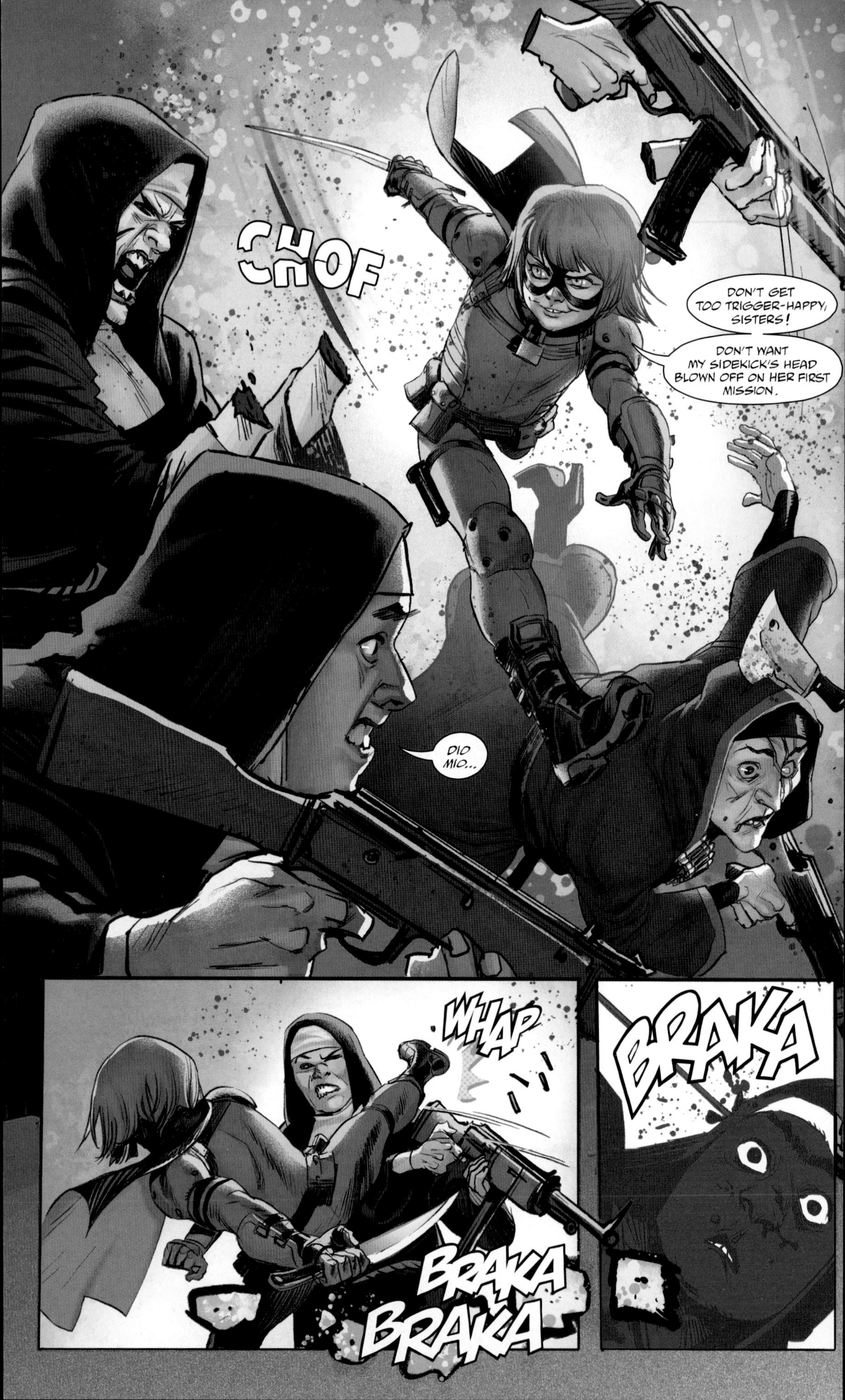
CHOF
DON'T GET TOO TRIGGER-HAPPY, SISTERS!
DON'T WANT MY SIDEKICK'S HEAD BLOWN OFF ON HER FIRST MISSION.
DIO MIO...
WHAP
BRAKA BRAKA
BRAKA

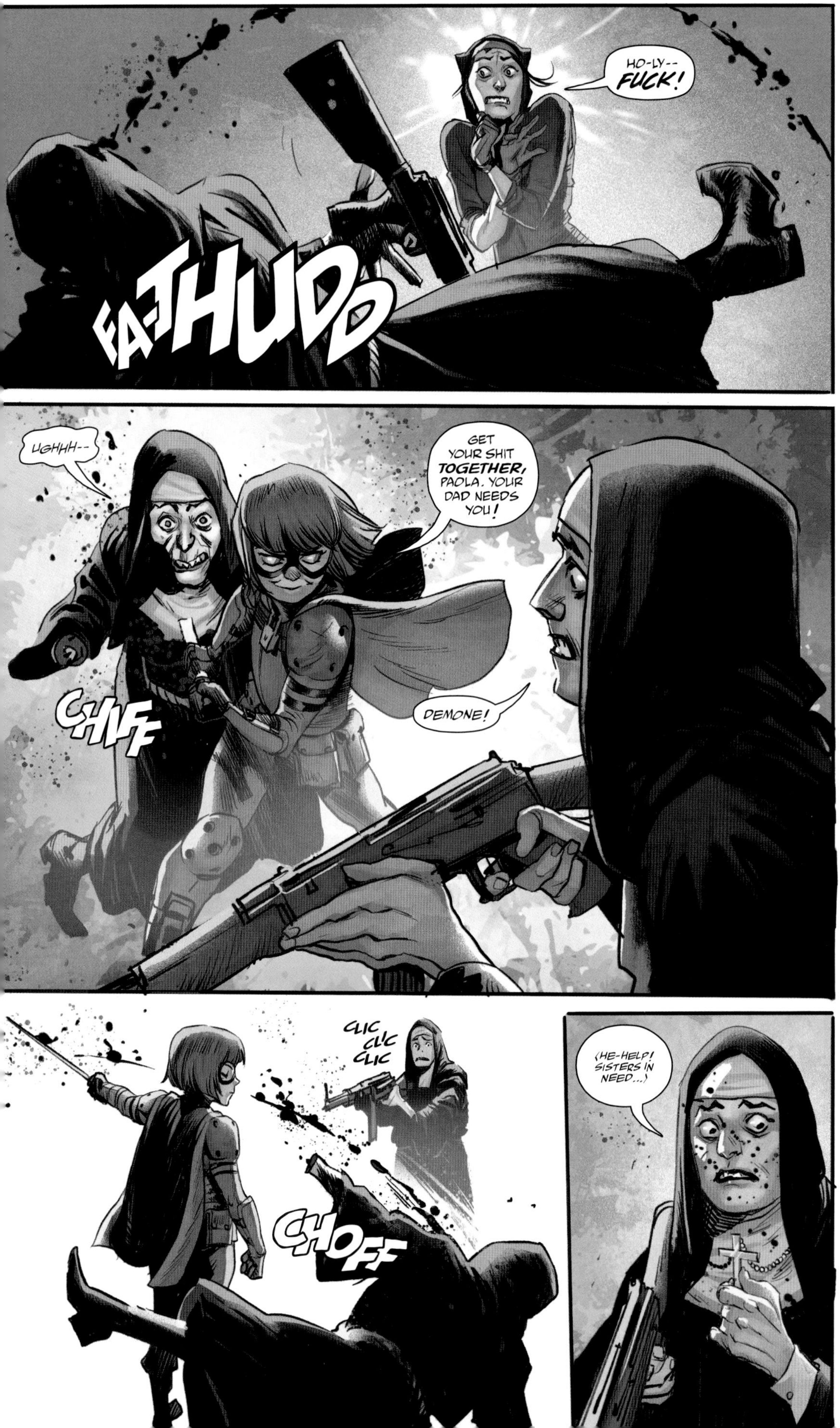
HO-LY--
FUCK!
FA-THUDD
UGHHH--
GET YOUR SHIT TOGETHER, PAOLA. YOUR DAD NEEDS YOU!
CHUFF
DEMONE!
CLIC CLIC CLIC
CHOFF
(HE-HELP! SISTERS IN NEED...)

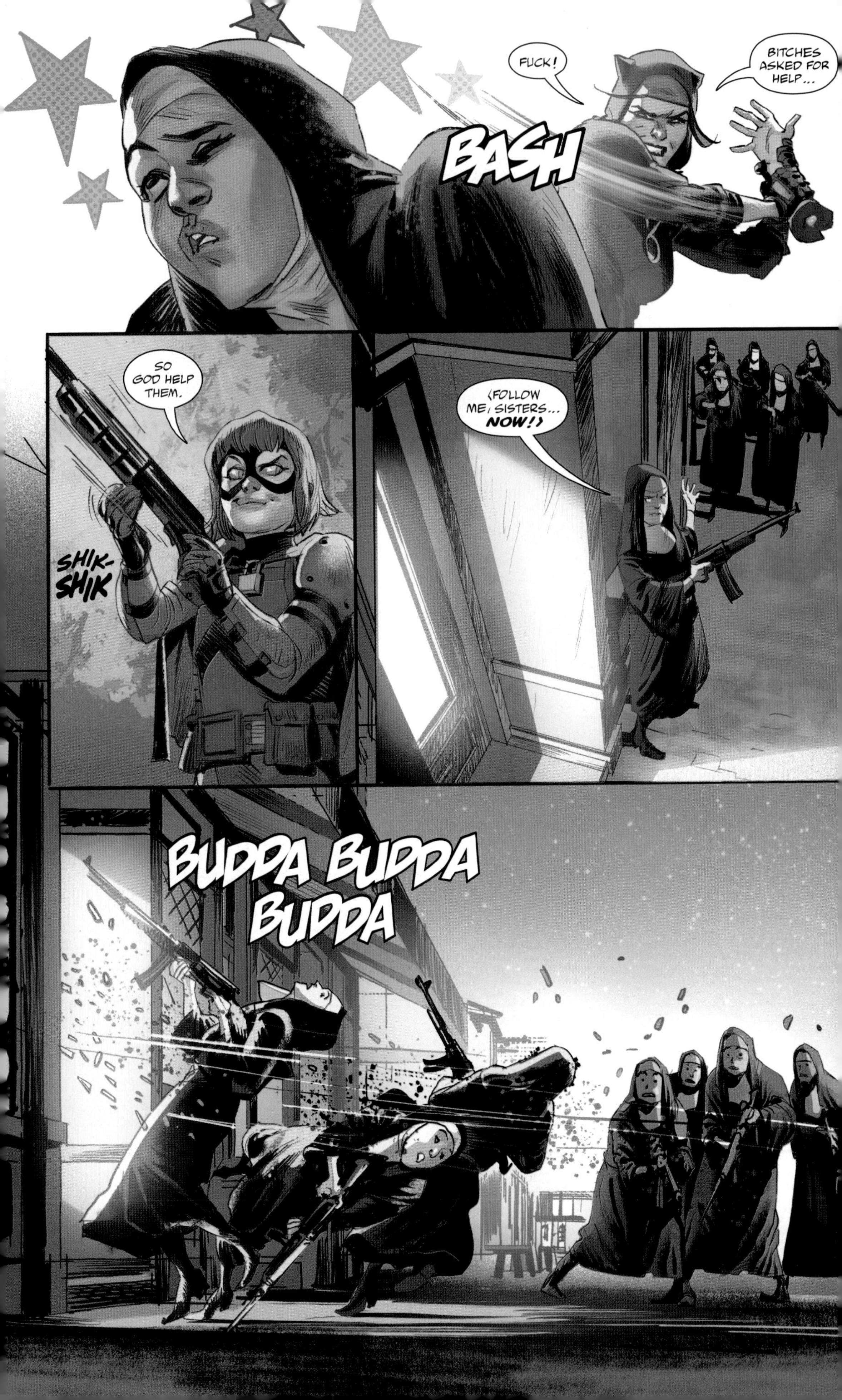
BASH
FUCK!
BITCHES ASKED FOR HELP...
SO GOD HELP THEM.
SHIK-SHIK
‹FOLLOW ME, SISTERS... NOW!›
BUDDA BUDDA BUDDA

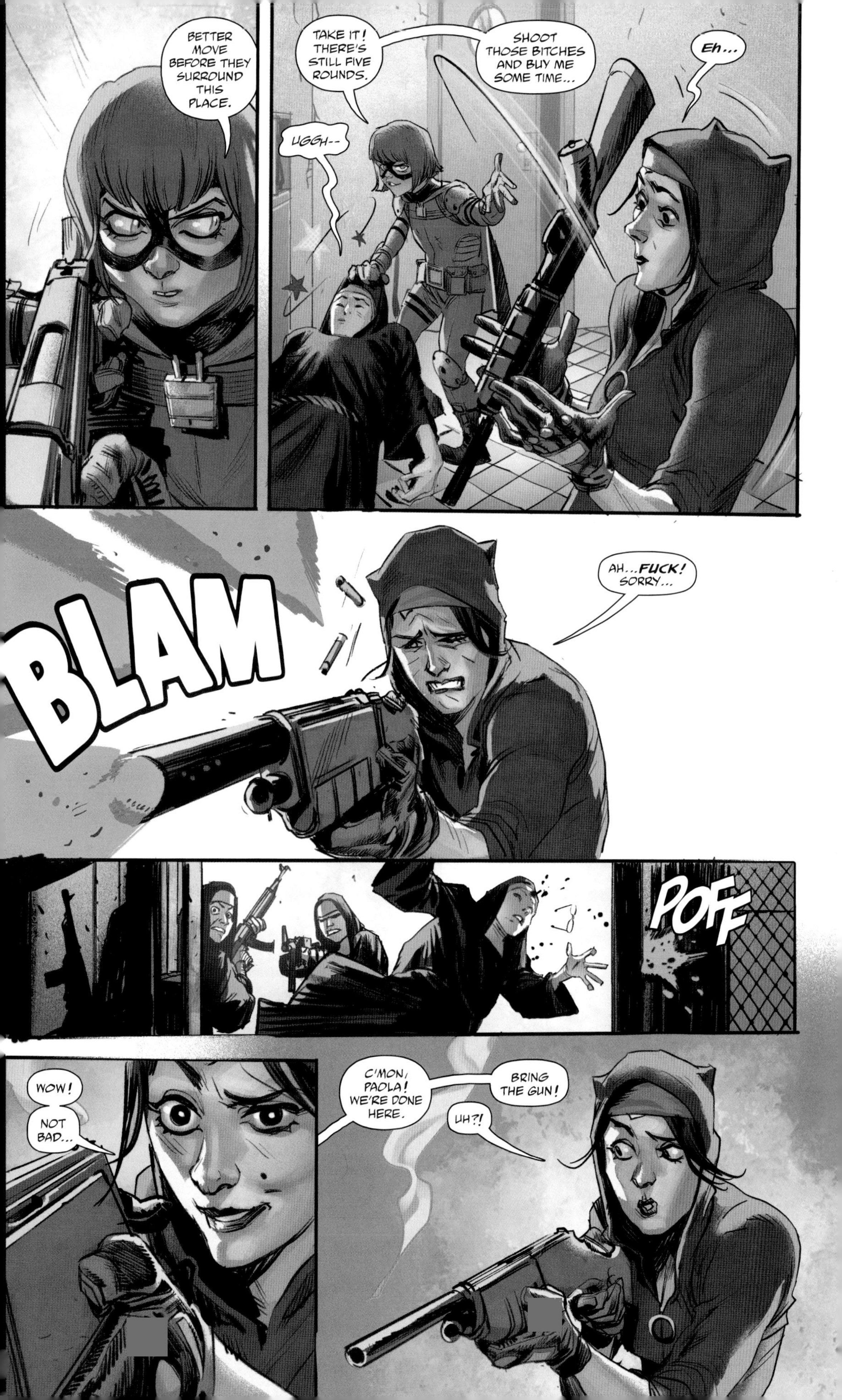
BETTER MOVE BEFORE THEY SURROUND THIS PLACE.
TAKE IT! THERE'S STILL FIVE ROUNDS.
SHOOT THOSE BITCHES AND BUY ME SOME TIME...
Eh...
UGGH--
BLAM
AH...FUCK! SORRY...
POFF
WOW!
NOT BAD...
C'MON, PAOLA! WE'RE DONE HERE.
BRING THE GUN!
UH?!

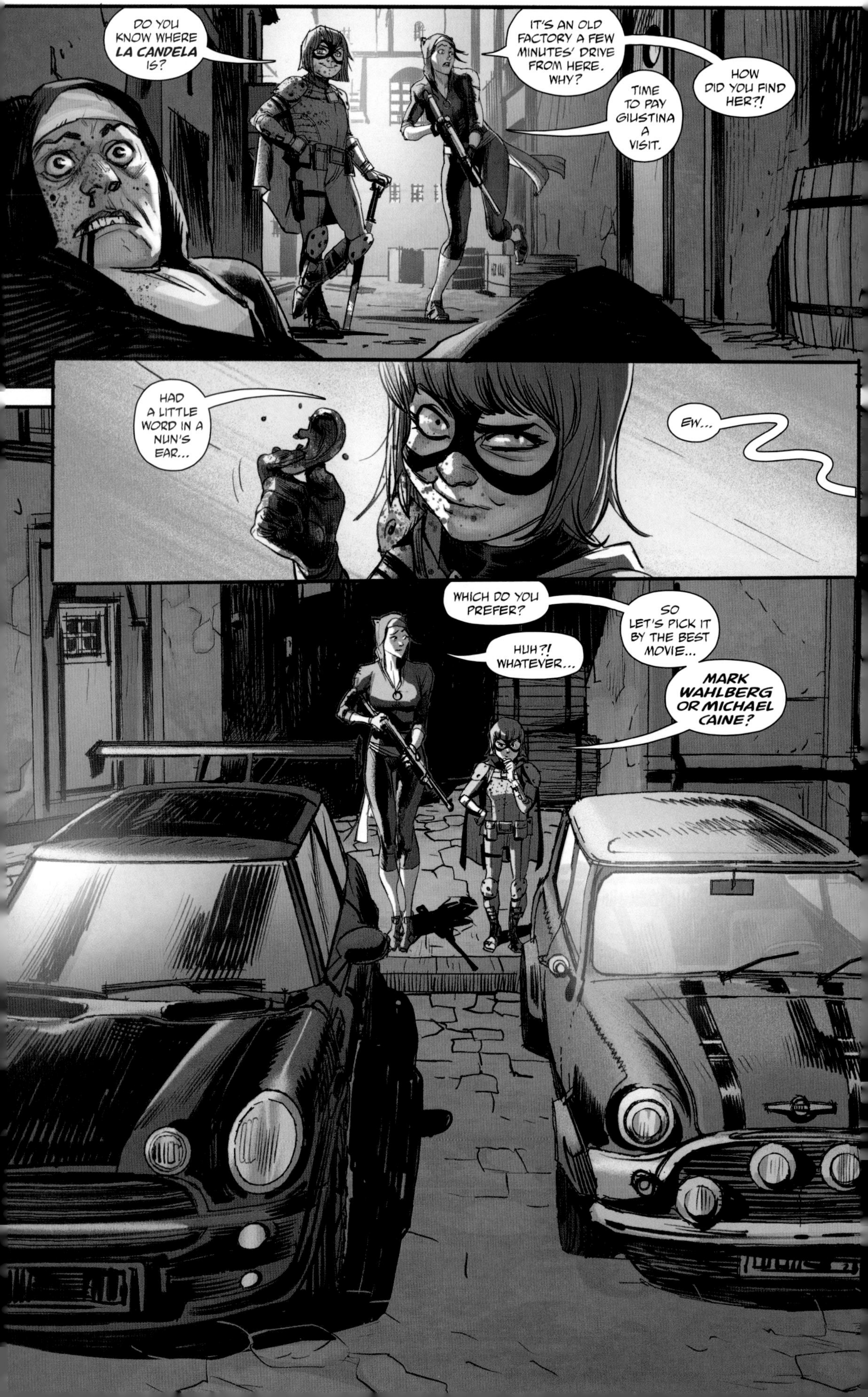

DO YOU KNOW WHERE LA CANDELA IS?
IT'S AN OLD FACTORY A FEW MINUTES' DRIVE FROM HERE. WHY?
TIME TO PAY GIUSTINA A VISIT.
HOW DID YOU FIND HER?!
HAD A LITTLE WORD IN A NUN'S EAR...
EW...
WHICH DO YOU PREFER?
HUH?! WHATEVER...
SO LET'S PICK IT BY THE BEST MOVIE...
MARK WAHLBERG OR MICHAEL CAINE?

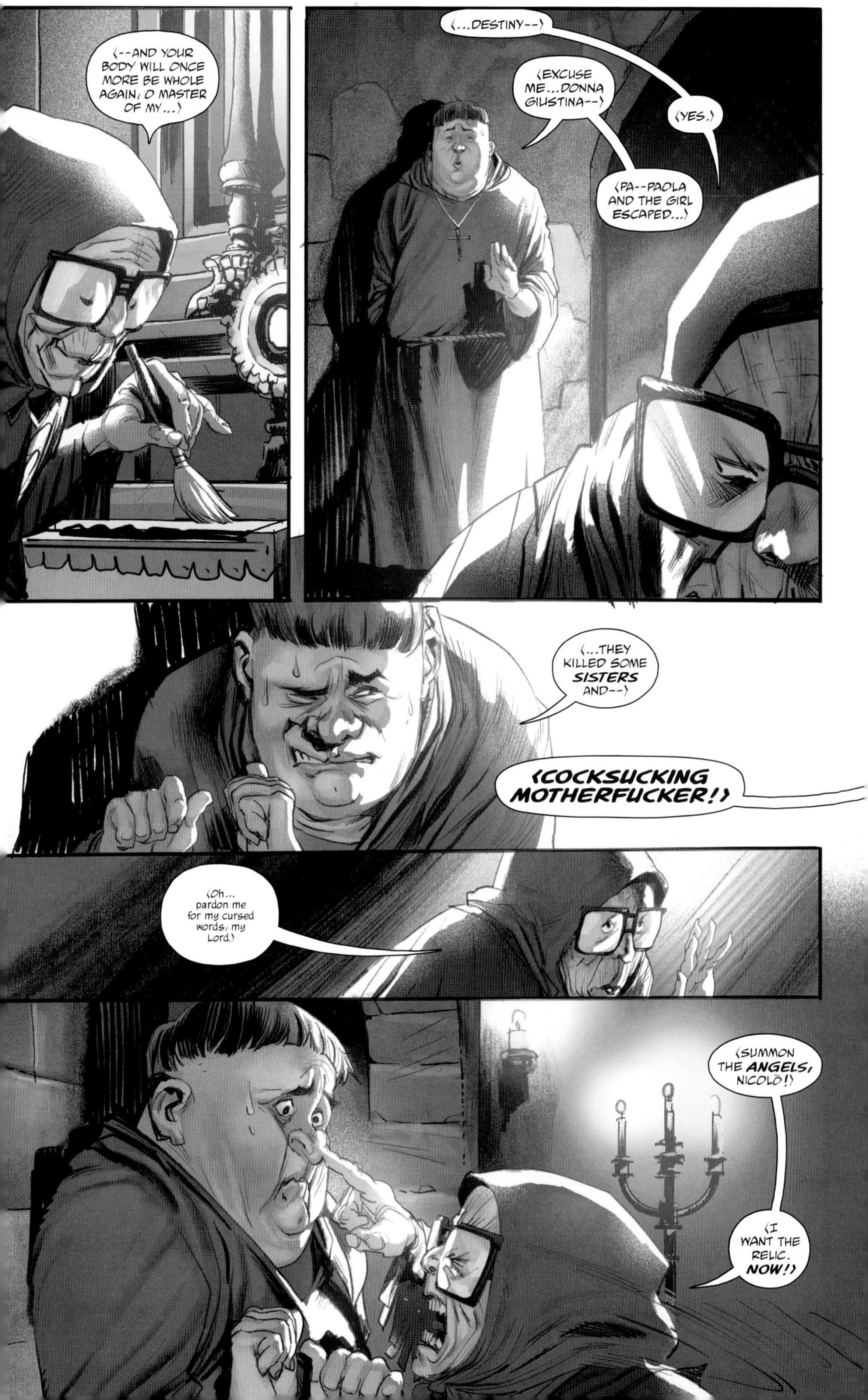
‹--AND YOUR BODY WILL ONCE MORE BE WHOLE AGAIN, O MASTER OF MY...›
‹...DESTINY--›
‹EXCUSE ME...DONNA GIUSTINA--›
‹YES.›
‹PA--PAOLA AND THE GIRL ESCAPED...›
‹...THEY KILLED SOME SISTERS AND--›
‹COCKSUCKING MOTHERFUCKER!›
‹Oh... pardon me for my cursed words, my Lord.›
‹SUMMON THE ANGELS, NICOLÒ!›
‹I WANT THE RELIC. NOW!›

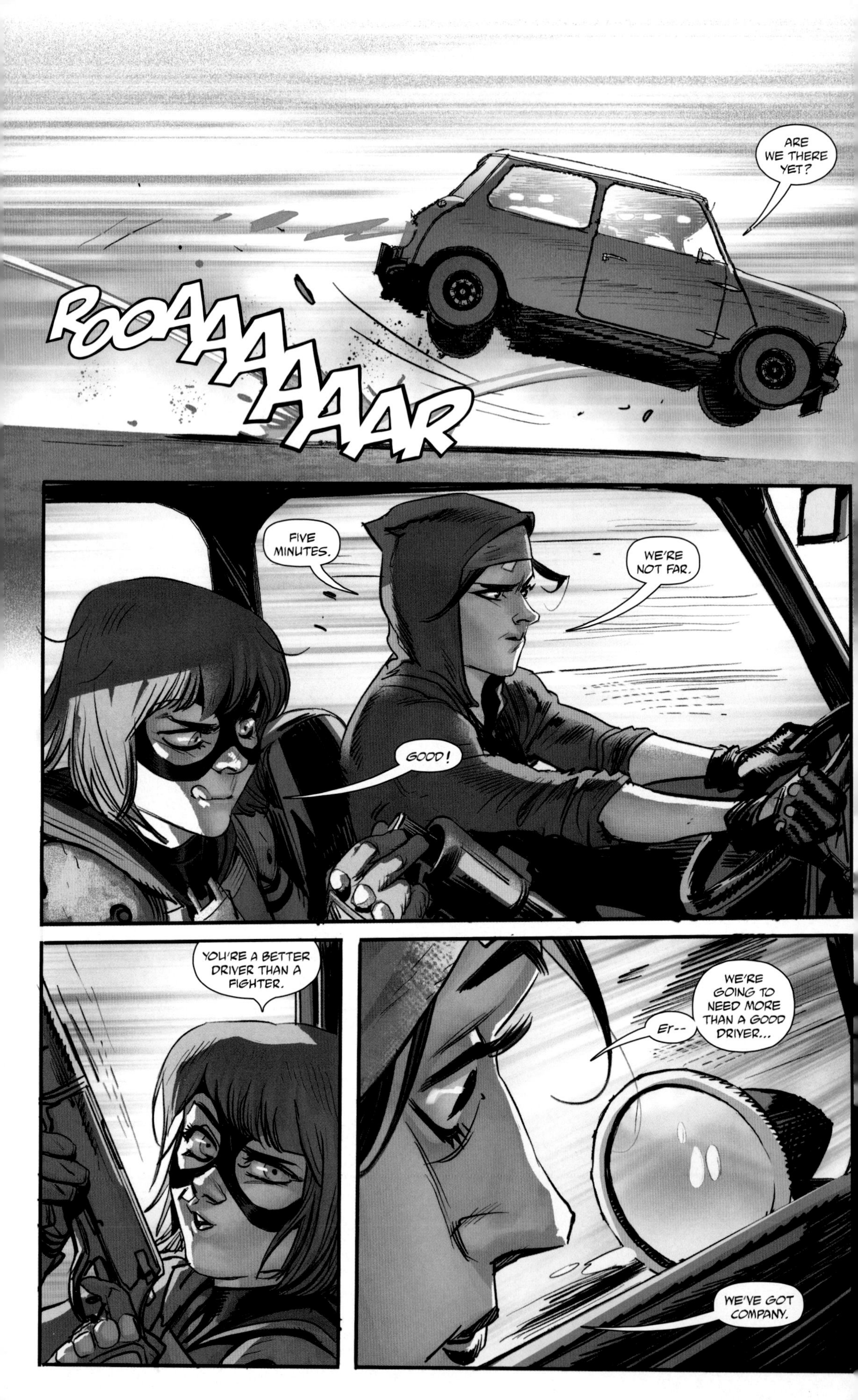
ARE WE THERE YET?
ROOAAAAAAAAR
FIVE MINUTES.
WE'RE NOT FAR.
GOOD!
YOU'RE A BETTER DRIVER THAN A FIGHTER.
WE'RE GOING TO NEED MORE THAN A GOOD DRIVER...
Er--
WE'VE GOT COMPANY.

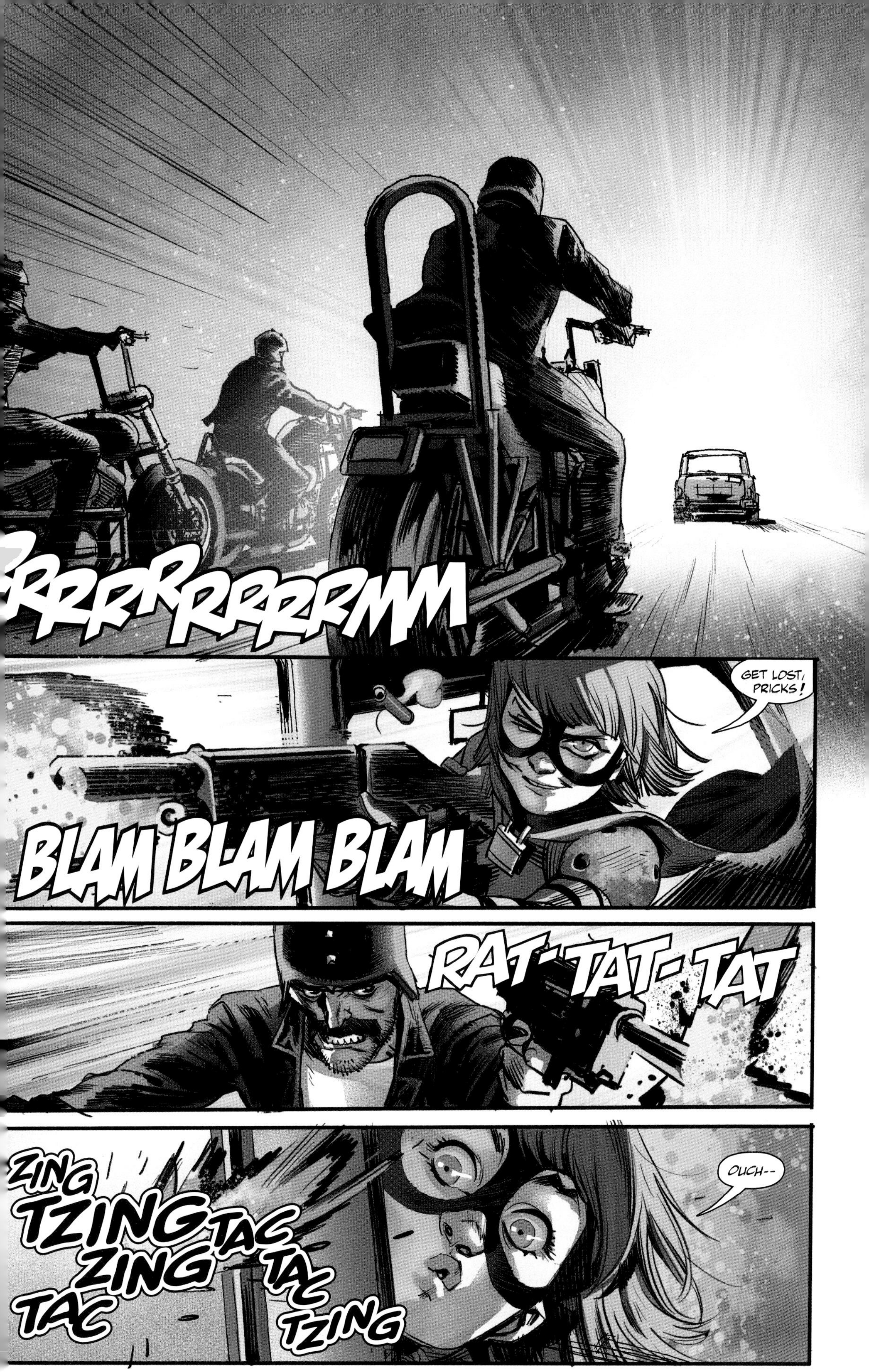
RRRRRRRRRMM
GET LOST, PRICKS!
BLAM BLAM BLAM
RAT-TAT-TAT
ZING
TZING
ZING
TAC
TAC
TAC
TZING
OUCH--

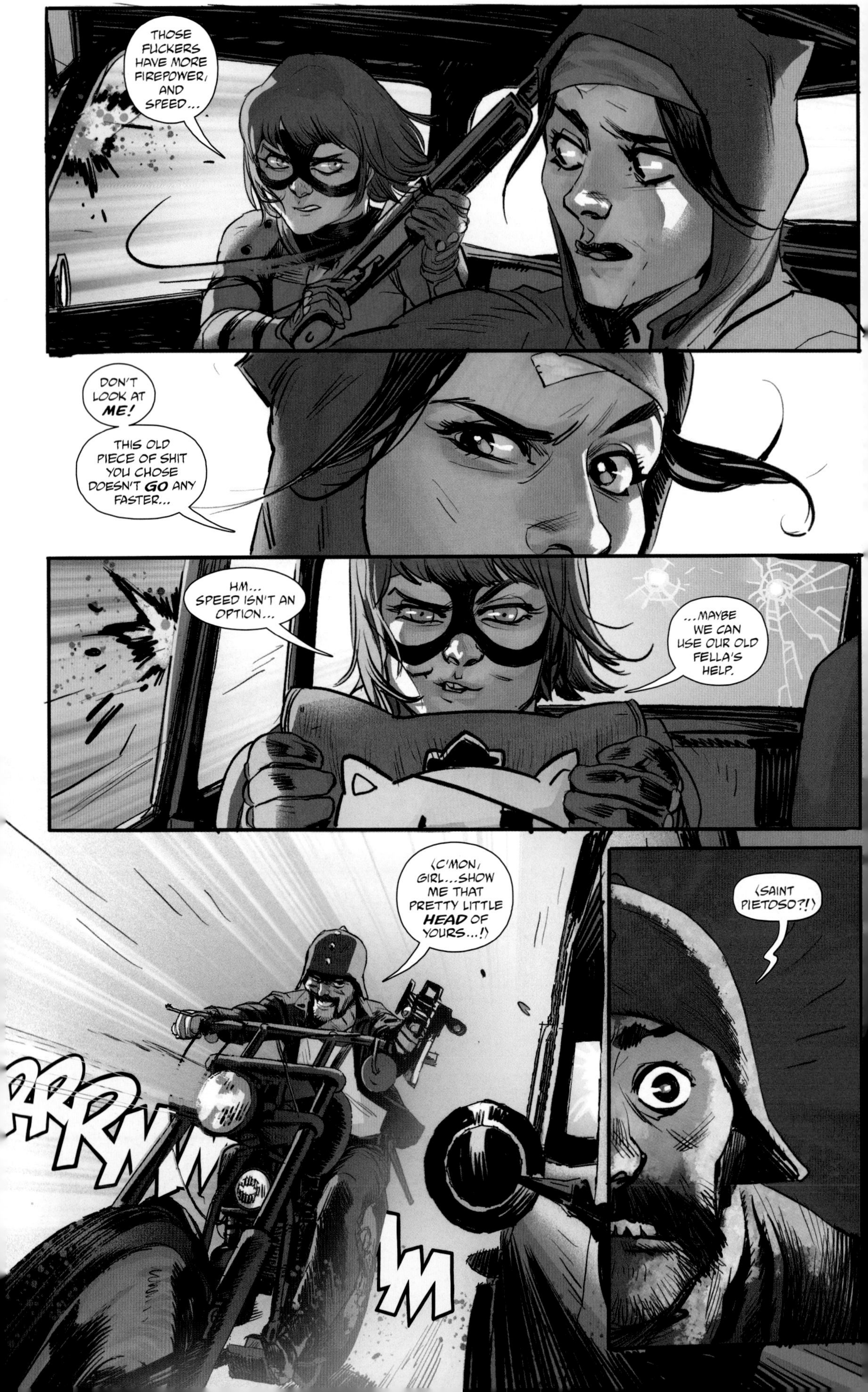
THOSE FUCKERS HAVE MORE FIREPOWER, AND SPEED...
DON'T LOOK AT ME!
THIS OLD PIECE OF SHIT YOU CHOSE DOESN'T GO ANY FASTER...
HM... SPEED ISN'T AN OPTION...
...MAYBE WE CAN USE OUR OLD FELLA'S HELP.
‹C'MON, GIRL...SHOW ME THAT PRETTY LITTLE HEAD OF YOURS...!›
‹SAINT PIETOSO?!›

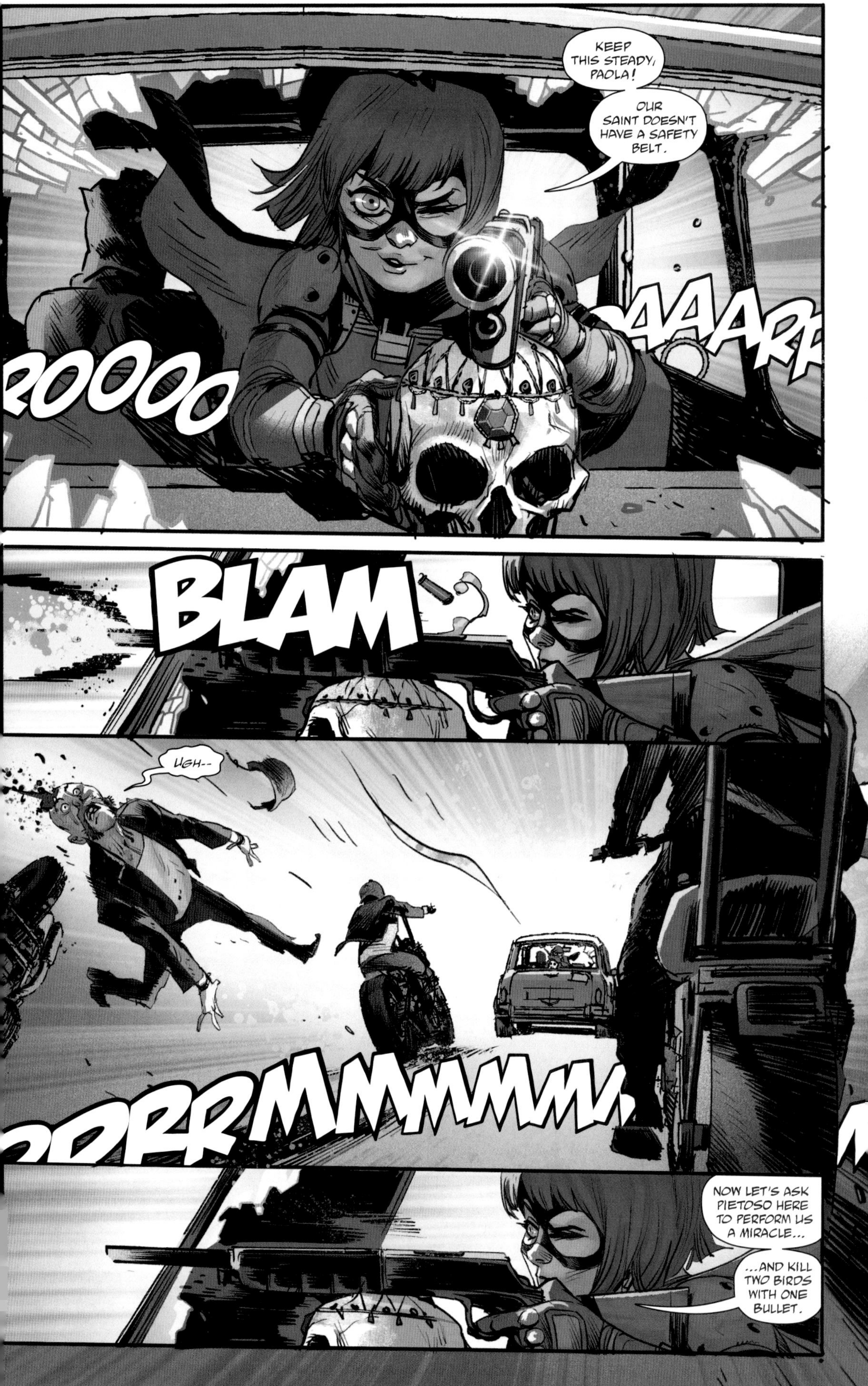
KEEP THIS STEADY, PAOLA!
OUR SAINT DOESN'T HAVE A SAFETY BELT.
ROOOO
AAAARR
BLAM
UGH--
RRRMMMMM
NOW LET'S ASK PIETOSO HERE TO PERFORM US A MIRACLE...
...AND KILL TWO BIRDS WITH ONE BULLET.

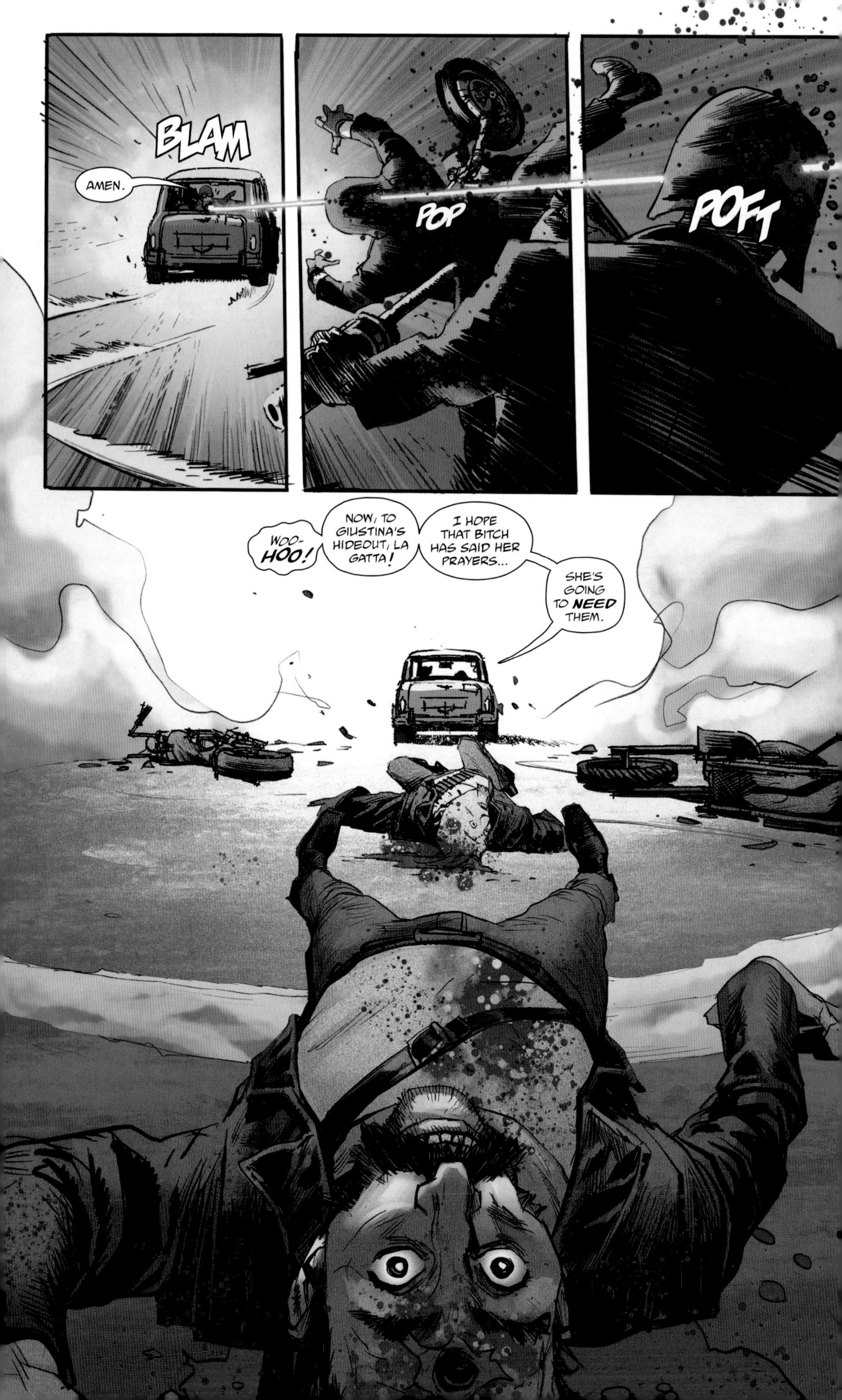
BLAM
AMEN.
POP
POFT
WOO-HOO!
NOW, TO GIUSTINA'S HIDEOUT, LA GATTA!
I HOPE THAT BITCH HAS SAID HER PRAYERS...
SHE'S GOING TO NEED THEM.

FOUR

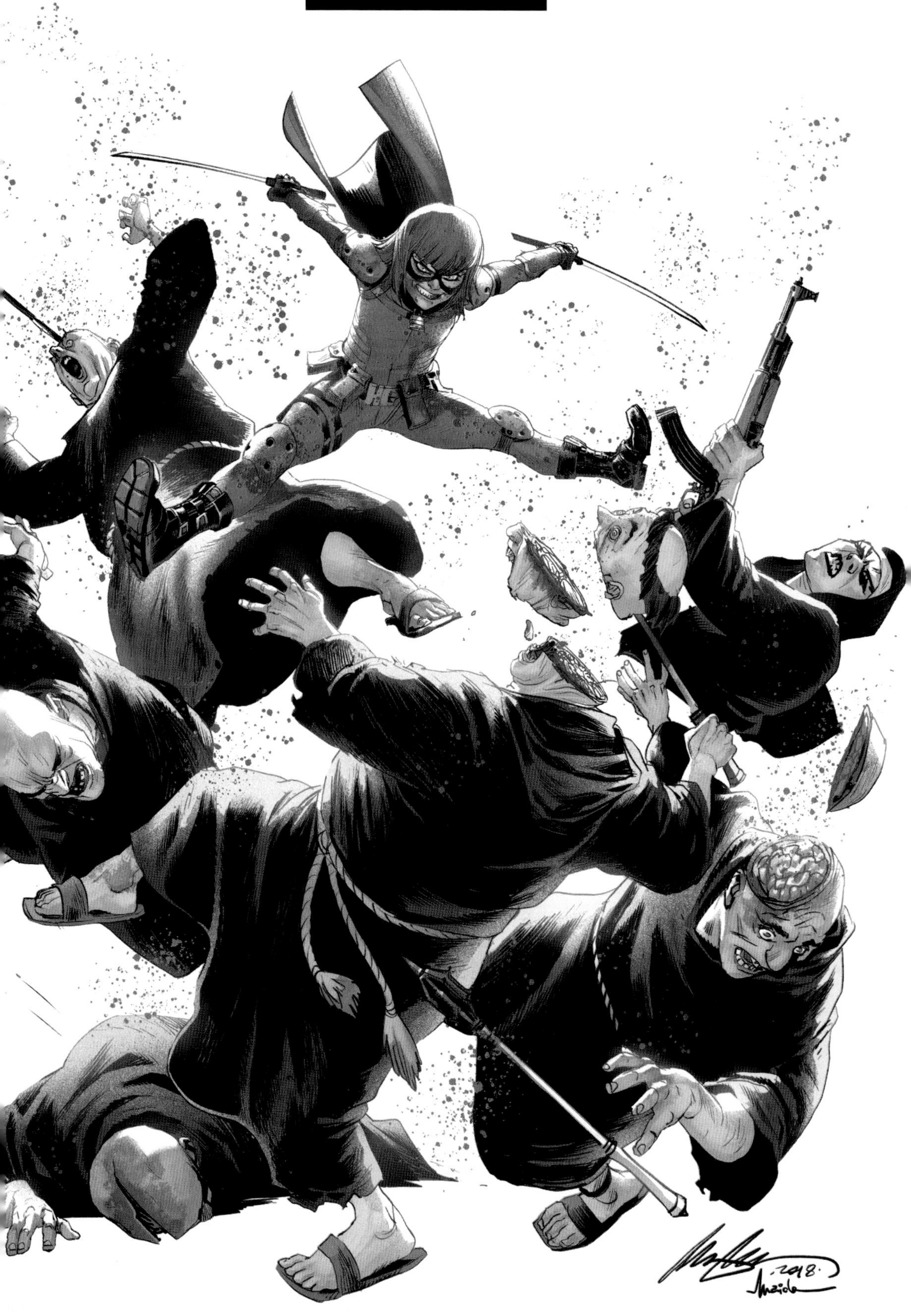

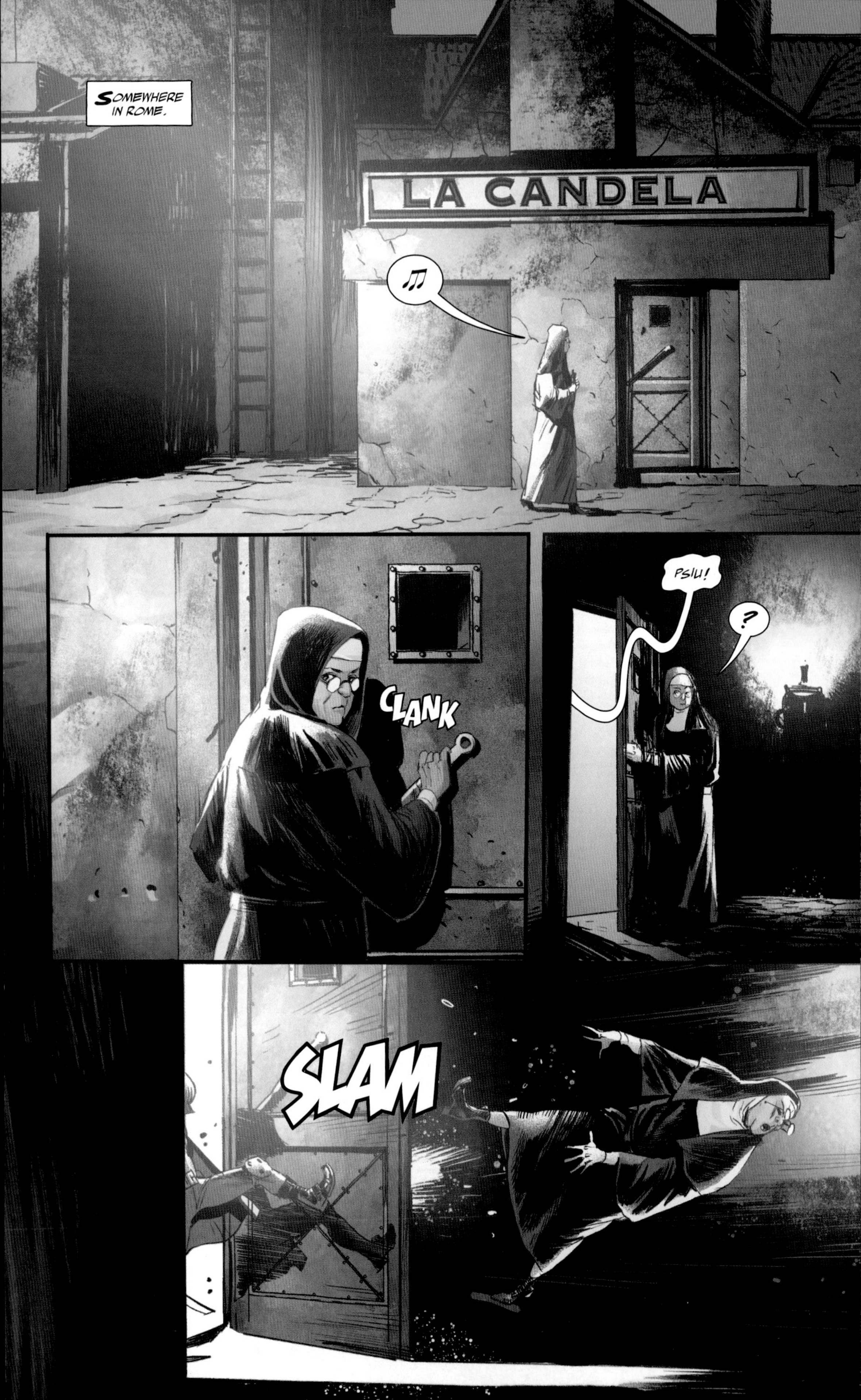
SOMEWHERE IN ROME.
LA CANDELA
♫
CLANK
PSIU!
?
SLAM

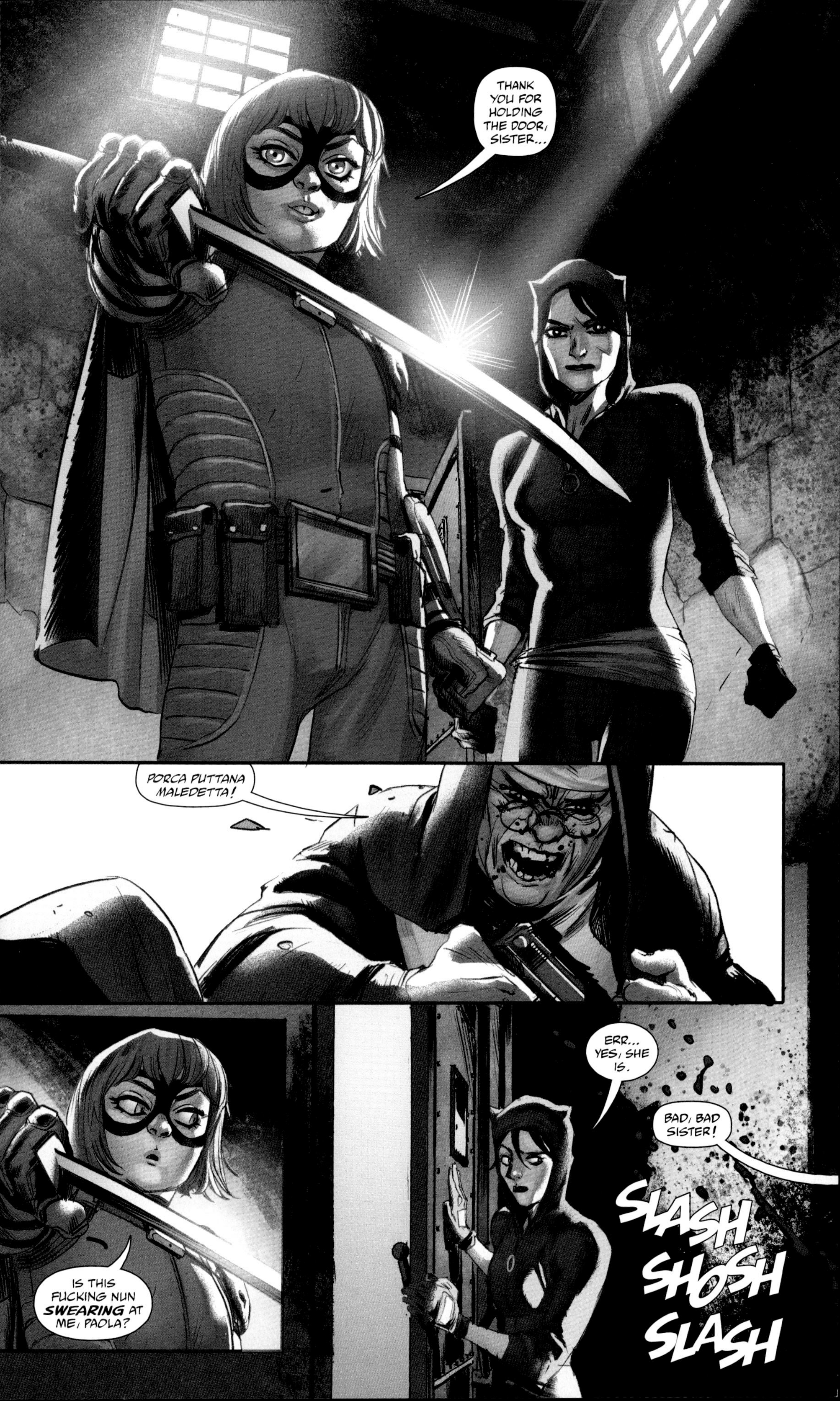
THANK YOU FOR HOLDING THE DOOR, SISTER...
PORCA PUTTANA MALEDETTA!
IS THIS FUCKING NUN SWEARING AT ME, PAOLA?
ERR... YES, SHE IS.
BAD, BAD SISTER!
SLASH
SHOSH
SLASH

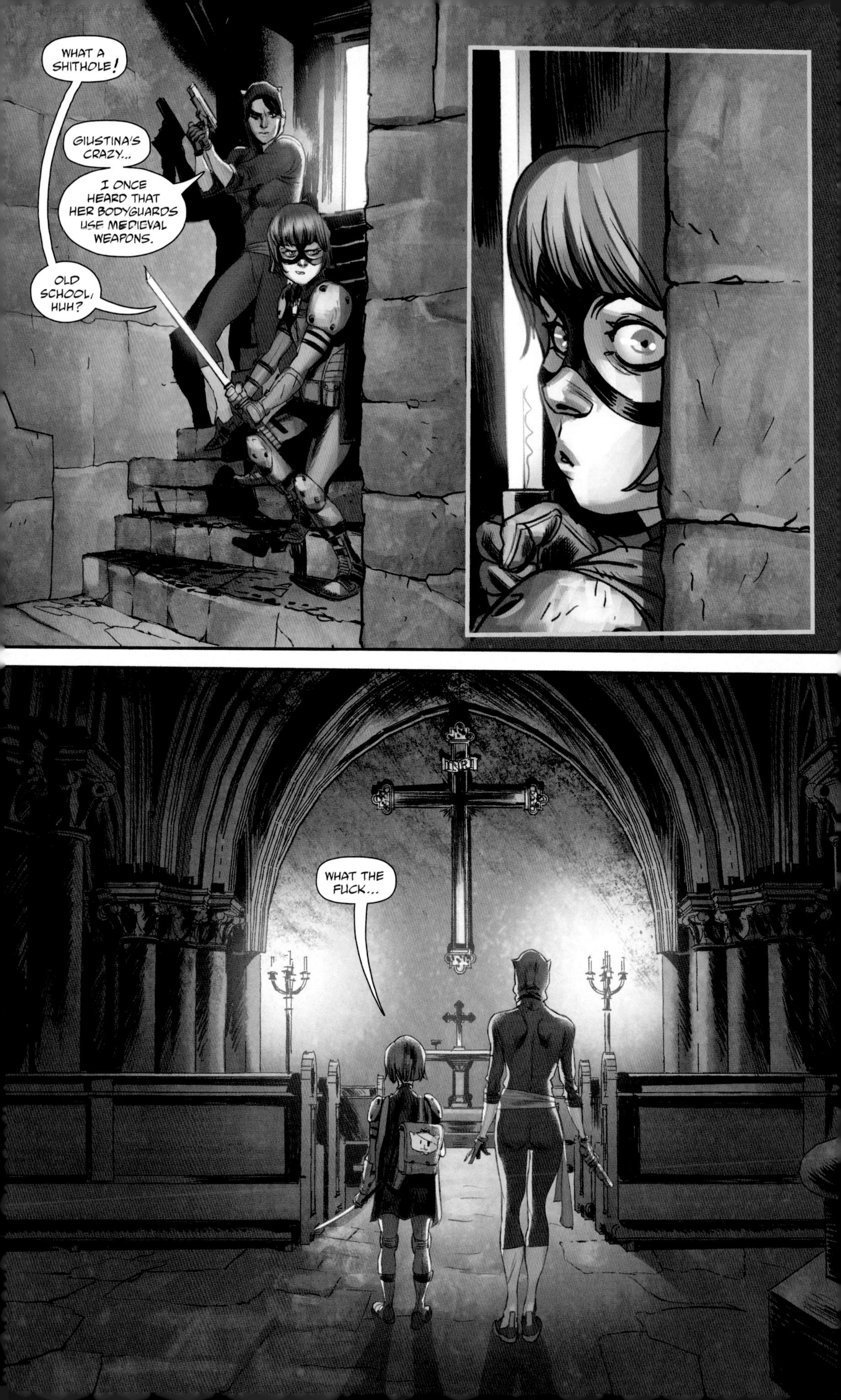
WHAT A SHITHOLE!
GIUSTINA'S CRAZY...
I ONCE HEARD THAT HER BODYGUARDS USE MEDIEVAL WEAPONS.
OLD SCHOOL, HUH?
INRI
WHAT THE FUCK...

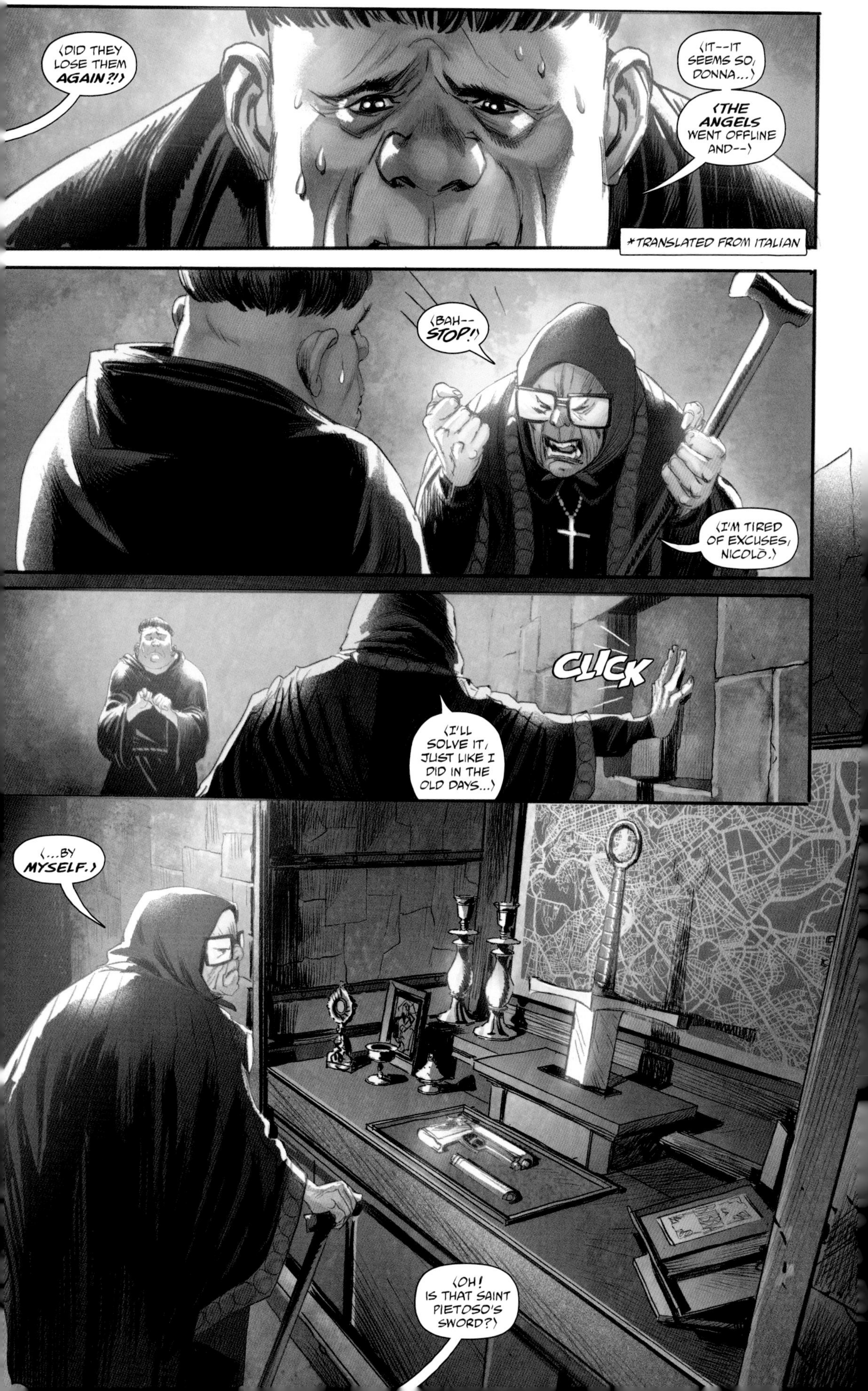
‹DID THEY LOSE THEM AGAIN?!›
‹IT--IT SEEMS SO, DONNA...›
‹THE ANGELS WENT OFFLINE AND--›
*TRANSLATED FROM ITALIAN
‹BAH-- STOP!›
‹I'M TIRED OF EXCUSES, NICOLÒ.›
CLICK
‹I'LL SOLVE IT, JUST LIKE I DID IN THE OLD DAYS...›
‹...BY MYSELF.›
‹OH! IS THAT SAINT PIETOSO'S SWORD?›

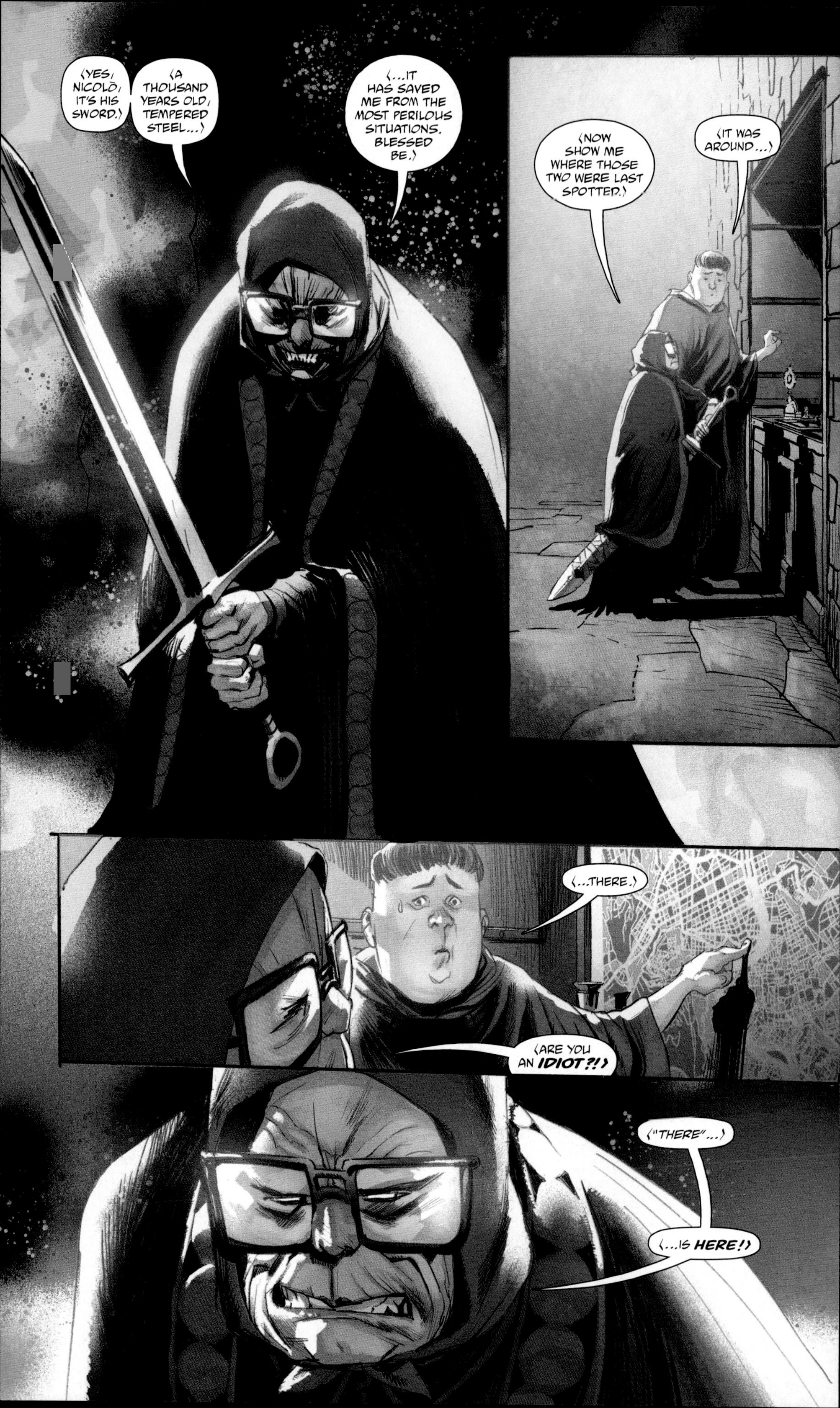
‹YES, NICOLÒ, IT'S HIS SWORD.›
‹A THOUSAND YEARS OLD, TEMPERED STEEL...›
‹...IT HAS SAVED ME FROM THE MOST PERILOUS SITUATIONS. BLESSED BE.›
‹NOW SHOW ME WHERE THOSE TWO WERE LAST SPOTTED.›
‹IT WAS AROUND...›
‹...THERE.›
‹ARE YOU AN IDIOT?!›
‹"THERE"...›
‹...IS HERE!›

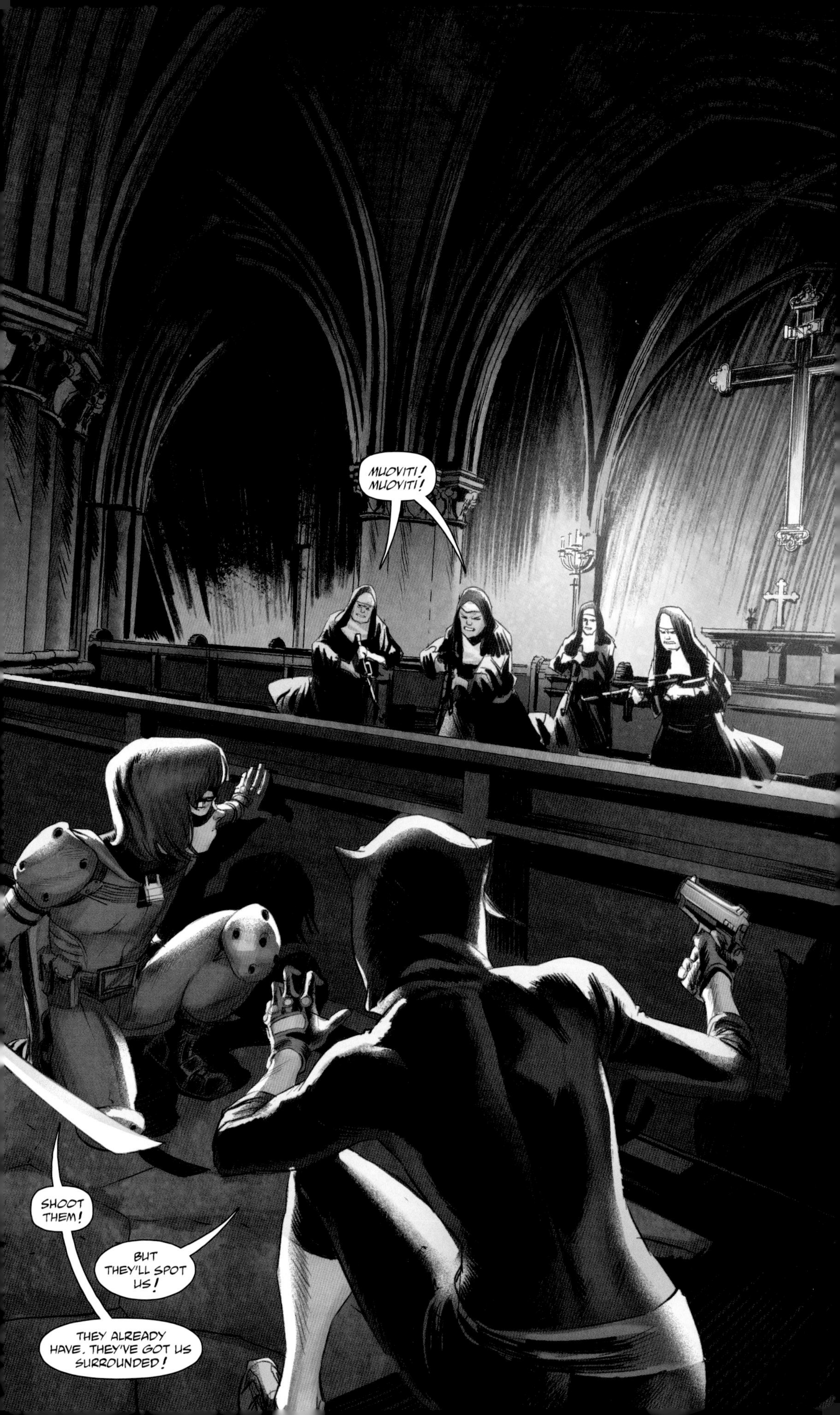
MUOVITI! MUOVITI!
SHOOT THEM!
BUT THEY'LL SPOT US!
THEY ALREADY HAVE. THEY'VE GOT US SURROUNDED!

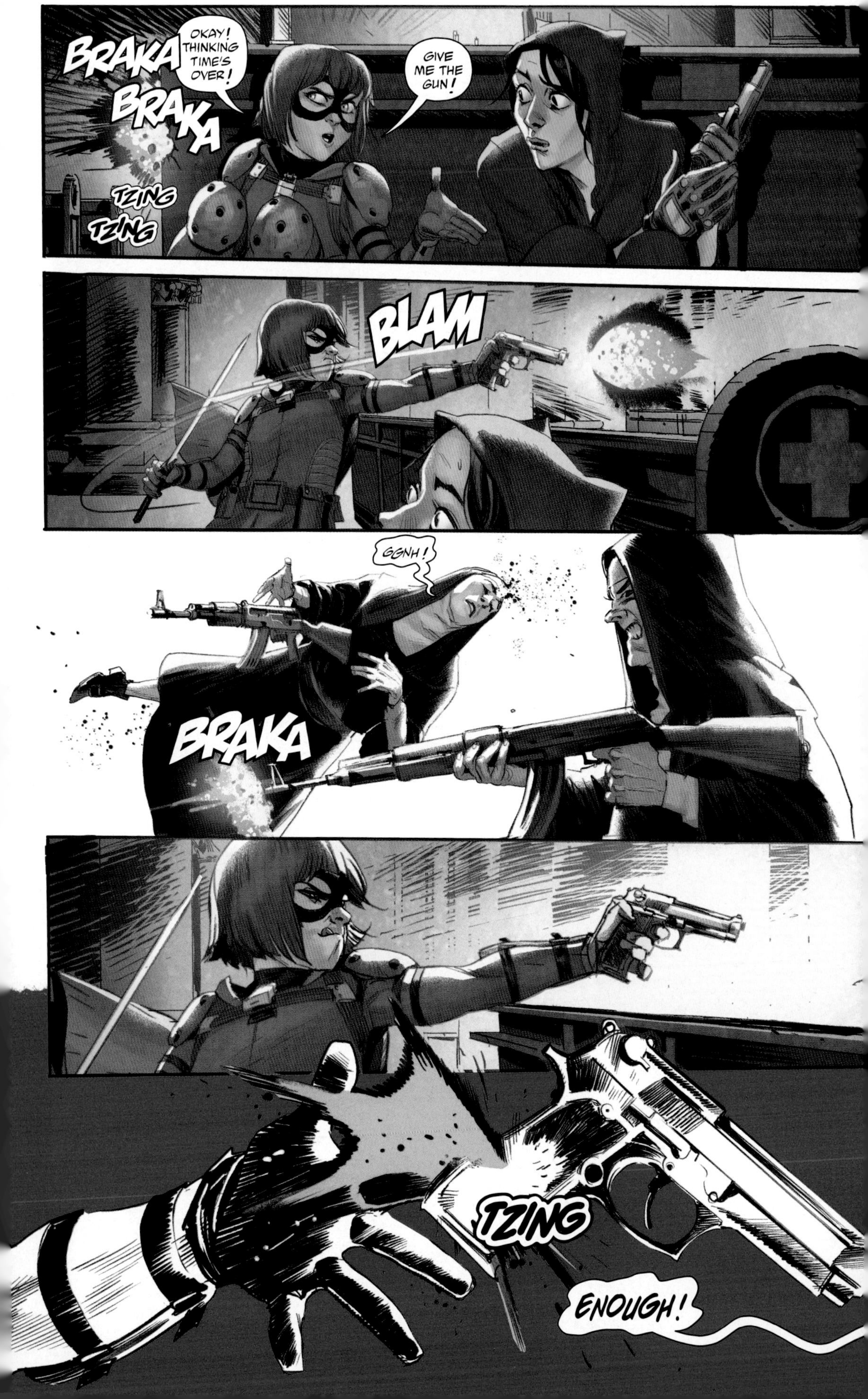
BRAKA
BRAKA
OKAY! THINKING TIME'S OVER!
GIVE ME THE GUN!
TZING
TZING
BLAM
GGNH!
BRAKA
TZING
ENOUGH!

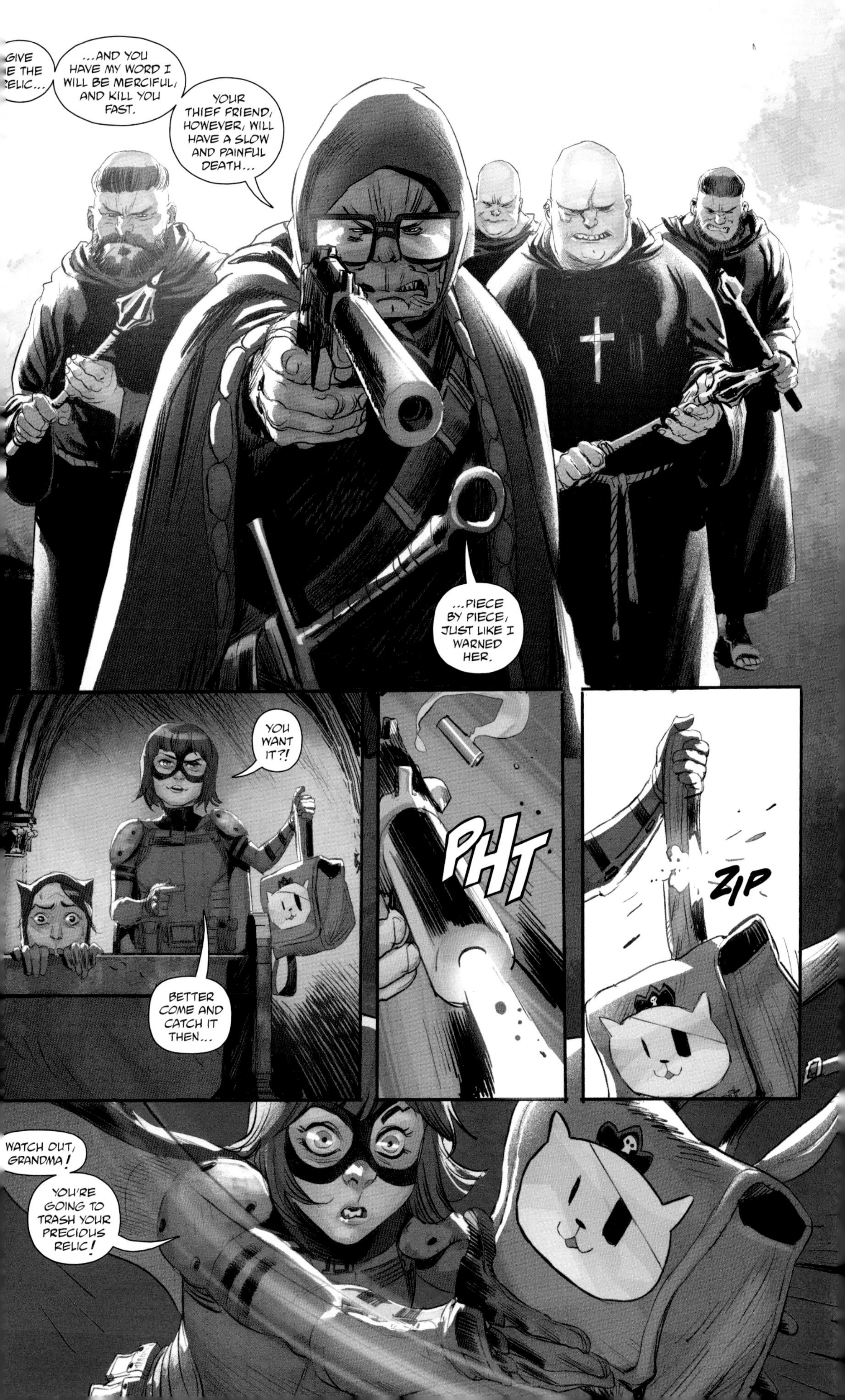
GIVE
E THE
RELIC...
...AND YOU HAVE MY WORD I WILL BE MERCIFUL, AND KILL YOU FAST.
YOUR THIEF FRIEND, HOWEVER, WILL HAVE A SLOW AND PAINFUL DEATH...
...PIECE BY PIECE, JUST LIKE I WARNED HER.
YOU WANT IT?!
BETTER COME AND CATCH IT THEN...
PHT
ZIP
WATCH OUT, GRANDMA!
YOU'RE GOING TO TRASH YOUR PRECIOUS RELIC!

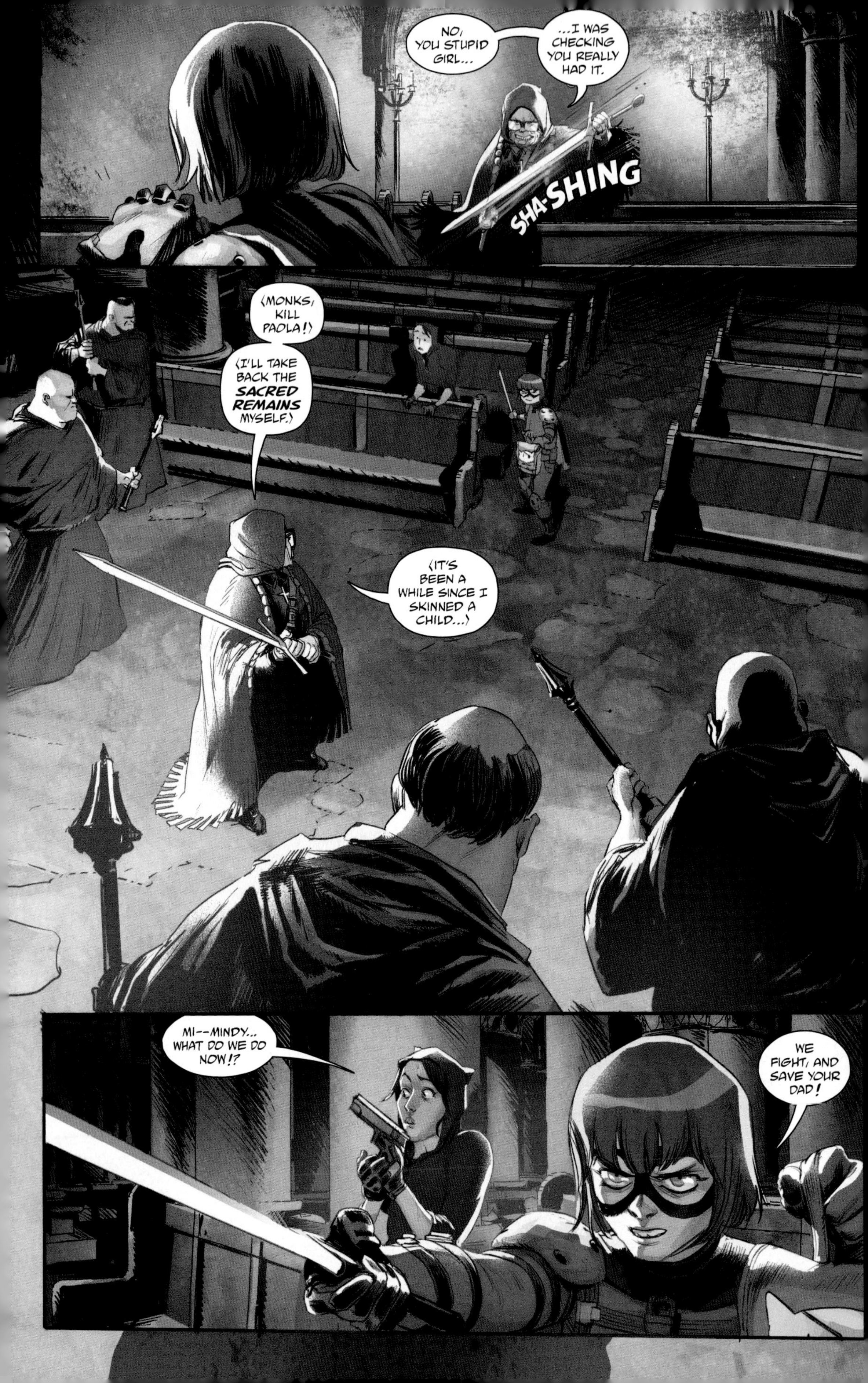
NO, YOU STUPID GIRL...
...I WAS CHECKING YOU REALLY HAD IT.
SHA-SHING
‹MONKS, KILL PAOLA!›
‹I'LL TAKE BACK THE **SACRED REMAINS** MYSELF.›
‹IT'S BEEN A WHILE SINCE I SKINNED A CHILD...›
MI--MINDY... WHAT DO WE DO NOW!?
WE FIGHT, AND SAVE YOUR DAD!

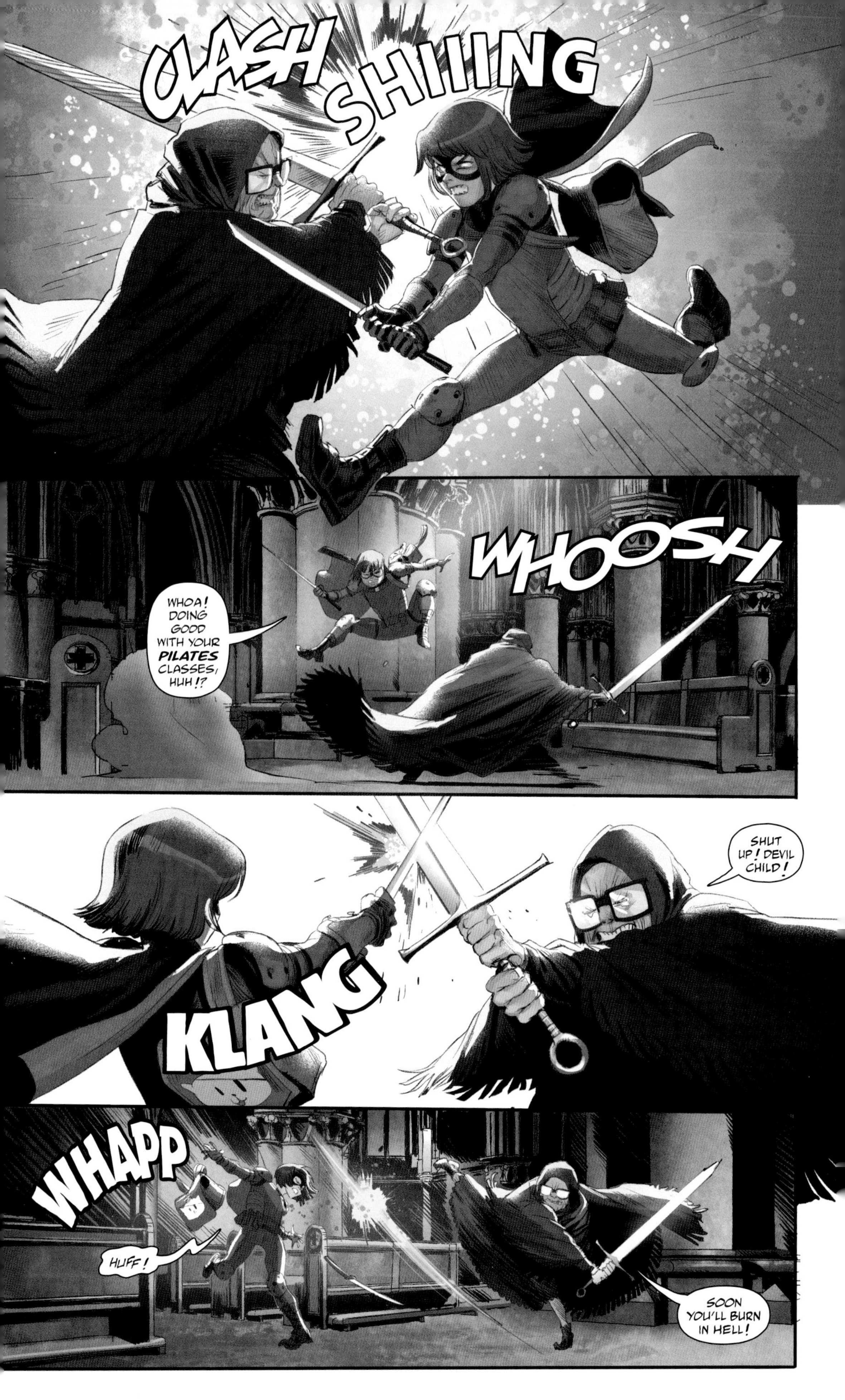
CLASH
SHIIING
WHOOSH
WHOA! DOING GOOD WITH YOUR PILATES CLASSES, HUH!?
SHUT UP! DEVIL CHILD!
KLANG
WHAPP
HUFF!
SOON YOU'LL BURN IN HELL!

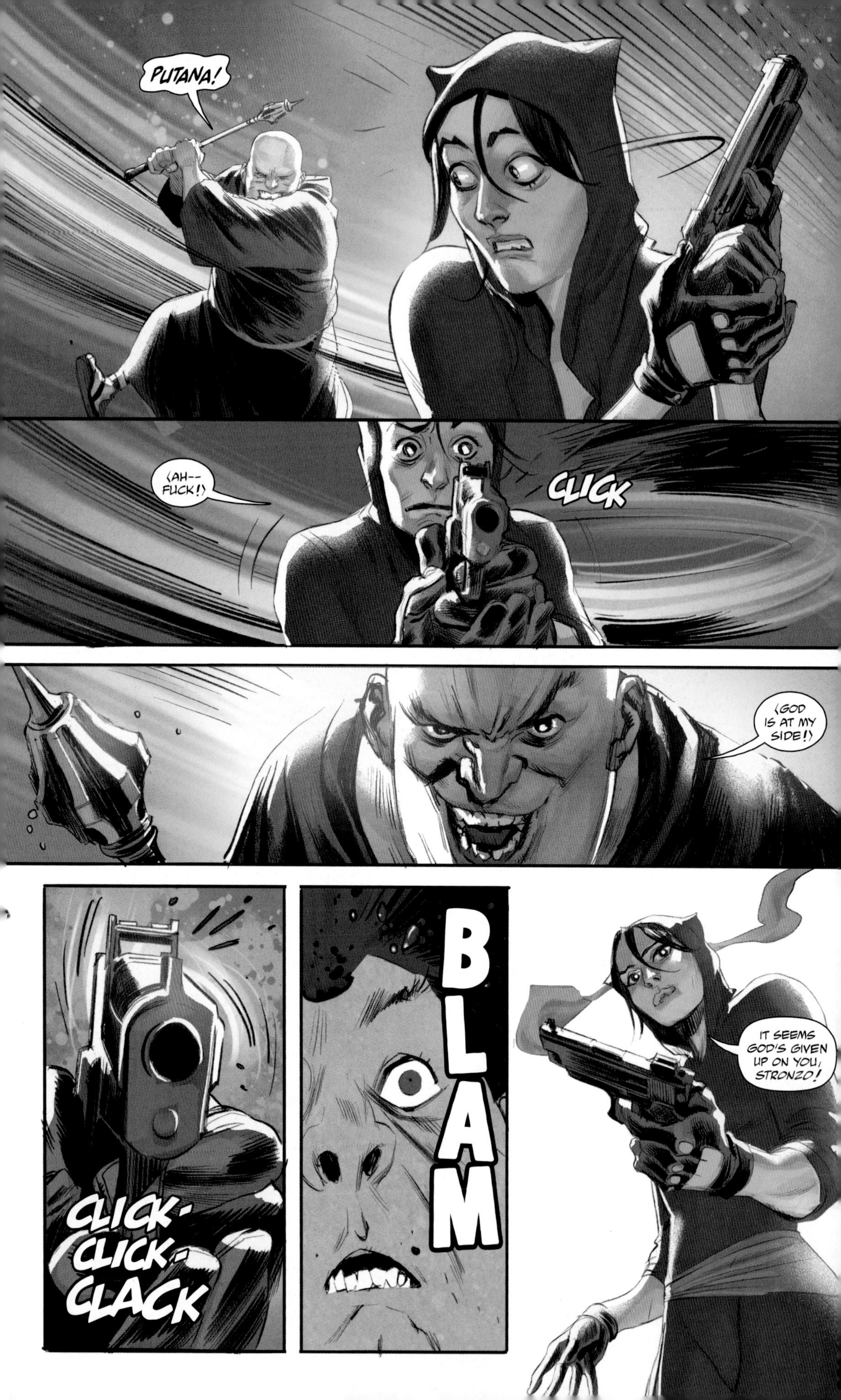

PUTANA!
‹AH--
FUCK!›
CLICK
‹GOD
IS AT MY
SIDE!›
CLICK-
CLICK-
CLACK
BLAM
IT SEEMS
GOD'S GIVEN
UP ON YOU,
STRONZO!

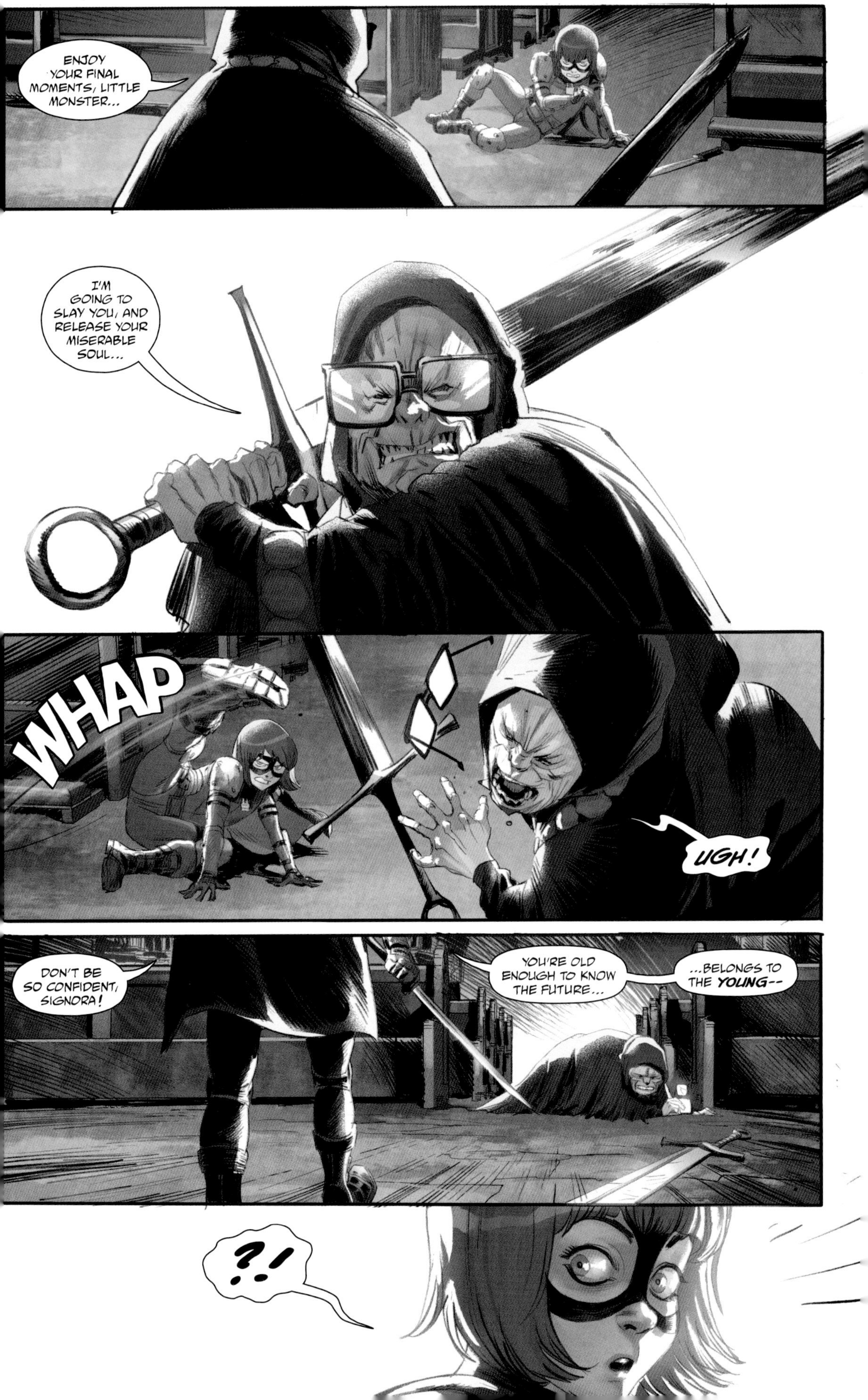
ENJOY YOUR FINAL MOMENTS, LITTLE MONSTER...
I'M GOING TO SLAY YOU, AND RELEASE YOUR MISERABLE SOUL...
WHAP
UGH!
DON'T BE SO CONFIDENT, SIGNORA!
YOU'RE OLD ENOUGH TO KNOW THE FUTURE...
...BELONGS TO THE YOUNG--
?!

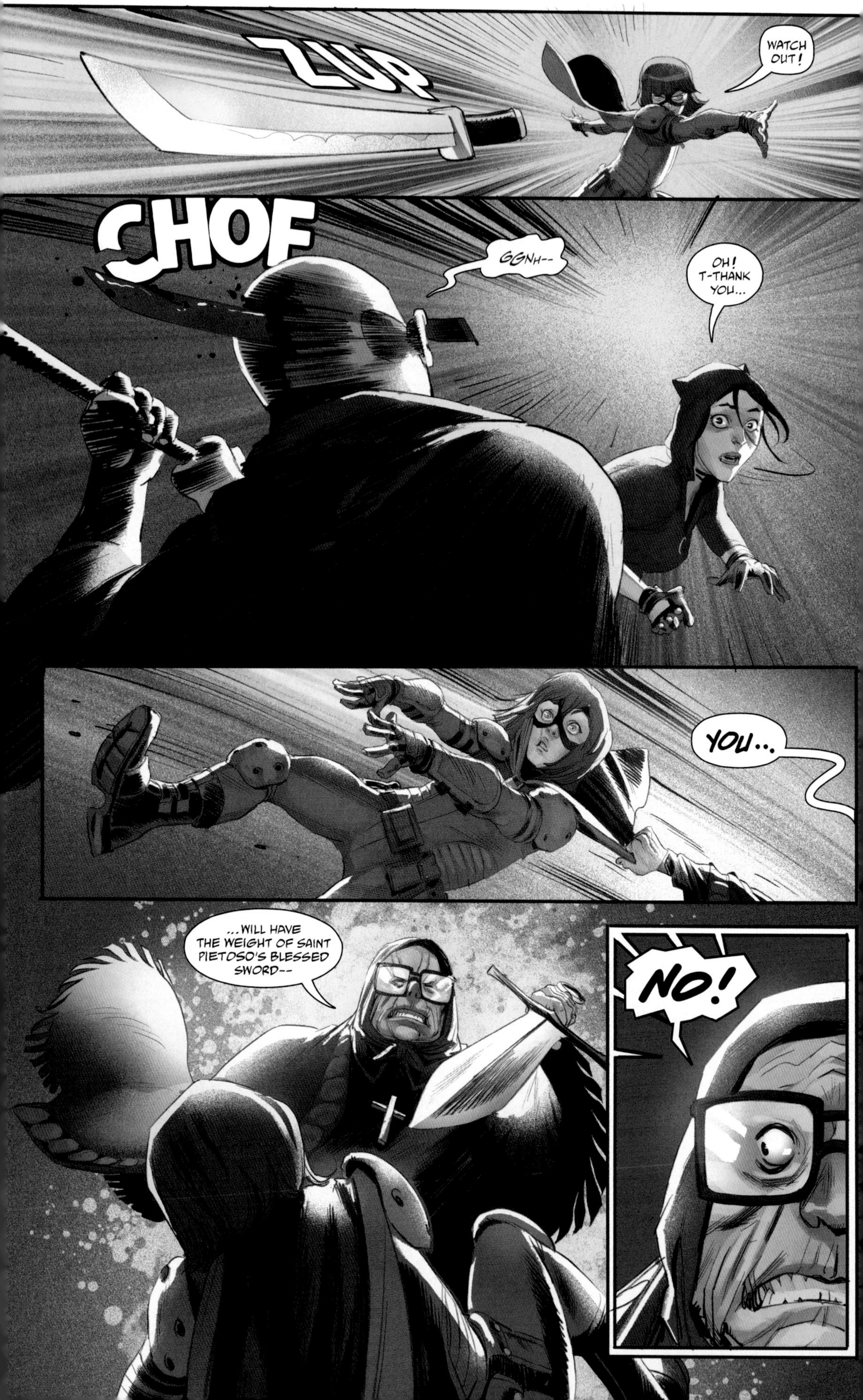
ZLUP
WATCH OUT!
CHOF
GGNH--
OH! T-THANK YOU...
YOU...
...WILL HAVE THE WEIGHT OF SAINT PIETOSO'S BLESSED SWORD--
NO!

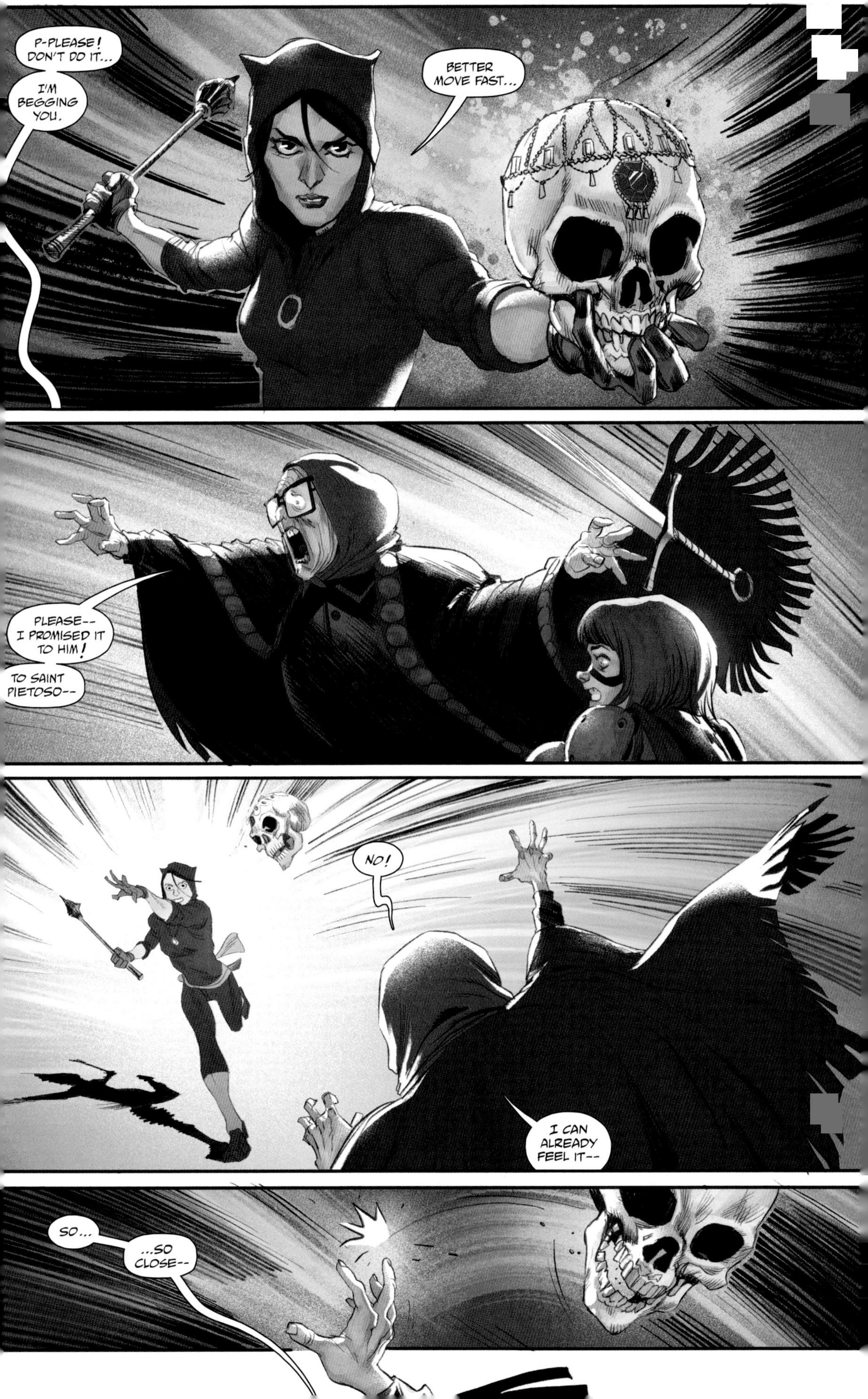
P-PLEASE! DON'T DO IT...
I'M BEGGING YOU.
BETTER MOVE FAST...
PLEASE-- I PROMISED IT TO HIM!
TO SAINT PIETOSO--
NO!
I CAN ALREADY FEEL IT--
SO...
...SO CLOSE--

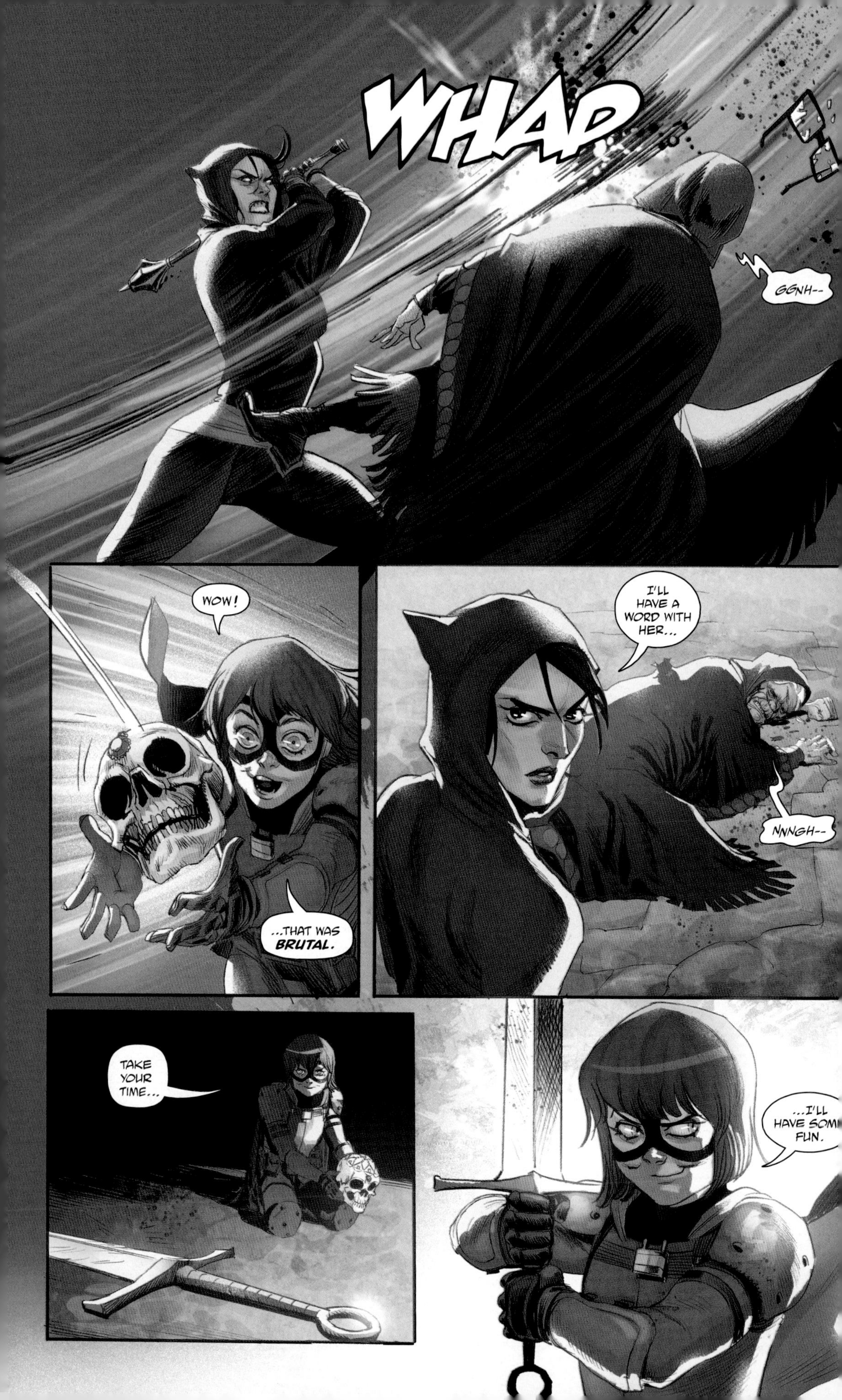
WHAD
GGNH--
WOW!
...THAT WAS BRUTAL.
I'LL HAVE A WORD WITH HER...
NNNGH--
TAKE YOUR TIME...
...I'LL HAVE SOM FUN.

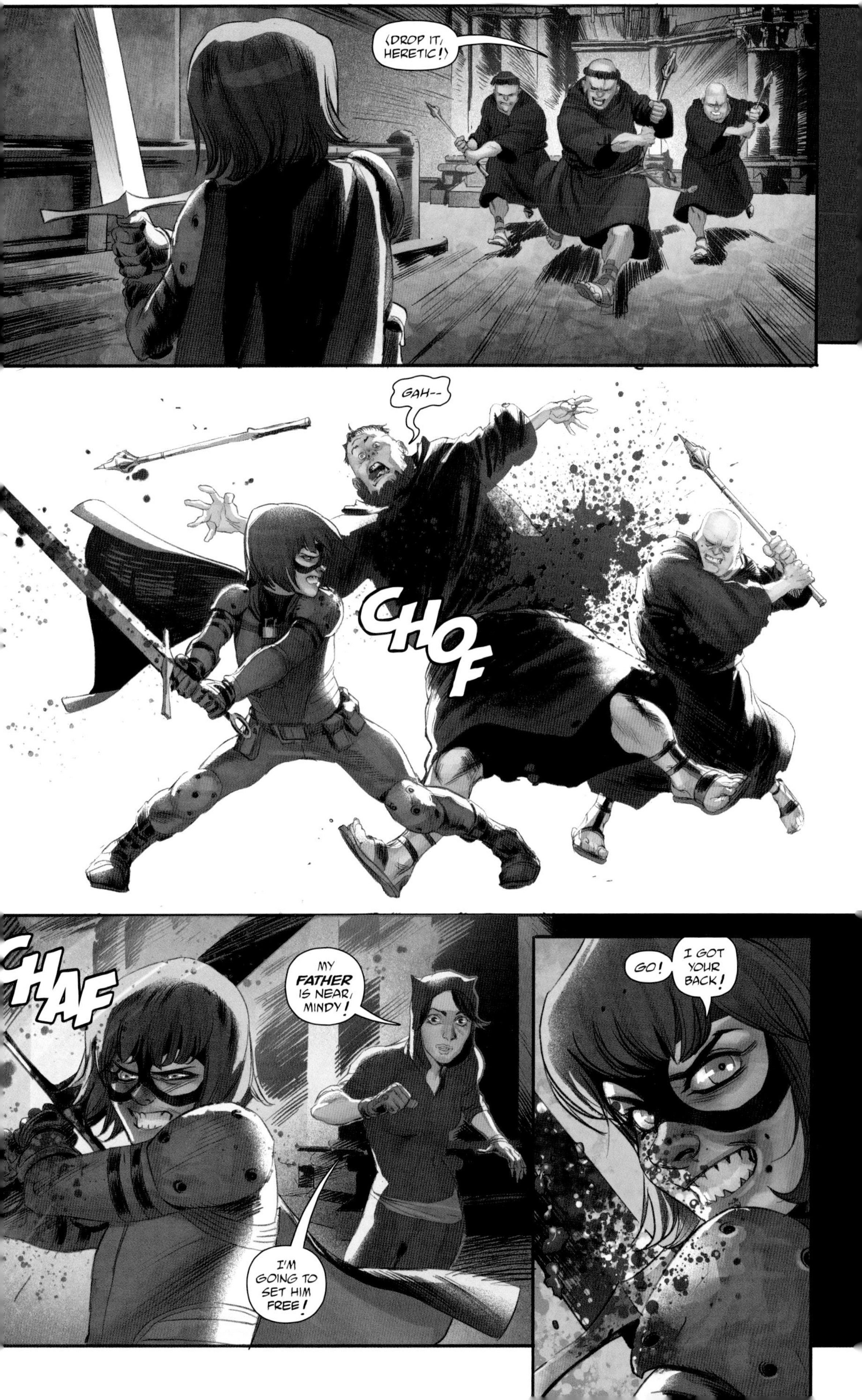
‹DROP IT, HERETIC!›
GAH--
CHOF
CHAF
MY FATHER IS NEAR, MINDY!
I'M GOING TO SET HIM FREE!
GO!
I GOT YOUR BACK!

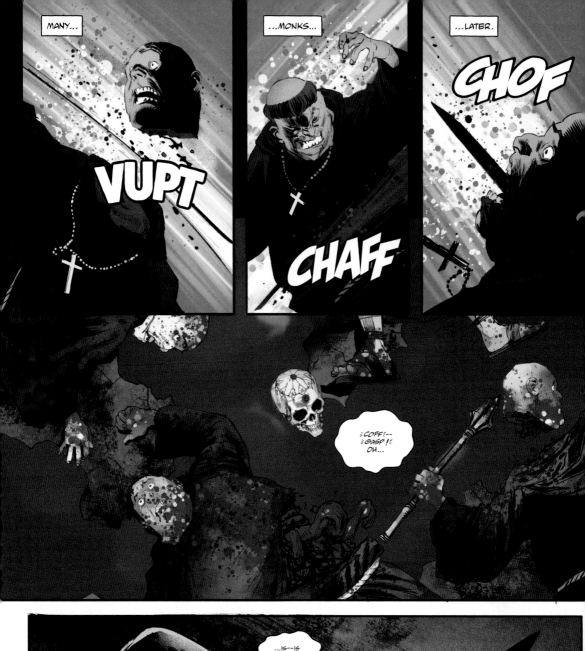

MANY...

...MONKS...

...LATER.

VUPT

CHAFF

CHOF

‡COFF‡-- ‡GASP!‡ OH...

...IS--IS IT OVER?

NO, GIUSTINA...

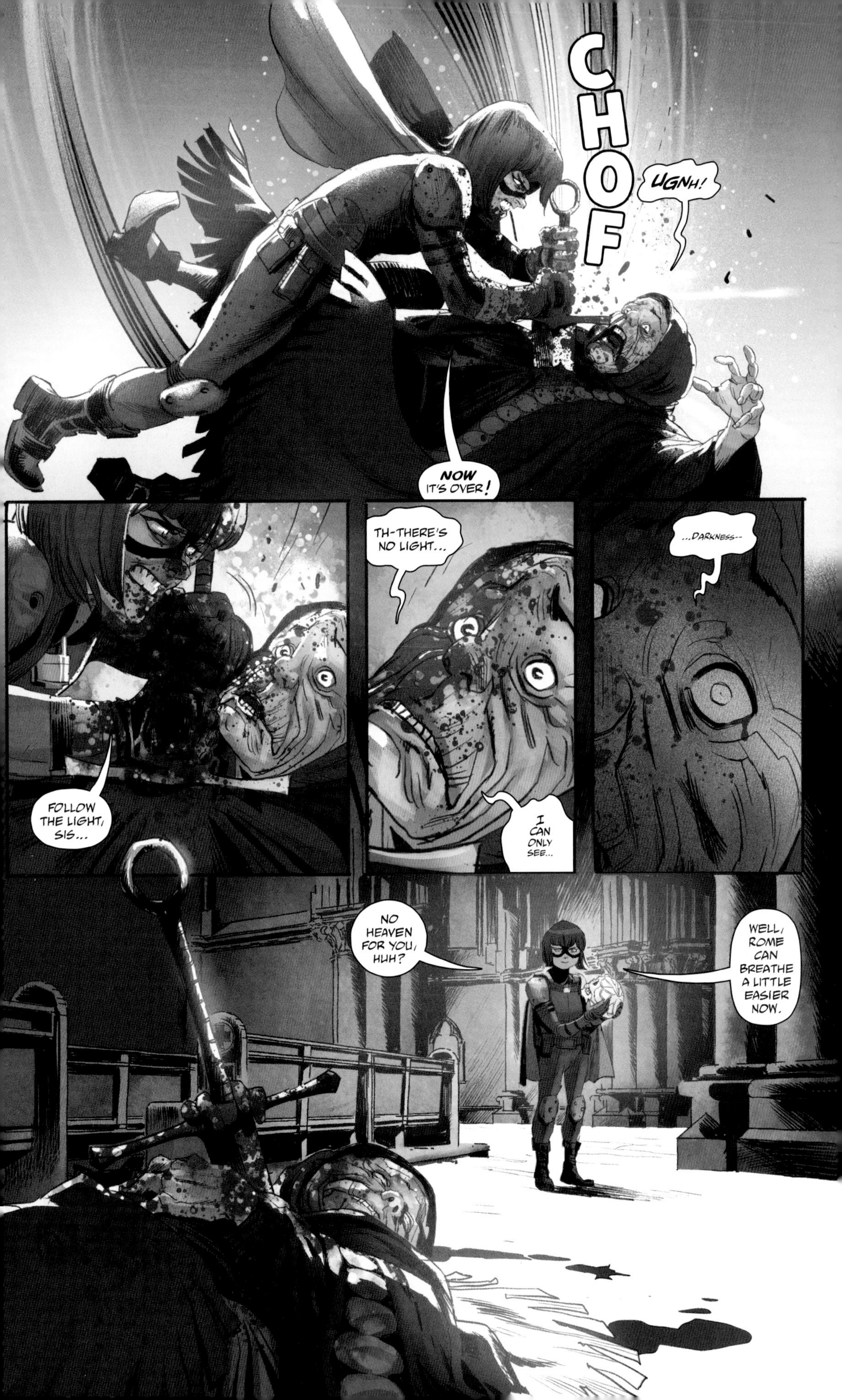
CHOF
UGNH!
NOW IT'S OVER!
FOLLOW THE LIGHT, SIS...
TH-THERE'S NO LIGHT...
I CAN ONLY SEE...
...DARKNESS--
NO HEAVEN FOR YOU, HUH?
WELL, ROME CAN BREATHE A LITTLE EASIER NOW.

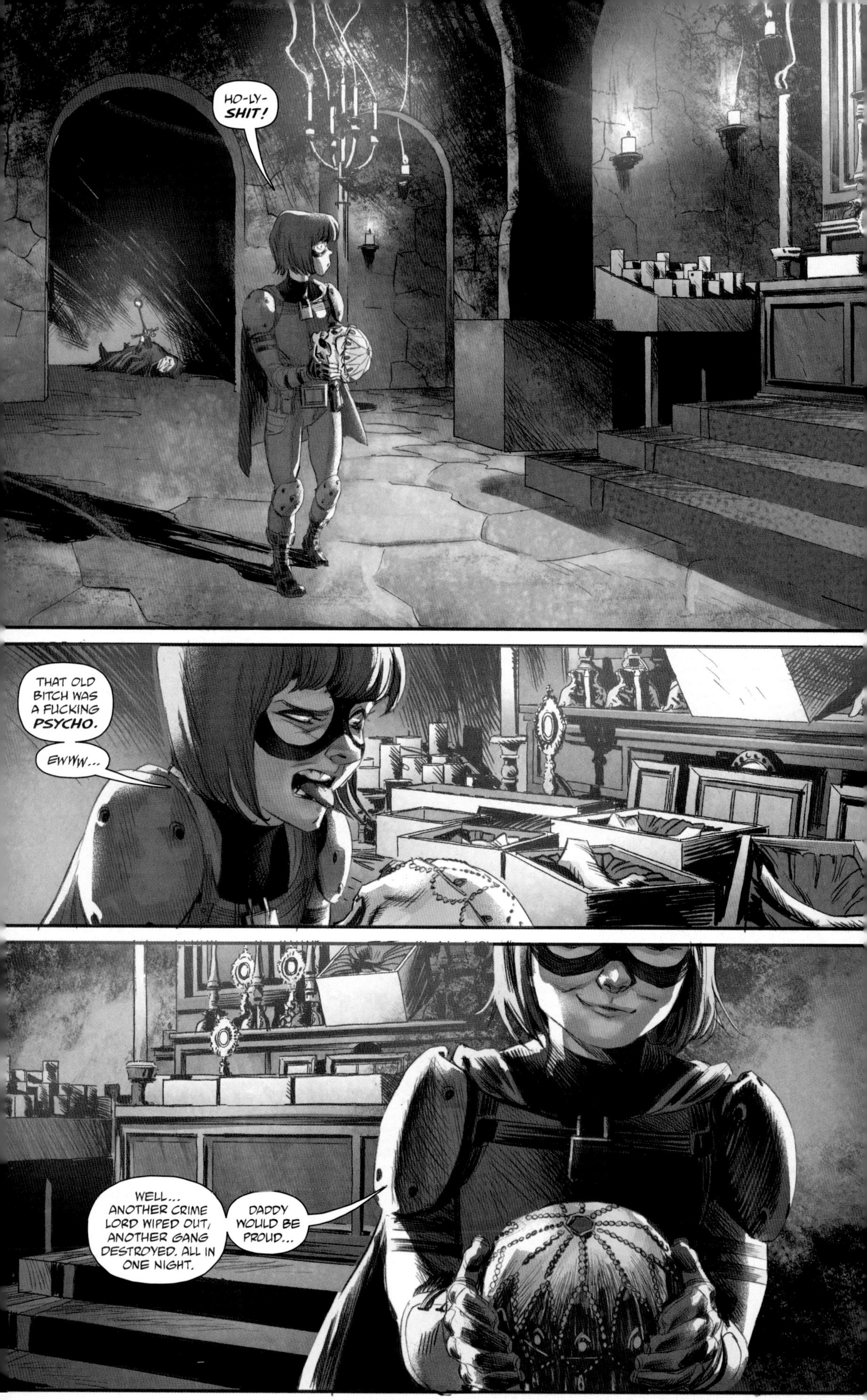
HO-LY-SHIT!
THAT OLD BITCH WAS A FUCKING PSYCHO.
EWWW...
WELL... ANOTHER CRIME LORD WIPED OUT, ANOTHER GANG DESTROYED. ALL IN ONE NIGHT.
DADDY WOULD BE PROUD...

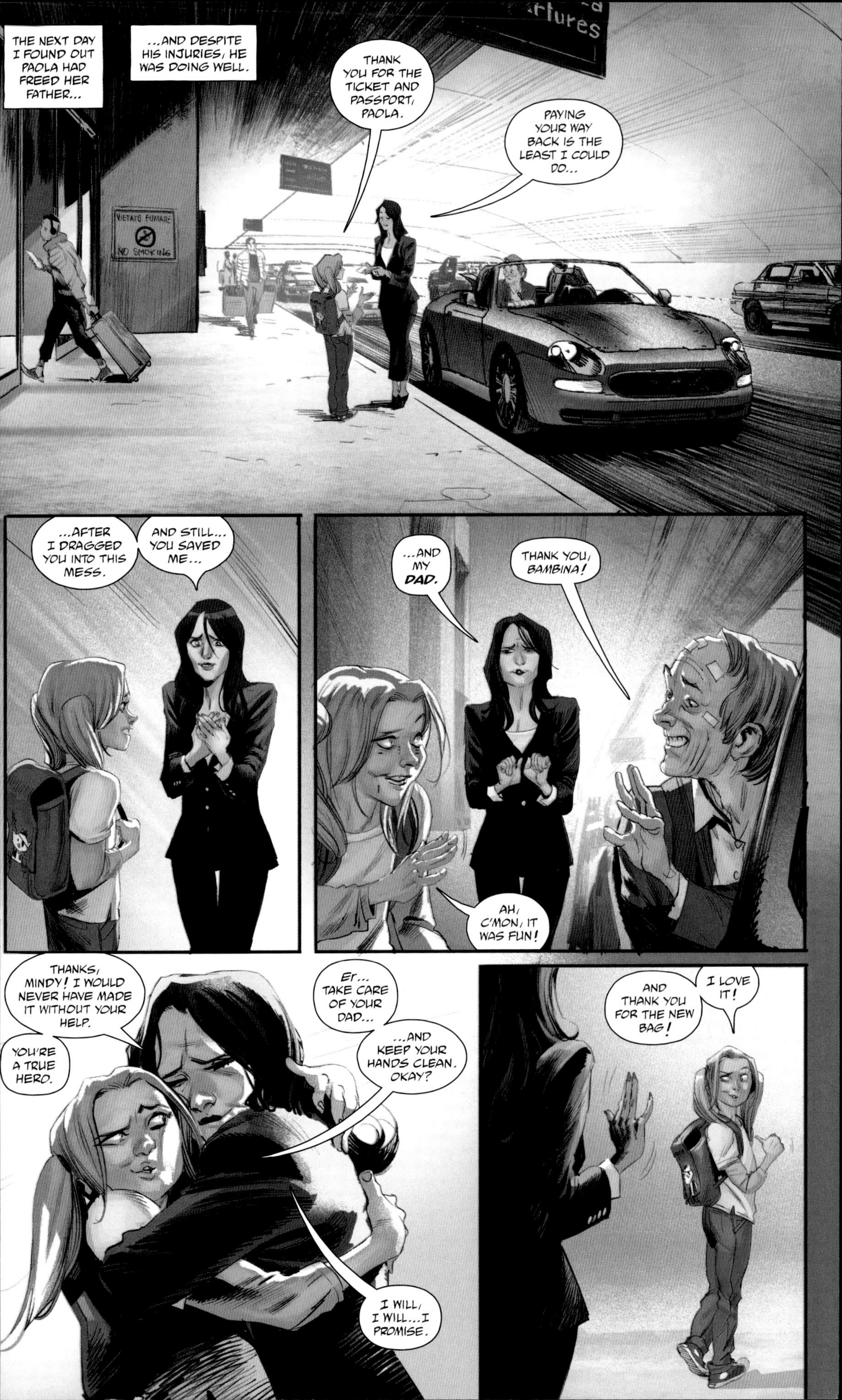
THE NEXT DAY I FOUND OUT PAOLA HAD FREED HER FATHER...
...AND DESPITE HIS INJURIES, HE WAS DOING WELL.
THANK YOU FOR THE TICKET AND PASSPORT, PAOLA.
PAYING YOUR WAY BACK IS THE LEAST I COULD DO...
VIETATO FUMARE
NO SMOKING
...AFTER I DRAGGED YOU INTO THIS MESS.
AND STILL... YOU SAVED ME...
...AND MY DAD.
THANK YOU, BAMBINA!
AH, C'MON, IT WAS FUN!
THANKS, MINDY! I WOULD NEVER HAVE MADE IT WITHOUT YOUR HELP.
YOU'RE A TRUE HERO.
Er... TAKE CARE OF YOUR DAD...
...AND KEEP YOUR HANDS CLEAN. OKAY?
I WILL, I WILL...I PROMISE.
AND THANK YOU FOR THE NEW BAG!
I LOVE IT!

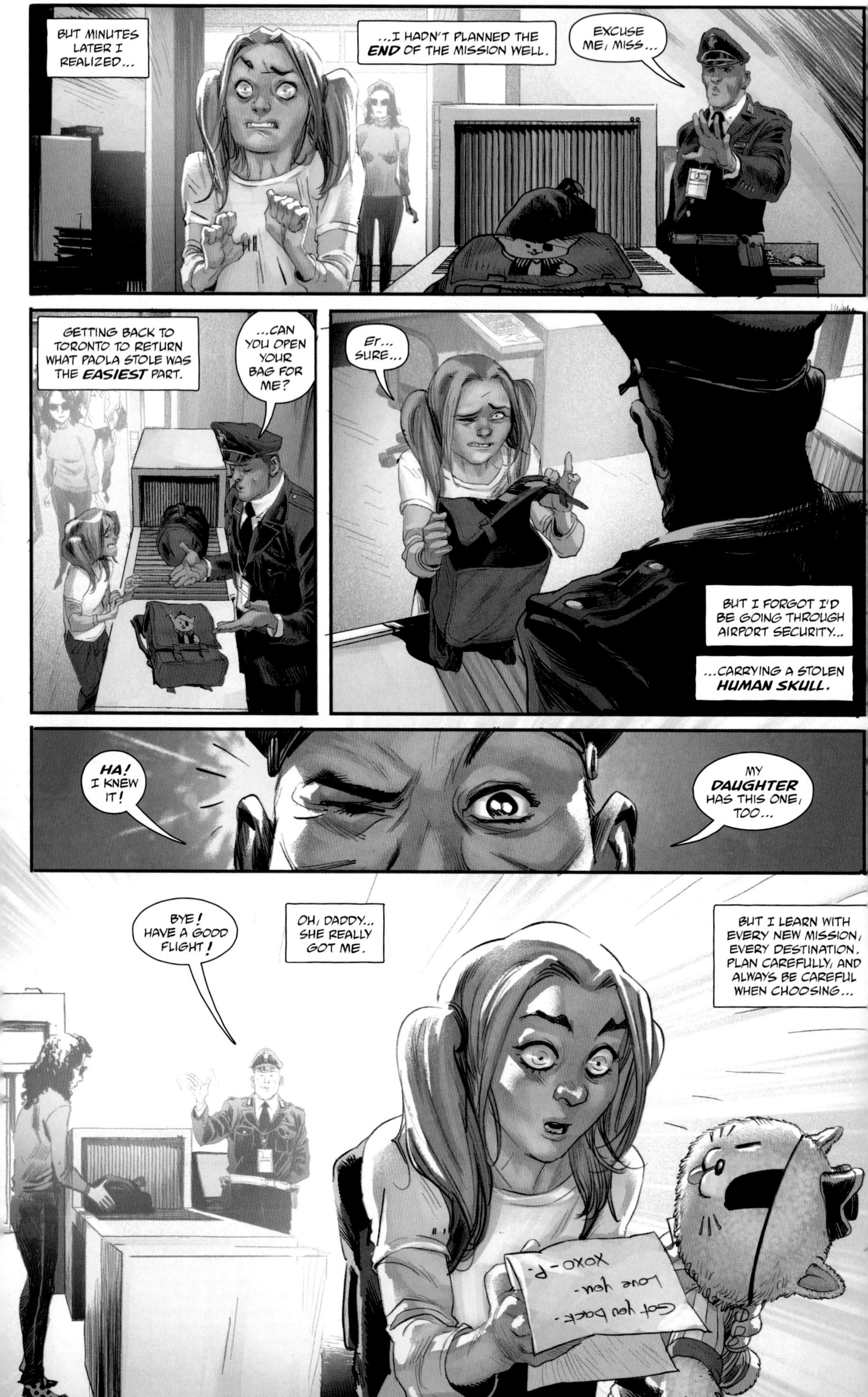
BUT MINUTES LATER I REALIZED...
...I HADN'T PLANNED THE **END** OF THE MISSION WELL.
EXCUSE ME, MISS...
GETTING BACK TO TORONTO TO RETURN WHAT PAOLA STOLE WAS THE **EASIEST** PART.
...CAN YOU OPEN YOUR BAG FOR ME?
Er... SURE...
BUT I FORGOT I'D BE GOING THROUGH AIRPORT SECURITY...
...CARRYING A STOLEN **HUMAN SKULL.**
HA! I KNEW IT!
MY **DAUGHTER** HAS THIS ONE, TOO...
BYE! HAVE A GOOD FLIGHT!
OH, DADDY... SHE REALLY GOT ME.
BUT I LEARN WITH EVERY NEW MISSION, EVERY DESTINATION. PLAN CAREFULLY, AND ALWAYS BE CAREFUL WHEN CHOOSING...
Got you back - Love you - XOXO -P.

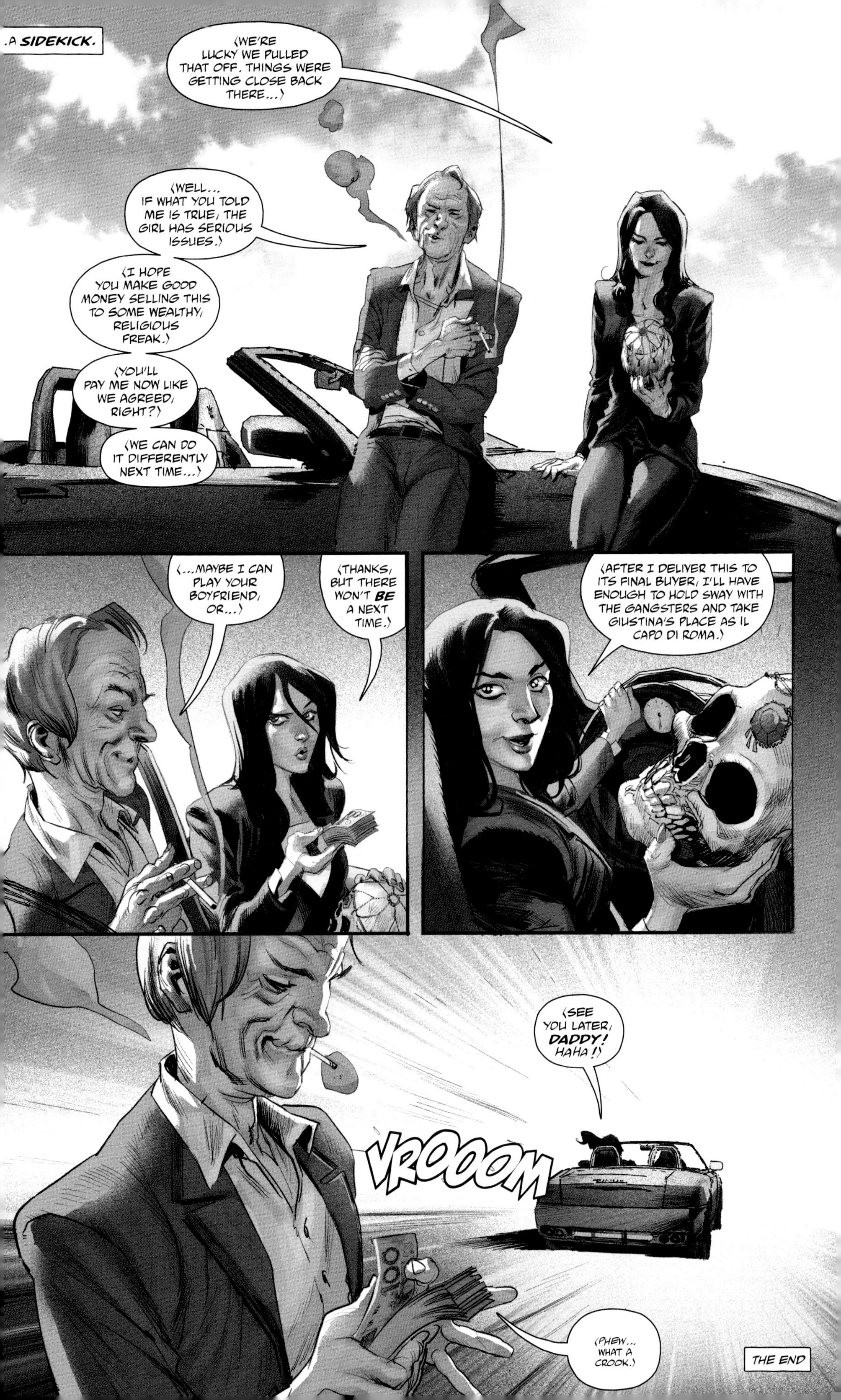
...A SIDEKICK.
‹WE'RE LUCKY WE PULLED THAT OFF. THINGS WERE GETTING CLOSE BACK THERE...›
‹WELL... IF WHAT YOU TOLD ME IS TRUE, THE GIRL HAS SERIOUS ISSUES.›
‹I HOPE YOU MAKE GOOD MONEY SELLING THIS TO SOME WEALTHY, RELIGIOUS FREAK.›
‹YOU'LL PAY ME NOW LIKE WE AGREED, RIGHT?›
‹WE CAN DO IT DIFFERENTLY NEXT TIME...›
‹...MAYBE I CAN PLAY YOUR BOYFRIEND, OR...›
‹THANKS, BUT THERE WON'T BE A NEXT TIME.›
‹AFTER I DELIVER THIS TO ITS FINAL BUYER, I'LL HAVE ENOUGH TO HOLD SWAY WITH THE GANGSTERS AND TAKE GIUSTINA'S PLACE AS IL CAPO DI ROMA.›
‹SEE YOU LATER, DADDY! HAHA!›
VROOOM
‹PHEW... WHAT A CROOK.›
THE END

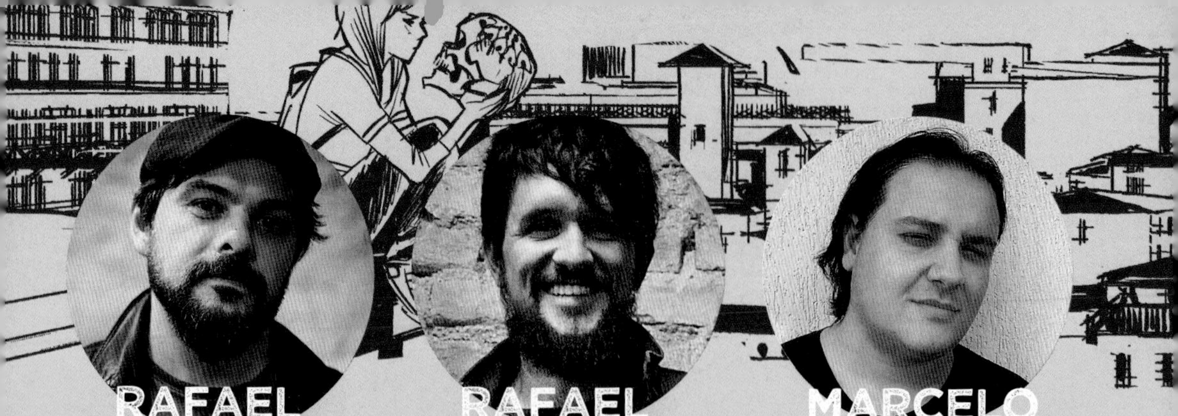

RAFAEL ALBUQUERQUE

was born in Porto Alegre, Brazil. He has been working in the American comic book industry since 2005. Best known for his work on **ALL STAR BATMAN**, **ANIMAL MAN**, and **BATGIRL**, he has also published the creator-owned books **MONDO URBANO** (2010), **EIGHT** (2015), and **HUCK** (2015).

Rafael is an Eisner, Harvey, and Inkpot Award winner for the NY Times bestseller **AMERICAN VAMPIRE** (DC Comics/Vertigo, 2010), written by Scott Snyder and Stephen King. His recent projects include the adaptation of the popular Neil Gaiman tale **A STUDY IN EMERALD**, and Mark Millar's **HIT-GIRL**.

RAFAEL SCAVONE

started his comics career in 2014, translating and editing comic books alongside Rafael Albuquerque within their own publishing house. Since then he has worked for DC Comics, writing popular characters such as **WONDER WOMAN** and **BATMAN**. He also recently adapted the award-winning story **A STUDY IN EMERALD**, from Neil Gaiman, for Dark Horse Comics. He lives in Brazil, loves to hear and tell stories, and spends most of his time among books, music, and friends.

MARCELO MAIOLO

is best known for his work at DC Comics on such titles as **I, VAMPIRE**, **GREEN ARROW**, **TEEN TITANS**, and, most recently, **JUSTICE LEAGUE OF AMERICA**. His work for other publishers includes **TRUE BLOOD** for IDW, **KING** for Jet City Comics, **PACIFIC RIM** for Legendary, **ALL-NEW X-MEN** and **OLD MAN LOGAN** for Marvel, **LIBERTALIA** for Glénat, and **SPIDER** for Delcourt/Soleil. He lives and works in Brazil.

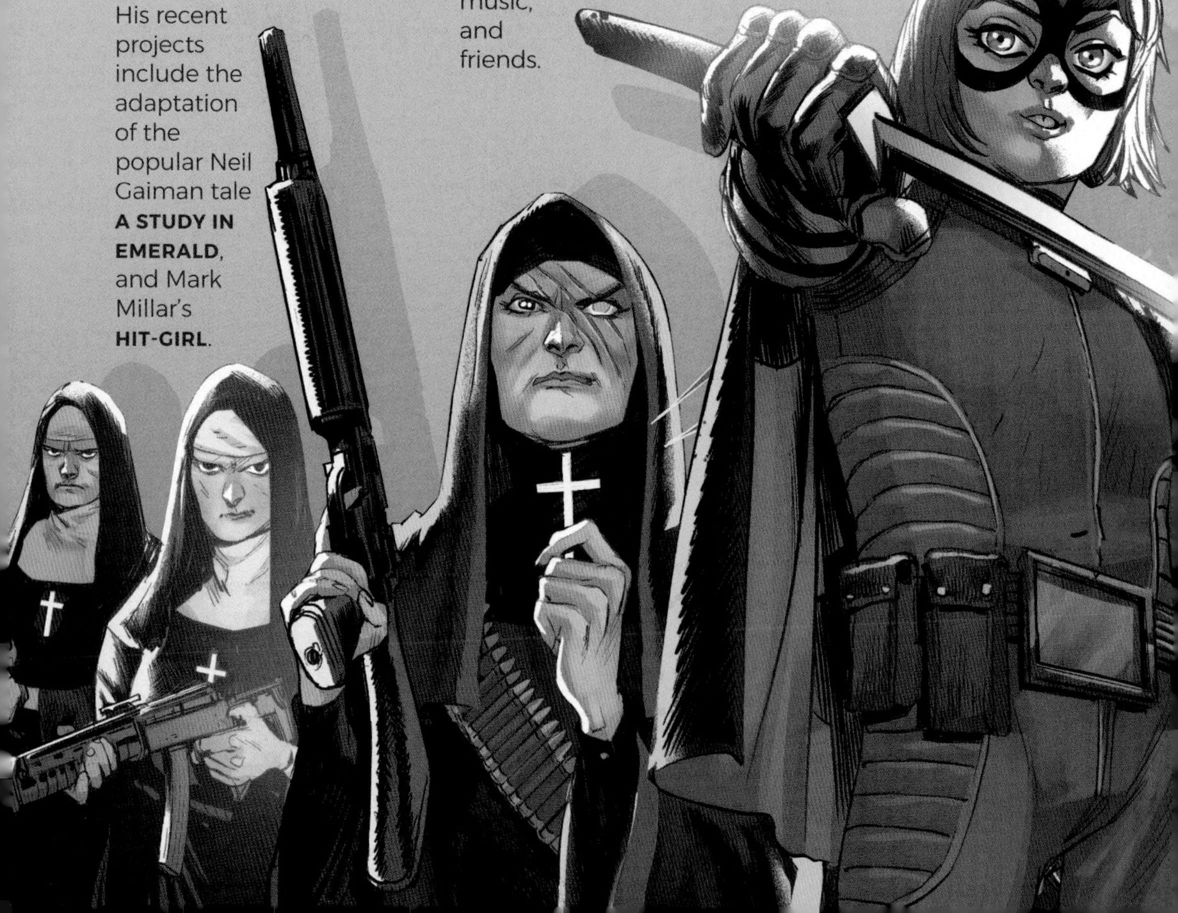

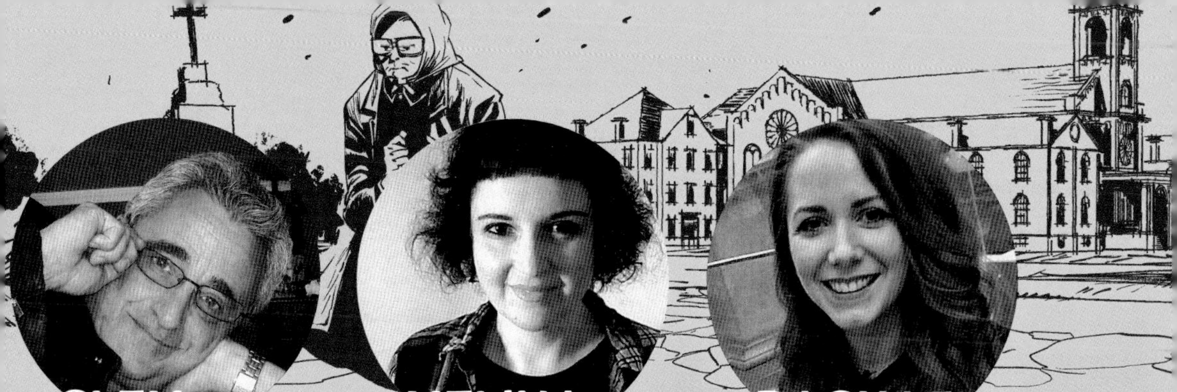

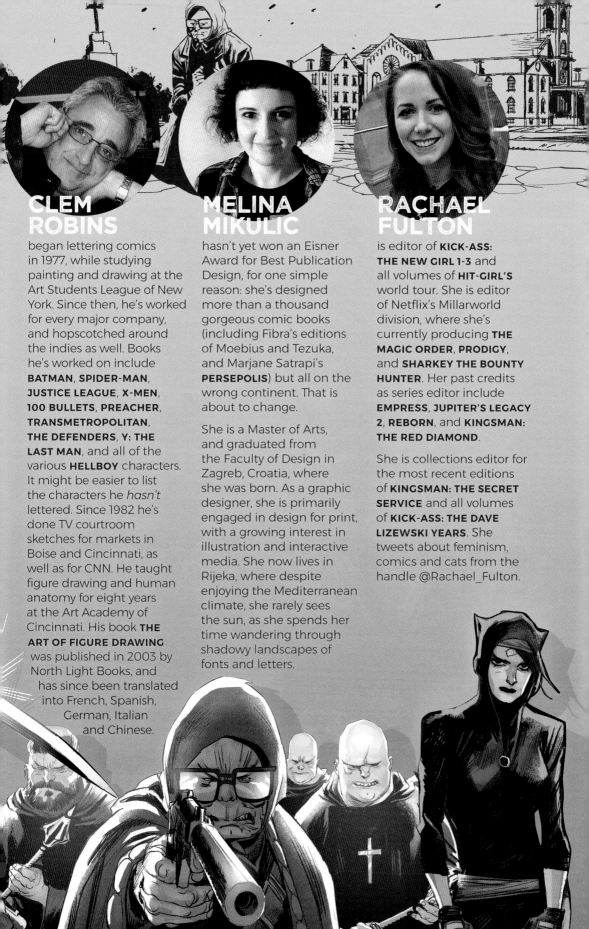

CLEM ROBINS

began lettering comics in 1977, while studying painting and drawing at the Art Students League of New York. Since then, he's worked for every major company, and hopscotched around the indies as well. Books he's worked on include **BATMAN**, **SPIDER-MAN**, **JUSTICE LEAGUE**, **X-MEN**, **100 BULLETS**, **PREACHER**, **TRANSMETROPOLITAN**, **THE DEFENDERS**, **Y: THE LAST MAN**, and all of the various **HELLBOY** characters. It might be easier to list the characters he *hasn't* lettered. Since 1982 he's done TV courtroom sketches for markets in Boise and Cincinnati, as well as for CNN. He taught figure drawing and human anatomy for eight years at the Art Academy of Cincinnati. His book **THE ART OF FIGURE DRAWING** was published in 2003 by North Light Books, and has since been translated into French, Spanish, German, Italian and Chinese.

MELINA MIKULIC

hasn't yet won an Eisner Award for Best Publication Design, for one simple reason: she's designed more than a thousand gorgeous comic books (including Fibra's editions of Moebius and Tezuka, and Marjane Satrapi's **PERSEPOLIS**) but all on the wrong continent. That is about to change.

She is a Master of Arts, and graduated from the Faculty of Design in Zagreb, Croatia, where she was born. As a graphic designer, she is primarily engaged in design for print, with a growing interest in illustration and interactive media. She now lives in Rijeka, where despite enjoying the Mediterranean climate, she rarely sees the sun, as she spends her time wandering through shadowy landscapes of fonts and letters.

RACHAEL FULTON

is editor of **KICK-ASS: THE NEW GIRL 1-3** and all volumes of **HIT-GIRL'S** world tour. She is editor of Netflix's Millarworld division, where she's currently producing **THE MAGIC ORDER**, **PRODIGY**, and **SHARKEY THE BOUNTY HUNTER**. Her past credits as series editor include **EMPRESS**, **JUPITER'S LEGACY 2**, **REBORN**, and **KINGSMAN: THE RED DIAMOND**.

She is collections editor for the most recent editions of **KINGSMAN: THE SECRET SERVICE** and all volumes of **KICK-ASS: THE DAVE LIZEWSKI YEARS**. She tweets about feminism, comics and cats from the handle @Rachael_Fulton.

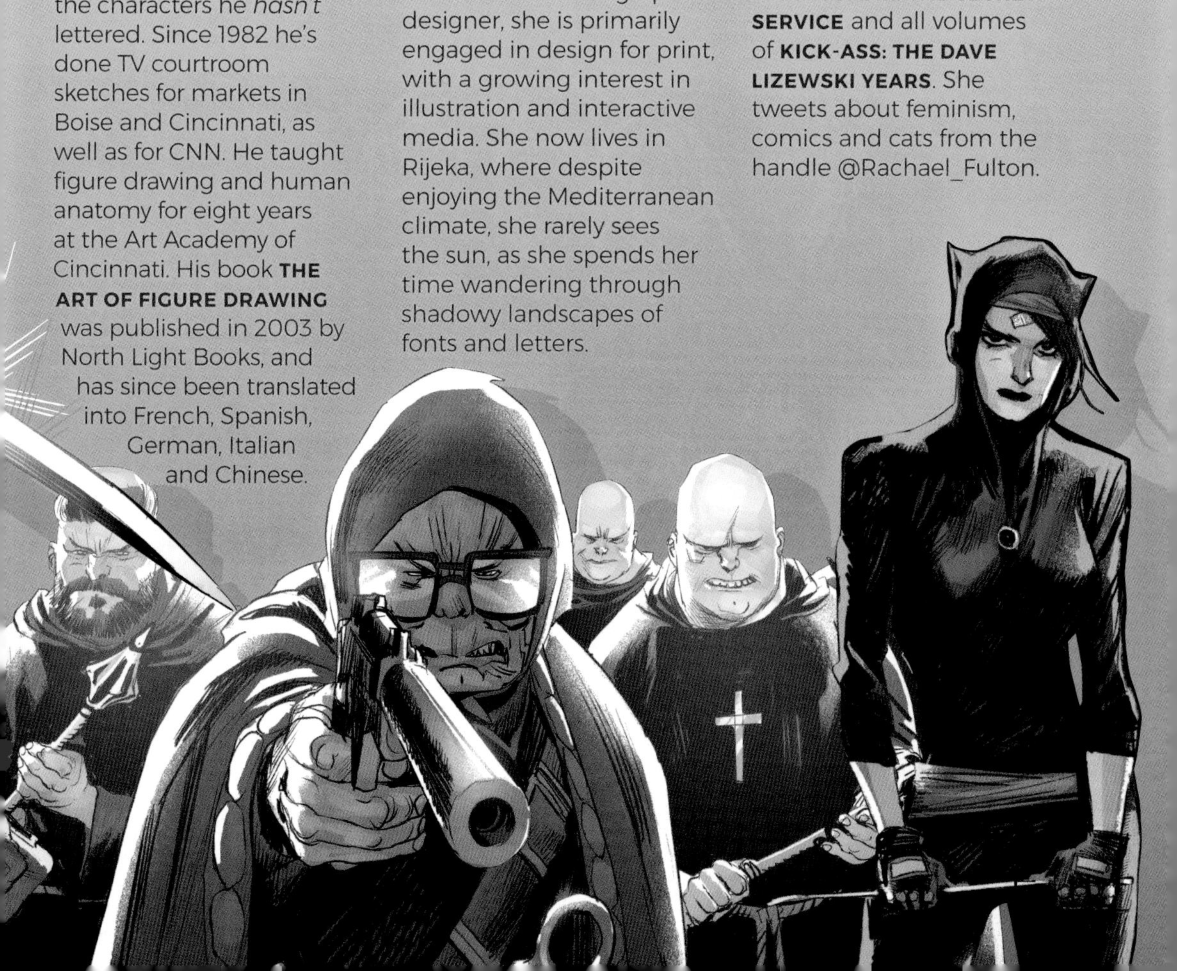

RAFAEL ALBUQUERQUE

CHARACTER SKETCHES

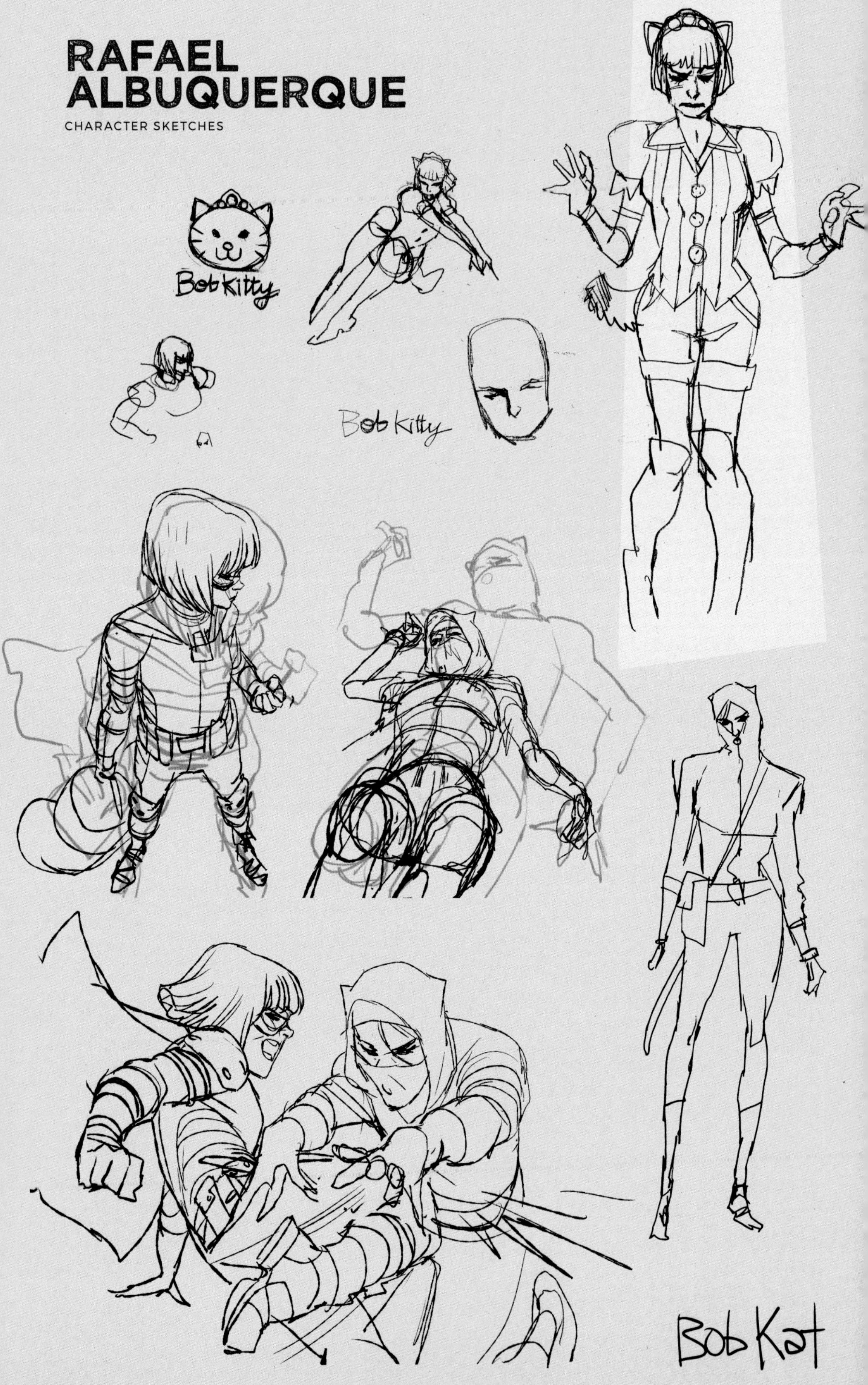
Bob Kitty
Bob Kitty
Bob Kat

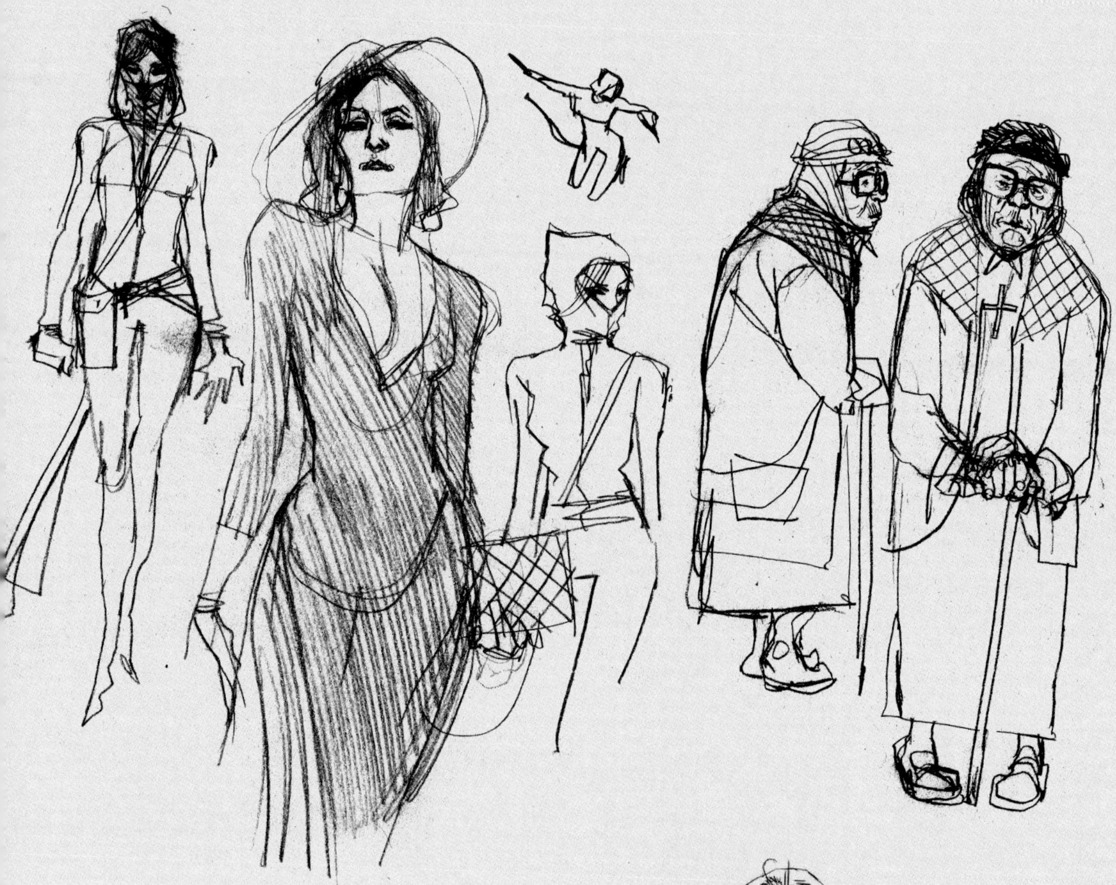

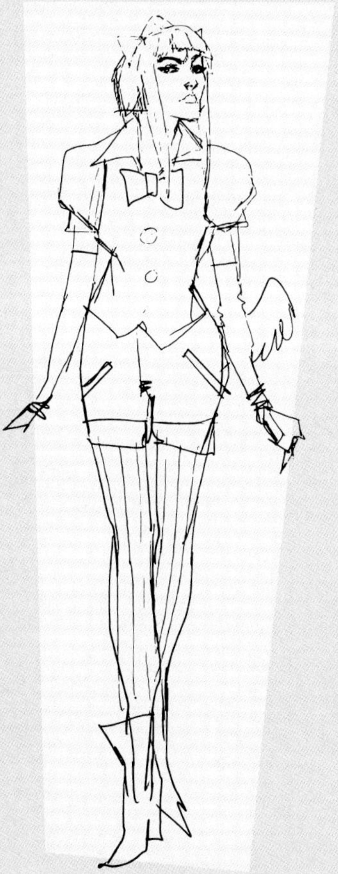

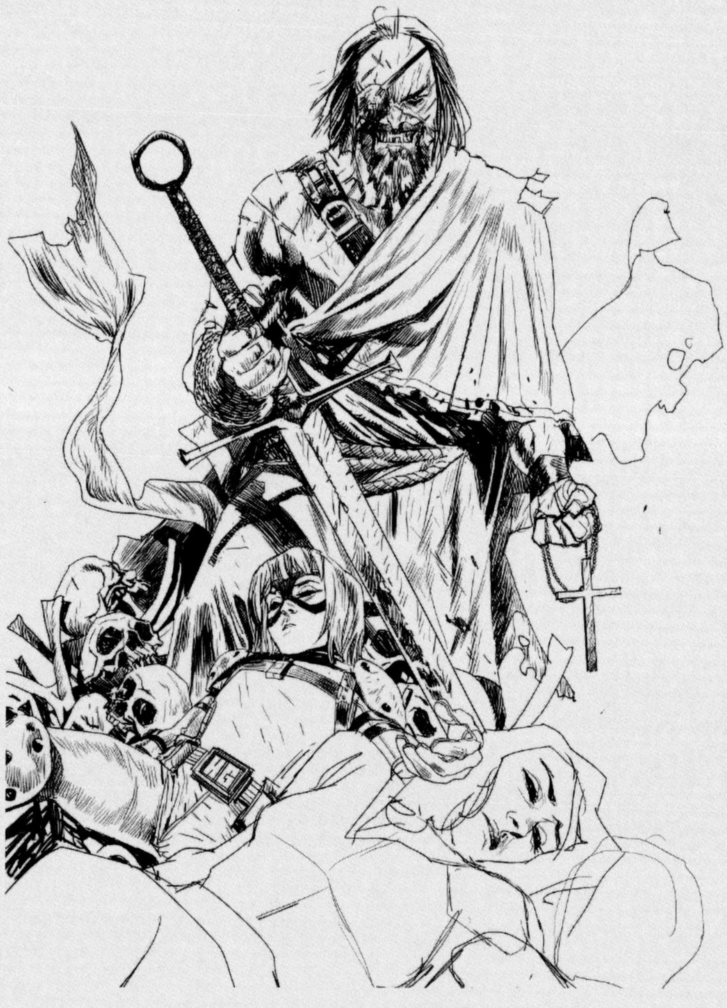

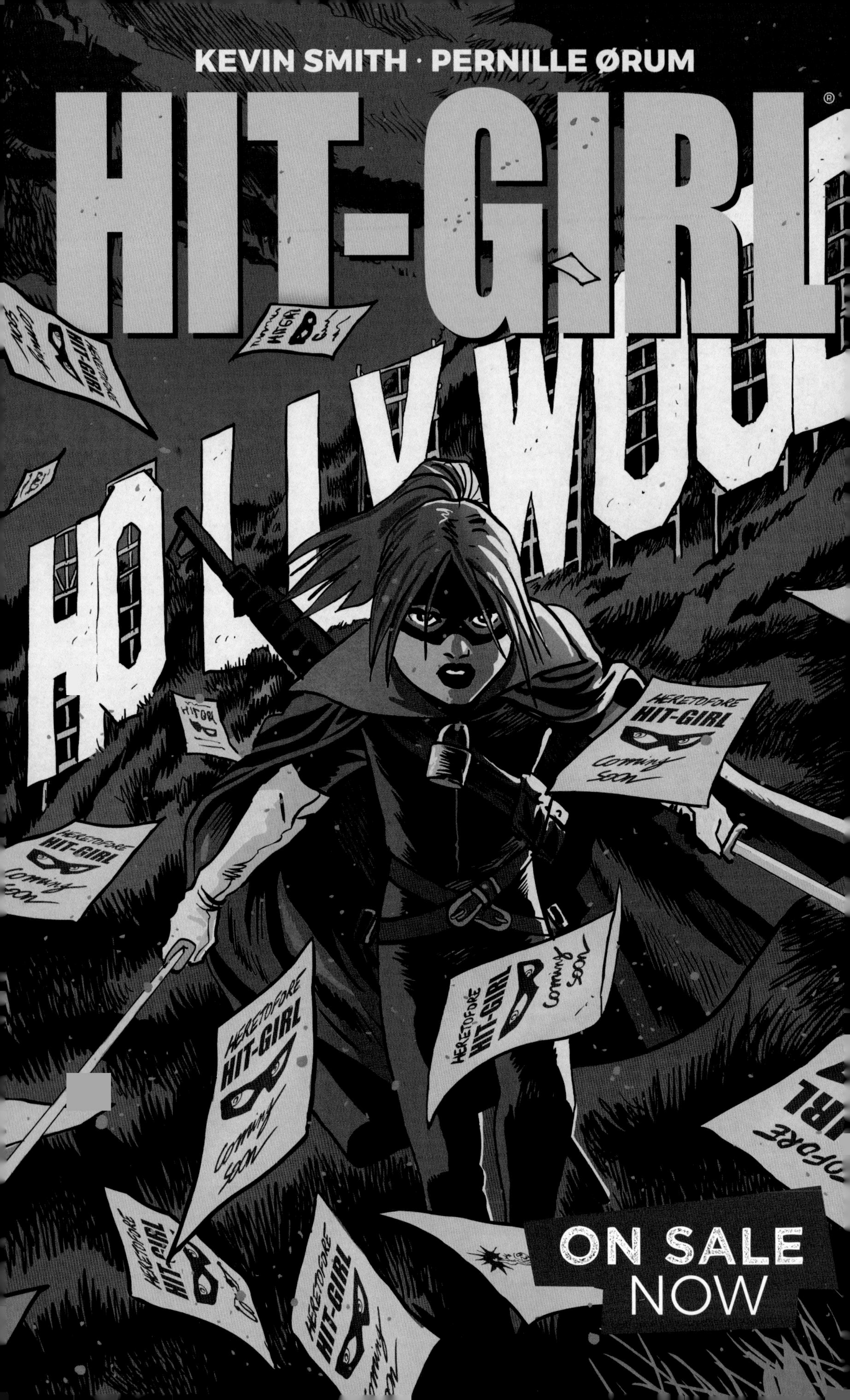
KEVIN SMITH · PERNILLE ØRUM
HIT-GIRL®
HERETOFORE HIT-GIRL Coming soon
ON SALE NOW

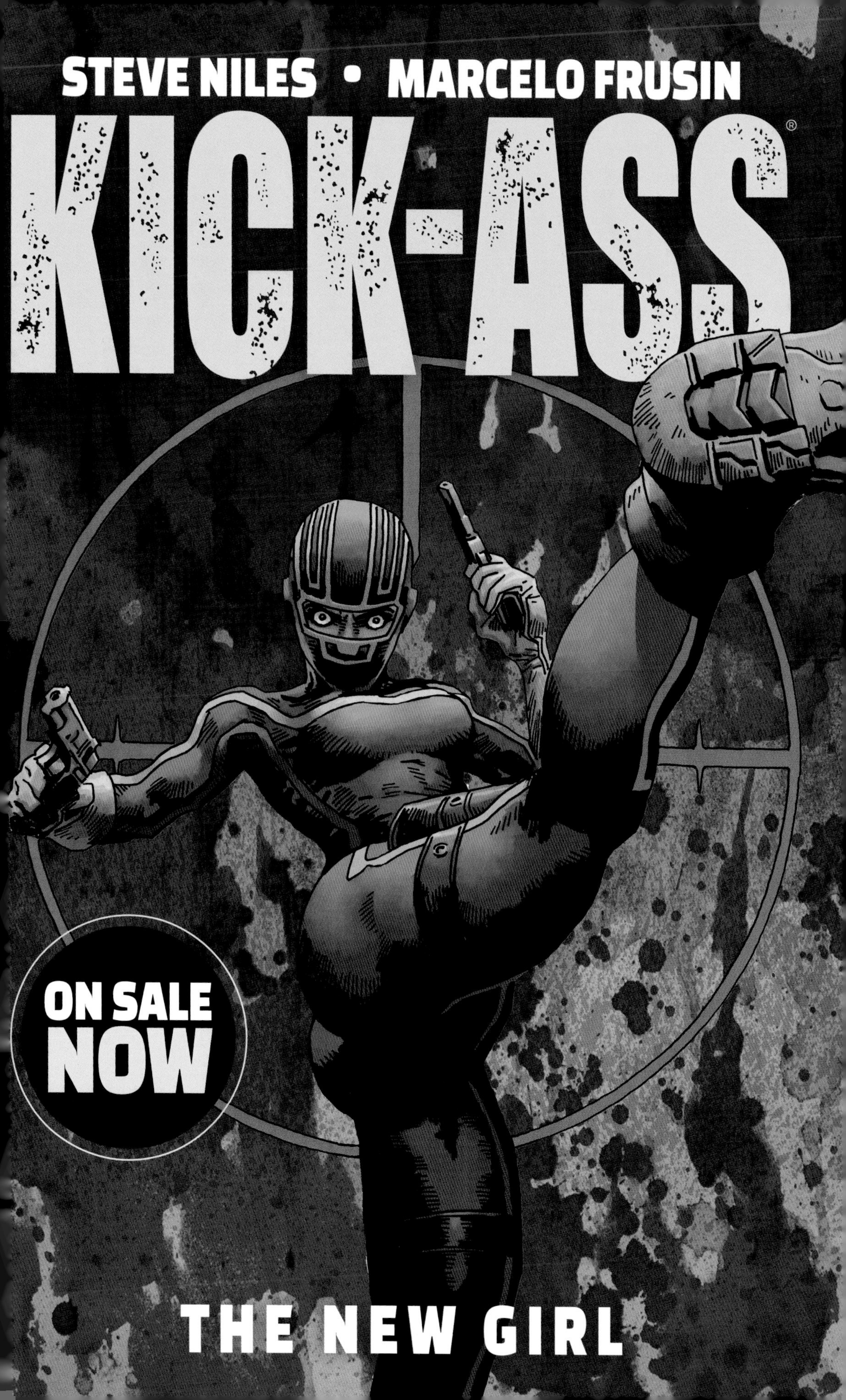

STEVE NILES • MARCELO FRUSIN
KICK-ASS®
ON SALE NOW
THE NEW GIRL

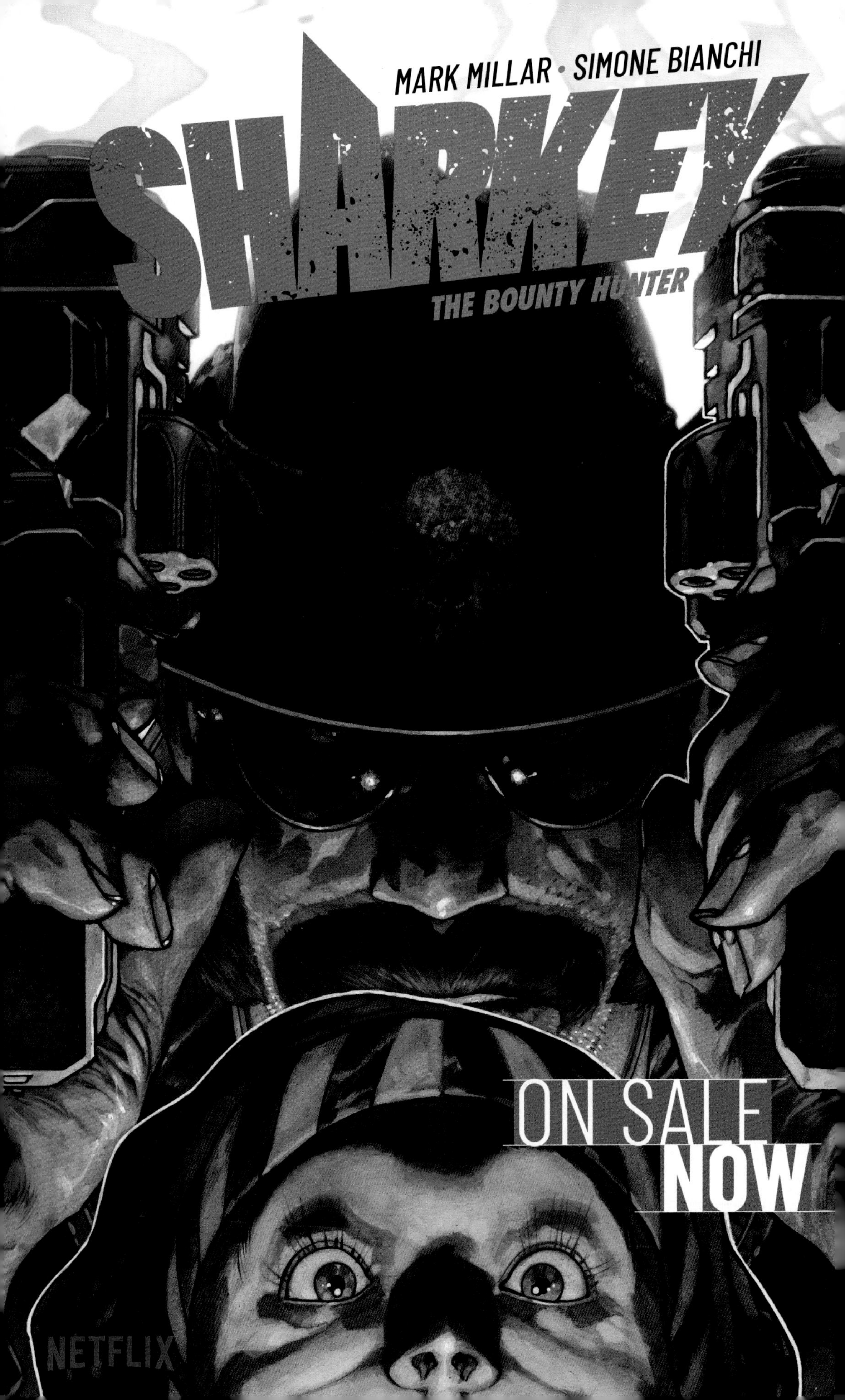
MARK MILLAR • SIMONE BIANCHI
SHARKEY
THE BOUNTY HUNTER
ON SALE
NOW
NETFLIX

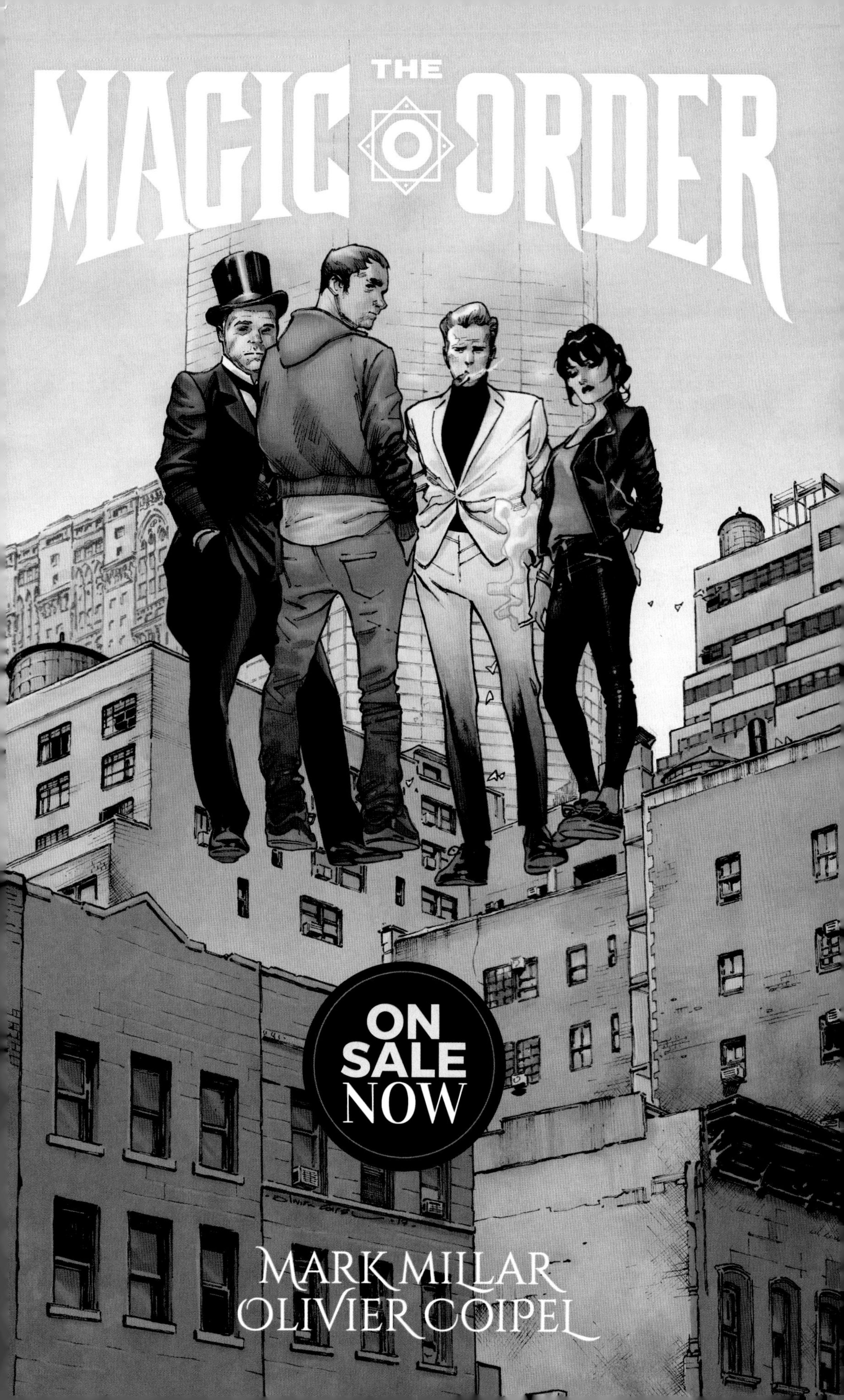
THE
MAGIC ORDER
ON SALE NOW
MARK MILLAR
OLIVIER COIPEL

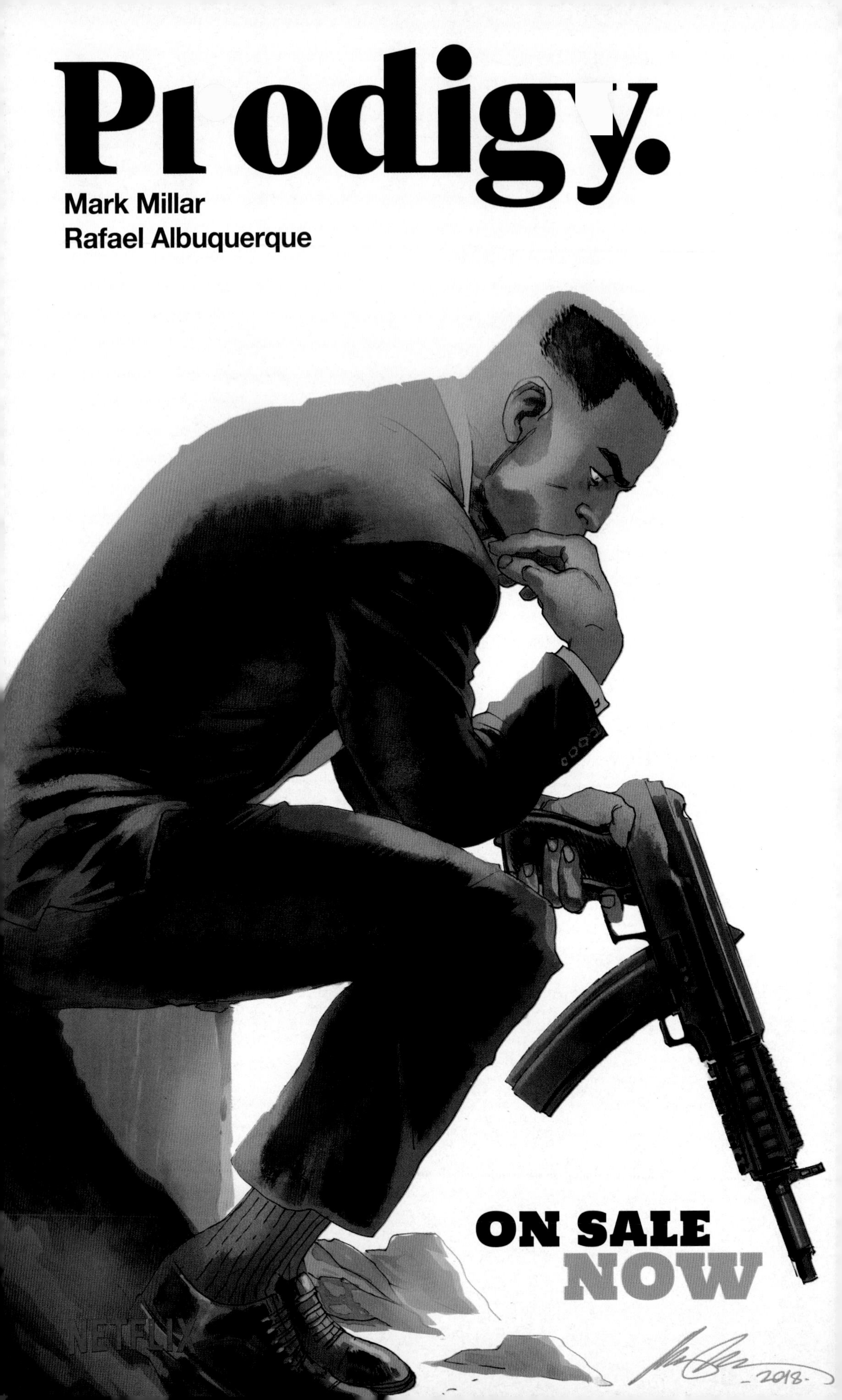

Prodigy.
Mark Millar
Rafael Albuquerque
ON SALE
NOW
NETFLIX
2018

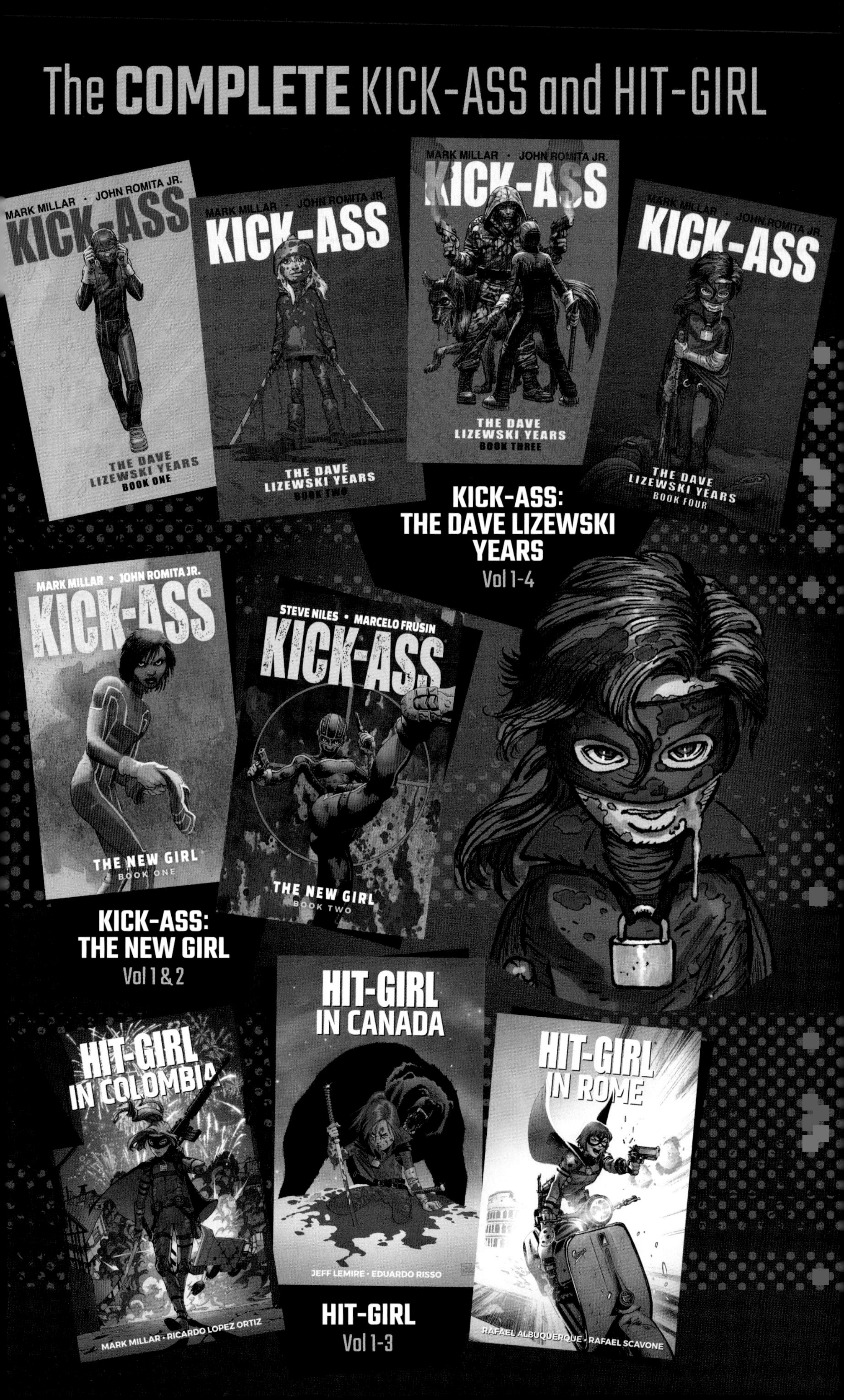
The COMPLETE KICK-ASS and HIT-GIRL
MARK MILLAR • JOHN ROMITA JR.
KICK-ASS
THE DAVE LIZEWSKI YEARS
BOOK ONE
MARK MILLAR • JOHN ROMITA JR.
KICK-ASS
THE DAVE LIZEWSKI YEARS
BOOK TWO
MARK MILLAR • JOHN ROMITA JR.
KICK-ASS
THE DAVE LIZEWSKI YEARS
BOOK THREE
MARK MILLAR • JOHN ROMITA JR.
KICK-ASS
THE DAVE LIZEWSKI YEARS
BOOK FOUR
KICK-ASS: THE DAVE LIZEWSKI YEARS
Vol 1-4
MARK MILLAR • JOHN ROMITA JR.
KICK-ASS
THE NEW GIRL
BOOK ONE
STEVE NILES • MARCELO FRUSIN
KICK-ASS
THE NEW GIRL
BOOK TWO
KICK-ASS: THE NEW GIRL
Vol 1 & 2
HIT-GIRL IN COLOMBIA
MARK MILLAR • RICARDO LOPEZ ORTIZ
HIT-GIRL IN CANADA
JEFF LEMIRE • EDUARDO RISSO
HIT-GIRL IN ROME
RAFAEL ALBUQUERQUE • RAFAEL SCAVONE
HIT-GIRL
Vol 1-3

MILLARWORLD®

THE COLLECTION CHECKLIST

EMPRESS
MARK MILLAR STUART IMMONEN

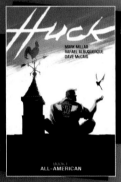

EMPRESS
Art by Stuart Immonen

Huck
MARK MILLAR
RAFAEL ALBUQUERQUE
DAVE McCAIG
BOOK 1
ALL-AMERICAN

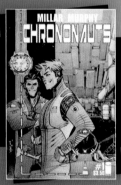

HUCK
Art by Rafael Albuquerque

MILLAR MURPHY
CHRONONAUTS
#1
$3.50

CHRONONAUTS
Art by Sean Gordon Murphy

MARK MILLAR DUNCAN FEGREDO
MPH

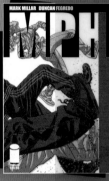

MPH
Art by Duncan Fegredo

MARK MILLAR · GORAN PARLOV
STARLIGHT

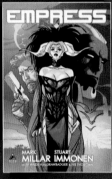

STARLIGHT
Art by Goran Parlov

MILLAR·TORRES·GIANFELICE
JUPITER'S CIRCLE
BOOK ONE

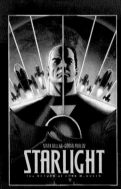

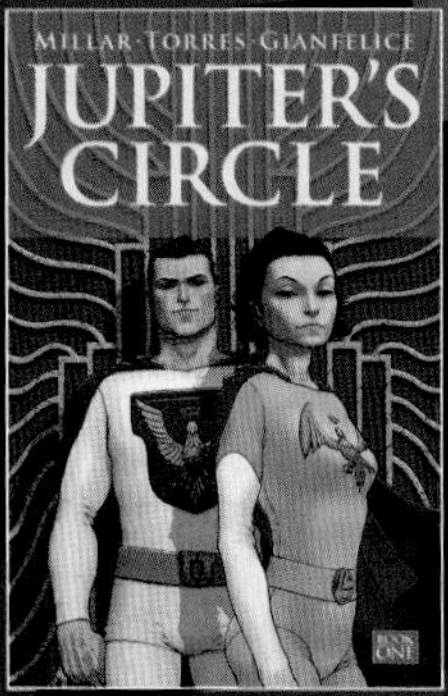

JUPITER'S CIRCLE 1 & 2
Art by Wilfredo Torres

MARK MILLAR · FRANK QUITELY
JUPITER'S LEGACY
BOOK ONE

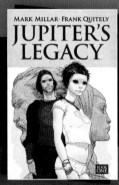

JUPITER'S LEGACY
Art by Frank Quitely

MARK MILLAR LEINIL YU
SUPER CROOKS
THE HEIST

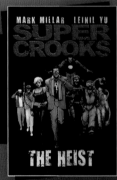

SUPER CROOKS
Art by Leinil Yu

MARK MILLAR & LEINIL YU
SUPERIOR
FROM THE WRITER OF KICK-ASS

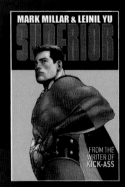

SUPERIOR
Art by Leinil Yu

MILLAR & McNIVEN'S
NEMESIS

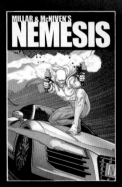

NEMESIS
Art by Steve McNiven

REBORN

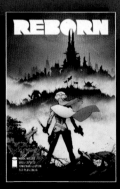

REBORN
Art by Greg Capullo

AMERICAN JESUS
BOOK ONE : CHOSEN
MARK MILLAR

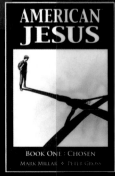

AMERICAN JESUS
Art by Peter Gross